Ruth Gogoll
L as in Love
Book One

I0608193

Ruth Gogoll

L as in Love
Book One

Translated from the German by
Susan Way

Chapter 1
Marlene, Chris, and Sabrina

"**O**h, come on." Marlene waved her off. "Knock it off with the love stuff already! There's no such thing."

"Whatever makes you think that?" asked Chris.

"Nerve-wracking relationship crises, stressful come-ons, one misunderstanding after another ..." sighed Marlene.

"Maybe you just pick the wrong women," Chris suggested cautiously.

"Me? The wrong women?" Marlene exploded.

"Well, yeah, I mean ... maybe you should try one sometime who has more brains than ... umm ... boobs."

Marlene drummed her fingers on the table impatiently. "That's not the problem."

"You don't think so?" Chris shrugged. "When I look back over your last three ... *liaisons* ..." *And really, all of the ones before those three, too*, she thought to herself, but she didn't want to enrage Marlene again. Then she'd get nowhere at all with her.

"Coincidence." Marlene shook her head violently.

"Coincidence?" Chris's eyebrows rose. "If I remember correctly, you dove right in with every one of those women on purpose. Not one of them accidentally stumbled into your bed."

Marlene stopped her drumming. "It's just that they were so sweet ... somehow." She looked like a bewildered dachshund.

"You never saw past their exteriors," Chris sighed. "You didn't pay attention to anything else. Maybe you should've had them spell the word 'love' first, as a basic qualifier." *At least two of them wouldn't've been able to do that*, she thought spitefully, but she refrained from sharing such snarky thoughts with Marlene.

"I do everything I can." Marlene held up her hands helplessly. "I buy all my women shoes."

Chris could barely hold back her laughter, but she tried to suppress it. "And what do you hope to accomplish by that?"

"Women have a thing for shoes, everybody knows that," Marlene mumbled.

Chris glanced down at Marlene's worn-out sneakers, which she had the feeling might be the same ones Marlene had been wearing when they'd first met – years ago. "If that's true, then you're not a woman," she said.

"Well, yeah ..." Marlene pulled her feet back so the table hid them from Chris's eagle eyes. "I'm just ... not that kind of woman."

"Neither are some other women you could meet," Chris agreed. "How would it be if you tried one of those for a change? You'd have a lot in common. Maybe even the same concept of love."

"That would never work!" Marlene stared at Chris, flabbergasted. "Someone who dresses like me?"

"She doesn't have to dress like you, but at least you might have some common interests if you chose someone more similar. Wouldn't that be nice for a change? What do you talk about with these females of yours, anyway?"

"Umm ... talk?" Marlene looked confused.

"That's what I thought." Chris sighed. "You don't talk a lot, am I right?"

"No, it's more like ..." Marlene wrung her hands, "... a little."

"A little," Chris repeated. "Or not at all?"

"Yeah ..." Marlene made a face. "As soon as we start talking, I always get accused of not caring about her, of never listening to her –"

How could you listen if you never talk to each other? thought Chris.

"Of just not doing everything she expects." Marlene ran her hands through her hair. "But what does she expect? I never get told that."

"And then she accuses you of not doing what she's never told you to do?" asked Chris.

"More or less. It's always pretty much the same. And usually … she's already found someone else by then. That's why –" Marlene stared at the table. "That's why I don't like to talk. When she starts to talk –"

"You take her to bed," Chris finished her sentence. Marlene had told this tale so often that Chris pretty much knew it by heart. Only the individual woman changed.

"Yes." Marlene was staring at Chris again now. "That's a good thing, isn't it?"

"Hmm." Chris tried to find some way to explain to Marlene what this was all about. "Sure, it's good. But if you *only* do that –"

"I mean, when someone starts in on me like that, it's the beginning of the end anyway, so why talk to her and speed it up? Besides, I don't even understand half of what she says."

"What don't you understand?"

"She says I don't respect her enough. That I only ever wanted sex from her. That I only came on to her because I wanted to get her in bed."

Chris frowned. "But that's true."

Marlene grimaced again. "Well, it doesn't seem to bother my ladies at first. They can't jump in bed fast enough."

"And you expect it to stay that way?"

"It doesn't change for me," Marlene answered blankly.

"But for her, it obviously does." Chris took a deep breath. "That's how it always is. In the beginning, when you don't know each other very well, everything is just so hot in bed. But after you get to know each other better, you might also want to do something else together once in a while."

"Like what?" asked Marlene.

"See a play, watch a movie, go out to eat?" Chris suggested. "You know. Outings? Conversation?"

"Why?" asked Marlene. "Sex makes me happy. And sex every day makes me even happier."

"Has it ever occurred to you that sex alone might not constitute the balanced use of your free time?" asked Chris with a sigh.

"No," said Marlene. "I slave away all day at the office. When I come home, I want to relax, maybe have something to eat, and then –"

"Off to bed." Chris nodded. Marlene had always been that way. The only new thing was that she had started equating this behavior with love.

"Yeah." Marlene's voice sounded irritated. "What's wrong with that?"

"Most women see it differently," said Chris. "And expect something different."

"Okay, but what the hell *do* they expect?" cried Marlene. "Why can't they just say what it is?"

"Sometimes I really do doubt that you're a woman," replied Chris, shaking her head. "No woman wants to have to *say* what she wants. She just wants you to know it."

"But how am I supposed to do that if she never says anything?"

"Have you ever tried a little romance?" asked Chris. "The two of you alone in front of the fireplace? You know – *Love Story* on television?"

"*Love Story*? What a hetero tearjerker!" Marlene gave Chris a mutinous look.

"That could be nice too, now and then. Or you could watch *Desert Hearts*. It doesn't matter. The important thing is the romance. The more tissues she needs, the better."

"I'm sure I don't even have that many tissues," muttered Marlene.

"Then buy some!" Chris threw up her hands. "No wonder they all leave you. You don't make the slightest effort."

"I buy them shoes," muttered Marlene in a huff.

"In the particular right size for each one?" Chris asked sarcastically. "Or do you buy them in advance by the dozen?"

"So what if I do?" snapped Marlene. "It's cheaper."

"Oh, man! I mean: woman." Chris was almost speechless. "Each woman is special – and she wants to be treated that way. You can't just give everyone the same gift, and in the wrong size! Do they ever give you the shoes back, and then you turn around and pass them on to the next one?"

Marlene looked at Chris as if that had happened at least once, but said nothing.

Chris was aghast. "You're mourning the loss of love, but you don't even know what love is," she declared with a sigh. "Love isn't something material. It comes from the heart. It has nothing to do with shoes *or* sex."

"Well, what *does* it have to do with, then?" asked Marlene, overwhelmed.

"Love is when you hold the door open for her, or when you help her into her coat. When you offer her the better seat in the restaurant and accept that you're the one who's going to be sitting facing the bathroom door all evening. Love is a feeling. It's not a thing you can buy or define. Love is when you don't have to stop and think about all the nice things you could do for your woman. You just do them of your own accord, based on what you feel in your gut."

"She said something similar." Marlene shook her head. "At least the part about just knowing things. But how am I supposed to do that?" She stood up. "There is no such thing as love, that's all. I just have to come to terms with that." She waved briefly and left Chris's living room and apartment, where the two of them had planned to spend a pleasant evening together.

"You handled that very nicely." A very familiar voice surprised Chris from behind.

She turned around in surprise. "I thought you were out with your old friends from school."

"I was." Sabrina sighed. "But it was boring." She sat down on the arm of Chris' overstuffed chair. "You said a lot of sweet things just now," she whispered with a smile, stroking Chris's hair.

"Oh . . ." Chris didn't know quite how she should answer. "Marlene was so desperate, I was trying to –"

"I met her girlfriend . . . or soon-to-be ex-girlfriend, if Marlene keeps treating her that way." Sabrina rolled her eyes.

"That . . . what's her name again?"

"Anita," replied Sabrina. "At first I thought she was another one of those . . . of Marlene's buxom wonders, but she isn't. She's actually really great. Not dumb at all."

"Oh, such compliments come from your lips," said Chris, grinning.

"Yeah, we never get to know any of Marlene's women, they come and go so fast," sighed Sabrina once again. "Maybe the ones before weren't so bad either."

"Maybe." Chris shrugged. "And what's she saying now, your Anita?"

"She's not *my* Anita; she's Marlene's Anita." Sabrina gave her a slightly critical look. "But probably not for long." She shook her head. "She really loves Marlene. I don't get it."

"I like Marlene too," said Chris. "She's one of my oldest friends."

"There's a world of difference between *like* and *love*," Sabrina pointed out. "Even you know that."

"What do you mean, even I?" asked Chris, unsettled.

"You don't see Marlene with the same eyes as Anita does, that's what I mean, you dope," teased Sabrina. "Anita is truly ... I don't know what she sees in Marlene, but she's really suffering. She's tried talking to Marlene, but Marlene —"

"Just drags her into bed," Chris surmised.

"Right." Sabrina shook her head once again. "Is she blind? Anita is yearning for her attention, for her love, but Marlene just wants to have sex with her."

Chris shrugged again, helpless. "I tried to explain that to Marlene, but she didn't seem to be listening. Or maybe she just truly doesn't get it. If Anita hasn't had any luck either ..."

"Well, you know ..." Sabrina grinned. "Anita has certain outstanding assets that are probably distracting Marlene from listening."

"That is true," Chris acknowledged.

"You remember *that* about her, but not her name?" Sabrina asked suspiciously.

"I was also somewhat distracted," Chris grinned, "by you."

"Hmm." Sabrina looked skeptical. "In any event, it was sweet, the way you tried to teach Marlene what love is." She smiled again. "Though it occurs to me that you haven't helped *me* into *my* coat in quite a while. Should I be worried?"

"Not a bit." Chris smiled back at her. "Or am I Marlene all of a sudden?"

"Fortunately, no." Sabrina's smile became tender. "Unless you've been faking it really well."

"I don't have that ability," Chris assured her earnestly. "I am what I am. I can't be any different."

"Maybe neither can Marlene." Sabrina stared musingly into space. "Poor Anita."

"Poor Marlene too," said Chris. "She gets dumped over and over and she can't figure out why."

"Yes, I sort of feel sorry for her, but more for Anita," said Sabrina. "I can empathize with her, I guess."

"Do you feel the same way about me that Anita feels about Marlene?" asked Chris, horrified.

"When you let your macho side hang out ..." Sabrina said cryptically, "you do bear a certain resemblance to Marlene."

"I let my macho side hang out?" Chris stared at her, aghast.

"Not exactly." Sabrina laughed. "Just sometimes, you're a little ... brusque. But there's really no comparing you to Marlene."

"What do you mean by 'brusque'?" Chris frowned.

"Don't you remember how we first got to know each other?" asked Sabrina with a grin.

"Hmm ... yes, I do." A feeling of uncertainty crept over Chris. "You think I dragged you off to bed exactly like Marlene would have?"

"I have no idea how Marlene does it." Sabrina shrugged. "But you seemed to know exactly what you wanted."

"And you ... didn't want it?" Chris hadn't felt this uneasy in a very long time. Why had Sabrina kept this from her until now? What else had Chris done wrong?

"I would've waited a little," said Sabrina. "But it was all right."

Oh, no! Chris wanted to tear her hair out until not a single strand was left. "All *right?*" she asked. "You thought it was all right? That's it? And you wouldn't have —" She was done for.

Sabrina's grin spread across her entire face. "I'll have to drop that one again in the future," she said. "It seems to unnerve you quite a bit."

"If that's what you wanted, you certainly hit the spot," said Chris wearily.

"Well, you're pretty cute when you're unsettled," said Sabrina softly. She brushed a kiss onto Chris's hair, then her ear, then her cheek. "You're pretty cute, period. And you bear no resemblance at all to Marlene."

Chris's cheeks glowed. So did her ears. She felt hot all over.

"Do you know what love is?" whispered Sabrina in her ear. "It's when to this day you still worry about whether you treated me considerately enough back then. When my happiness is more important to you than your own. When you hold back when you'd rather rush in. When you think of me first, and yourself second." She looked deep into Chris's eyes. "Love is always about the happiness of the other. I'm happy when you're happy; I couldn't be happy if you weren't. And I have the feeling it's exactly the same for you. That's what love is. Nothing else."

Chris cleared her throat. With a visible effort, she subdued the lump in her throat. "Our tape of *Love Story* – do you still know where it is?"

Sabrina smiled. "I think so, yes."

She stood up and left the room. Chris moved the sofa closer to the fireplace and adjusted the angle of the television.

Sabrina came back and held out the tape to Chris. "Put it in," she said. "I'll go get the tissues."

Chris got the tape ready, and waited. They'd sit close together on the sofa and bawl, then hold each other in their arms and feel close, and secure.

Yes, love, thought Chris. *It's the little things that count.*

Chapter 2
Marlene and Anita

"**M**arlene, is that you?"

"Who else would it be? Are you expecting someone else?" Marlene grumbled.

"No." Anita stood in the kitchen doorway and smiled. "Only you."

"So why are you asking?"

Anita's smile froze on her face. "I cooked. We can eat."

"You always cook," said Marlene. She turned and looked at Anita, though less at her face than at her breasts. "That's sexy, what you have on."

Anita's smile looked like it was engraved in stone. "A kitchen apron?"

"It'd be even sexier if you didn't have anything on under it." Marlene grinned. "But we can change that – later. Right now I'm hungry." She went across to the living room. "Can you bring me a plate? I want to see how the football game went."

"I set the table," said Anita softly.

"But I can't see the TV from there," said Marlene. She was already sitting in the armchair in front of the television. "Can't you get yourself a bigger screen? This thing is tiny. You can hardly see the ball."

"I hardly ever watch TV," said Anita, and went back to the kitchen.

"I don't get that," said Marlene, reaching for the remote control. "What do you do at night, then?" She grinned. "When I'm not here?"

Anita came into the room with a plate. The food on it was arranged like a small still life, in luminous colors, and smelled delicious.

Marlene grabbed the plate without even looking at it. Her eyes were fixed on the television, following the game she'd saved on Anita's VCR.

"I read," said Anita. "Usually."

"Hmm?" Marlene hadn't heard her. She picked carelessly at her food, quickly disrupting Anita's beautiful arrangement.

"I'm going to eat at the table," said Anita. Marlene didn't answer. Anita went over and sat down at the dining table, still set with two plates and gleaming silverware, and in the center the silver candelabra with the two candles that she hadn't lit yet. She'd been intending to light them when she and Marlene sat down to eat. Together.

Anita sighed and laid her head in her hands. She wasn't hungry anymore. And she'd been looking forward to this evening so much. *It can't go on like this*, she thought. *I have to talk to her*.

She remembered what Sabrina had said. Sabrina didn't like Marlene, even though Marlene was Chris's best friend. Chris and Sabrina – four years they'd been together now, and they still seemed so happy.

She and Marlene, on the other hand ... Anita sighed again. But they hadn't been together long at all; only three weeks. *People just have to get used to each other at first*. She always said that, but now she was no longer so sure that she wanted to get used to what was going on between her and Marlene.

"I can watch the rest of the game later." Marlene was standing next to her and regarding her with a covetous look.

What did I expect? thought Anita. *It's always like this.* "Don't you want to know how it turns out?" she asked wearily.

"I already know," said Marlene. "It's not that important." She laid a hand on Anita's breast. "Can you take your clothes off?" she whispered hoarsely. "And then –" she swallowed, "put just the apron back on?"

Anita closed her eyes for a brief moment. "Of course," she said. "Anything you want. What else am I here for?" She stood up.

"Exactly." Marlene grinned. "I'm so hot for you, I could just do you right here –" One hand slid down to Anita's butt, the other hand to her breast, massaging it roughly.

"Why don't you?" asked Anita. "You don't normally hold back. Why should you care about the good china?"

Marlene's expression made it clear that she wasn't even listening to Anita anymore. She was already too excited. Her hand ran under the apron and hastily unfastened Anita's pants. She pulled down the silk panties so that Anita was naked under the apron. "Turn around," she whispered roughly.

Anita turned around and braced herself against the table. She didn't know why she was complying. She never thought about why she felt so completely at the mercy of Marlene's commands, why she always submitted to them.

Marlene stroked her backside ardently and moaned. "You have such a hot ass. And such hot tits." She reached around and ripped

Anita's bra off her breasts. "Insanely hot."

Anita surrendered, in resignation. She wouldn't even try to keep up with Marlene, who was too fast for Anita's needs in any case – although at the beginning it had been enough, but only just. She simply let Marlene take her; a plate slid off the table and shattered as Marlene's thrusts grew harder, as she rubbed herself against Anita and came.

"Oh, man!" Marlene let herself fall panting onto her back. "That was hotter than a monkey's tits!" She laughed. "Especially the tits part!" She reached forward again and squeezed Anita's nipples so hard it hurt. "Babe, you're definitely the hottest thing on the market right now." She rose and smacked Anita on the backside. "We'll come back to this later. Now I'm gonna go watch the rest of the game. You can clean up and do the dishes in the meantime. It looks like a disaster area in here." She laughed again and went over to the television.

Anita pulled her pants back up and buttoned them. She knelt down and gathered up the fragments of the shattered plate. It was her grandmother's china, which she'd taken out especially for this evening.

Numbly, she regarded the individual pieces. What would her grandmother have said about how she had treated her expensive heirloom dishes?

But it's too late now. What was I supposed to do?

She laid the shards on the table and pieced them back together. Little bits were missing and would probably never be found. Even if she were able to glue the plate back together, she'd never be able to use it again.

The telephone rang.

"Hey, can you get that? It's annoying!" Marlene called from in front of the TV.

"Yes, I'm ... going." Anita pulled up her zipper and stumbled slightly as she rushed to the phone.

"Chris here," said a voice Anita had heard only a few times before. "Is Marlene there? I tried her place, but nobody's picking up."

"Yes, she –" Anita swallowed. "She's here."

"Sabrina gave me your number." Chris laughed in a very friendly

15

way. "I didn't have it. But the two of you exchanged numbers recently."

"Yes." Anita was still a bit dazed. "We did." She tried to pull herself together. "I'm sorry, I . . . I'll get you Marlene right away."

There was a second of silence on the line. "Are you okay?" Chris asked. "You don't sound so good."

"No, no." Anita cleared her throat. "I'm fine. I just have a scratchy throat."

"You poor thing," said Chris. "A cold?"

Anita was irritated. She didn't even know Chris. Why was she asking about her health? "No, just . . . I don't know," she said quickly. "It just happens sometimes." She glanced over at Marlene, who was again staring intently at the TV screen. "Marlene is watching the game right now," she said uncertainly.

"So she doesn't want to be disturbed, I know." Chris laughed. "Just tell her I called, when she resurfaces. Sabrina and I are going to Sappho. I just wanted to ask if you two wanted to come along. You could come later. Carolin and Rick will be there, too."

"I'll tell her." From a distance, Anita contemplated the back of Marlene's head in front of the glimmering glass screen. "But I don't know if we'll . . . if we'll be able to come right away." *Depending on what else Marlene has in mind for me.* "Or at all."

"Tell her I will hold it against her personally if she doesn't come," said Chris, and her voice suddenly sounded serious. "If *you both* don't come."

"I'll try." Anita's uncertainty grew. "But I can't promise anything."

"I know," said Chris. "But I'd like it if we could chat sometime. Sabrina has told me a lot about you."

"Told you . . . what?" Anita's pulse began to race.

Chris laughed again. "That you're a really great woman. And now, of course, I'm jealous." Her laugh indicated that this wasn't meant in earnest. "How about you just come to Sappho," she added, "and if Marlene would rather rot in front of the television, leave her at home."

"Umm . . . yes." Anita didn't know what she ought to say. Chris was Marlene's friend, but she seemed more interested in Anita, which was slightly disconcerting.

"See you later," said Chris, and hung up.

"You were right," she said to Sabrina, who was sitting at her desk and scrolling through her e-mail.

"About what?" Sabrina looked up at her over the rims of her reading glasses, which Chris found exceptionally adorable.

"Anita and Marlene," explained Chris. "Or rather, Anita. I was just on the phone with her."

"So I heard," said Sabrina, putting away her glasses.

"Oh, too bad," said Chris. "You look so cute with glasses on."

"If you say so," said Sabrina. She smiled. "So what's up with Anita?"

"She sounded funny." Chris went over to Sabrina. "I mean, I don't know her, but if it had been anyone else on the phone, I would have thought she was just about to cry."

"Maybe she is. Maybe she was already crying. It'd be no wonder, the way Marlene behaves."

"Yeah, I think so, too." Chris sighed. "I'm really going to have to have another talk with her." She stroked Sabrina's cheek gently. "Maybe they'll come to Sappho. Then I can call Marlene on the carpet."

"Assuming there's any point to that," said Sabrina with a sigh. "I really feel sorry for Anita. Who knows what was happening between her and Marlene before you called. Marlene is over there, isn't she?"

"Yes." Chris nodded. "I don't think any woman wants to spend time in Marlene's apartment. Not even Marlene herself. She'd rather let her girlfriends cook for her."

"Anita said she cooks regularly." Sabrina nodded thoughtfully. "Which is, of course, convenient for Marlene."

"That's true." Chris sighed. "Why do women put up with that?"

Sabrina grinned. "Hey, *I* cook for *you*. Usually."

"Yes, I know." Chris looked at the floor, somewhat abashed. "But in return, I sit at your feet." She knelt in front of Sabrina and peered saucily up at her.

Sabrina laughed. "That's the least you can do!"

Chris rose. "Well, tonight I'm inviting you out for dinner. At

Sappho. So you don't have to cook."

"But someone else still has to do it. You're not doing it yourself," Sabrina rebuked.

"I'm just not very good at cooking," Chris apologized sheepishly. "But if you absolutely insist, I'll cook from now on. For both of us."

"Oh boy!" Sabrina laughed out loud. "Frozen pizza every day! Now that's really not my thing!" She smiled tenderly at Chris. "But it's nice of you to offer. I'm sure Marlene hasn't ever offered."

"No." Chris sighed. "I don't know why she doesn't get it. It's so simple."

"Maybe not for her." Sabrina frowned. "It must not be."

"So it seems." Chris smiled. "Tell me when you're finished. Then we can go to Sappho."

"Five minutes." Sabrina turned her chair to the computer and put her glasses back on.

"Sounds good. I'll call Sappho and order the food, so it'll be ready when we get there."

Sabrina laughed lightly. "You do that."

With a tender smile, Chris observed Sabrina's expression of concentration as she opened an e-mail.

Why do I have all the luck? she thought. *How did I come to deserve this?*

She picked up the receiver and dialed Sappho's number.

Chapter 3
The Sappho Gang

"**H**ey, you're already here." Chris waved a greeting at Rick and Carolin, who were sitting at a table inside the restaurant.

"I'm hungry . . ." growled Rick, rubbing her stomach.

Sabrina laughed. She sat down next to Carolin. "Guys are all the same," she said, grinning at her.

"Since when am I a guy?" protested Rick.

"Since always," said Carolin. "Since we were in school together." She and Rick had been best friends for years, but they'd never been a couple.

Rick grinned, but said nothing else.

"I'm hungry, too," said Chris. "Have you ordered yet?"

"Yes." Carolin nodded. "They're running a little slow today, and Rick didn't want to wait."

"Okay." Chris turned around and waved to the server. "Melly?"

Melly came over to their table. "What can I do for you, girls?"

"A few things," said Rick, letting her gaze travel over Melly's shapely figure.

"You never learn," said Melly, bending down and tapping Rick on the nose with one finger.

"You keep being too nice to me, so I keep getting my hopes up," grinned Rick.

"If everyone in this café did that, I'd have an awful lot to do – I mean, after quitting time," grinned Melly in return. "Chris, Sabrina, what would you like?"

"I already ordered over the phone," said Chris. "But you guys are so busy, it's probably not ready yet, right?"

"I'll find out." Melly nodded and disappeared in the direction of the kitchen.

"Have Marlene and Anita shown up yet?" asked Chris.

"Marlene and who?" Rick gave her a puzzled look.

"Anita, Marlene's new girlfriend," Sabrina enlightened her.

"Oh, the blonde with the incredible front end," said Rick, grinning again and making a corresponding gesture with both hands in front of her chest.

"Don't call her that." Sabrina gave Rick a chastising look. "She's very nice."

"I never denied that," replied Rick. "But 'nice' just isn't the first thing you notice when you look at her."

"See, you are a guy," Carolin grinned.

"Now really!" Rick defended herself. "Can I help how she's built?"

"No," said Chris. "But you can help the way you talk about it."

"You three aren't usually so prudish." Rick shrugged. "But okay. I won't say any more."

"Marlene always finds such … umm … well-built women," Carolin mused. "You hardly notice their faces anymore. Somehow they all look the same."

"I think we should stop talking about people behind their backs," said Sabrina. "It's not very polite."

"You're right," Carolin agreed. "But Marlene ... well, even though I've known her for quite a while now, I don't like the way she behaves."

"She can be a great pal," said Rick. She looked at Chris. "Don't you think so?"

"Yes." Chris nodded. "She's a great pal – as long as you're not sleeping with her. That's why you and I get along with her so well."

"Seeing as you two are such great pals," Carolin leaned in, "would you please take her aside and read her the riot act? Isn't that also a pal's job sometimes?"

"I already tried," sighed Chris. "But she doesn't understand it. For her, there are only two kinds of women, pals and ... well, the other kind."

"The ones she wants to lay." Carolin nodded.

"So what are we then?" Sabrina looked at Carolin with some irritation. "We're neither her pals nor ... no, really no!"

"Marlene has somewhat limited perception." Chris grinned. "Fortunately. Otherwise she might already have tried to get you to –" She looked affectionately at Sabrina.

"I think, with a B cup, I don't have a chance," Sabrina replied good-humoredly. "And I'm glad. I suspect Marlene can be pretty overpowering when she sets her sights on a woman."

"That's true." Chris sighed. "How often have I witnessed that before?"

"What did you witness? Did I miss something?"

All eyes shot up.

"Hi, girls," said Marlene with a grin, rapping on the table in greeting. She sat down next to Chris.

Only then did anyone see Anita, who had come in after her. She stood at the table, somewhat uncertain.

"Hello, Anita," smiled Sabrina. "Come, sit with us." She indicated the empty chair next to her.

Anita seemed unable to make up her mind. At that moment, Melly returned from the kitchen. "Your chateaubriand is almost ready," she said to Chris and Sabrina. "Marlene?" She looked questioningly at Marlene. "A beer? Something to eat, too?"

"Beer," said Marlene. "I already ate. Bring me a tall one." She glanced over at Anita, who still was still standing there undecided. "Well sit down, already," she said. "How long are you just gonna stand there?"

"Yeah." Anita spoke softly and scurried hastily behind the table. She sat tensely on the edge of the chair Sabrina had offered.

"How are you?" asked Sabrina, giving her a friendly smile. "Better? Chris said you might be coming down with a cold."

"I'm ... I'm fine," Anita answered quickly. She was still speaking softly. "It was nothing."

"You have a cold?" asked Marlene. "Couldn't you have told me that before I ate? Now I'm going to catch it, too. I can't afford that right now."

"I don't have a cold," said Anita, even quieter than before. "Everything is all right."

"Well, I hope so." Marlene shot her another resentful look.

Sabrina glanced at Chris. Chris nodded.

Carolin leaned forward so she could see Anita better. "This is the first time I've seen you at Sappho. What do you think?"

"Oh. Oh, yes." It seemed like Anita hadn't expected to be spoken to. She looked around quickly. "It's nice here."

"It's a little short on fresh meat, though" said Marlene, looking around as well. "I could use some about now."

Anita started and sank further down in her chair, as if she could no longer tolerate the tension.

"You're impossible, Marlene," said Chris angrily. "Is that really necessary?"

"What?" Marlene looked at her uncomprehendingly.

"Comments like that," said Chris. "This isn't some sleazy pick-up joint."

"For God's sake ..." Marlene shrugged. "What does that matter? Don't you all look around? Everyone does it."

"But you're not here alone," said Rick.

"What? Oh, Anita." Marlene gave a dismissive wave. "She doesn't care. She's used to it."

"Well, *I'm* not," Sabrina said sharply. "And I don't *want* to get used to it. So please, behave yourself."

"Oh, but Madame is sensitive today," grinned Marlene. "Does she give you hell like this at home, too?" She looked at Chris.

"Stop it, Marlene," said Chris quietly. "Sabrina is right. If you're going to behave like that, go somewhere else."

"Suit yourself." Marlene stood up. "If you don't want me, then I'm leaving. Have fun." She turned around and stomped out furiously.

Melly returned with the large beer. "Where's Marlene?"

"Gone," said Chris. "Give me the beer. I could use it about now."

Anita stood up.

"Where are you going?" asked Sabrina.

"I have to . . . go after her." Anita gazed helplessly at the door.

"I don't think so," said Sabrina. "It would be better if you stayed."

"But –"

"Good grief, Anita!" Carolin flared. "Why do you put up with that?"

"Put up with . . . what?" Anita looked like she didn't quite understand the question.

"She treats you like . . . like dirt, and you run after her?" Carolin shook her head. "You need to show some backbone."

"I . . . she . . ." Anita sat down again, flustered. "It was nothing."

"Nothing?" Carolin eyed her. "Well, you must have very thick skin. If my girlfriend treated me that way . . ."

"She had a hard day at the office," said Anita. "Her boss –"

"Who cares about that?" Carolin interrupted. "I don't care if she had a hard day at the office. That's her problem. And no reason at all to take her bad mood out on you."

Sabrina shook her head as well. "According to what you told me before, this is no exception. Trouble at work is not the reason. Marlene is the reason."

"She . . . she can't help it. She gets worked up about things so quickly," said Anita. "Then she just has to vent."

"All over you?" Carolin stared at her. "Are you her doormat or her garbage can or what?"

"She . . . she doesn't mean it that way," said Anita softly.

"But I mean it that way," said Carolin. "She can behave however she wants when she's alone, but that –" She took a deep breath to calm herself. "What would you like to drink?" she said amiably to Anita. "Let's not waste the evening. Sappho doesn't deserve that."

"I agree," said Chris. "Should we order a nice bottle of wine, for all of us?" She looked at Anita. "Do you drink wine?"

Anita was still sitting there, shoulders hunched. "Yes, I . . . drink wine," she said timidly.

Melly came to the table with an armload of plates. "Now everything is ready at once," she said, placing the dishes in front of each of the women.

"Melly, please bring us a bottle of that great merlot," said Chris, "that tastes so much like France." She laughed.

A few minutes later, they made a toast. "To a *harmonious* evening," said Carolin, laughing and rolling her eyes. "Which should no longer be a problem." She looked over at Anita. "Sorry."

Anita smiled shyly. "I'm sorry I caused so much trouble."

"You? Trouble?" Carolin laughed. "I think we have a lot more work to do on you, babe." She clinked glasses with Anita. "To start – enjoy the evening, and don't think about Marlene anymore."

"I'm glad you came," said Sabrina, smiling.

Anita's shy smile slowly blossomed. "Me too," she said quietly.

Chapter 4
Rick, Melly, Thea

"Here so early?" Melly wiped off the counter and put an espresso cup down. "You don't usually come in for breakfast."

"That's because I never eat breakfast," said Rick. "Not at home, either."

"So, now you want . . ." Melly raised her hands helplessly, "nothing?"

"No," said Rick, and gazed at her.

"Oh, Rick . . ." Melly sighed. "I have to take care of this." She picked up the espresso and took it to a woman at a table near the door.

When she returned, she avoided walking past Rick and began washing glasses behind the counter.

"I ate breakfast here once," said Rick. "One single time. With you."

"I know," said Melly. She didn't look up from the sink.

"Why not, Melly?" asked Rick.

"Why *yes?*" Melly lifted her gaze and looked Rick directly in the eye. "Does there always have to be an explanation for everything?"

"I can't force you to tell me," said Rick. "But ... did I do something wrong?"

Melly braced herself against the sink. "It was one night, Rick. One night like a thousand others." She looked at Rick, but she didn't smile. "You didn't do anything wrong, I'm just ... well, I'm not cut out for a relationship. I don't want one. That's all."

"One night like a thousand others?" Rick stared at her.

Melly took a deep breath. She dried her hands, crossed her arms, and leaned back against the cupboard. "Or a hundred ... or ten. Isn't it all the same?"

"Not really," replied Rick, blown away by Melly's offhand assessment.

"It's *my* life, Rick," said Melly, exasperated. "You have nothing to do with it."

"Unfortunately, that's true," sighed Rick. She slid onto a barstool. "Would you make me an espresso, too?"

Melly gave her an unwilling glance. "If you absolutely must have one." She turned to the espresso machine and tamped a fresh portion of ground coffee into the portafilter.

"So that night meant nothing to you," said Rick.

"Damn it!" Melly twisted the portafilter into place with a rough jerk, and pressed the button. "Are you never going to get it?" She was still speaking with her back to Rick.

"What is it that I'm supposed to get?" asked Rick.

Melly turned around. The coffee flowed into the demitasse behind her. "I'm not the love machine on duty here," she said resentfully. "You wanted something from me, and I gave it to you. Isn't that enough? What else do you want?"

"You," said Rick.

Melly shook her head. "I'm not for sale. I belong only to myself."

"I don't want to buy you. I only want . . . to be with you."

"That's the same thing. Or almost. Anything like that is out of the question for me; how many times do I have to tell you? Am I speaking Greek? Why am I not getting through to you?"

"Maybe my Greek really is a little rusty." Rick grinned crookedly.

"This isn't a joke, Rick!" Melly turned back to the espresso machine and took out the cup. She put it on a saucer, paused, and sighed. "What else am I supposed to do?" she asked. She turned around, placed the cup on the counter in front of Rick, and looked at her. "I like you, Rick. In fact, I like you a lot. That's why I slept with you, and it was very nice. But it's nothing more than that."

"One time and never again? Is that your motto?"

"More or less. It keeps a great deal of trouble at bay."

"Did you have trouble? With a girlfriend? Is that why?"

"You keep looking for an explanation," said Melly, "but there isn't one. Believe me, would you? It's simply the way it is."

"I *can't* believe it. Because I also like you . . . a lot."

"Good grief!" Melly took a few quick steps out from behind the counter, embraced Rick roughly, and kissed her.

The woman Melly had served the espresso to looked over from her table with interest.

"Don't you understand?" Melly gasped as she disengaged from Rick's mouth. "This has to stop. Or you can never come into the café again."

"You'll ban me?" asked Rick, still completely stunned by Melly's kiss.

"I could," said Melly, "and I will, if you don't drop it. If you don't leave me alone."

"How am I supposed to do that? After that kiss?"

"You're crazy." Melly shook her head. "And you'd better go now. I don't have anything more to say to you."

"Am I banned? Am I forbidden to enter the café?"

Melly sighed. "No. Come, if you want. But don't come alone."

"As you wish." Rick slid off the barstool. She looked at Melly. "But I can't promise you that I'll never look at you again. That is definitely too much to ask. If you want that, then please just throw me out completely."

"I'll think about it," said Melly. She turned around and went back into the kitchen.

Rick's gaze followed her. When she stopped staring at the empty doorway, she redirected her focus toward the exit.

"Having problems with your girlfriend?"

Rick turned. It was the woman who'd ordered the espresso.

"She's not my girlfriend," said Rick. "Unfortunately."

"Ah." The woman stood up. "Unrequited love. The most romantic kind."

"I don't know if it's love," said Rick. She crossed to the door, opened it, and left.

A few steps later, the woman was next to her again. "My name is Thea. Thea Funk. I'm a journalist."

"Really?" Rick replied absently. She was still thinking about Melly.

"I'm working on a series about ... hmm ... interpersonal relationships," continued Thea Funk. "Relationships between interesting people."

Rick stood still. "A gossip columnist." She laughed lightly. "Well, I'm no celebrity. None of us are."

"That's not what I'm writing about. Gossip isn't *exactly* the wrong idea. But aren't we all interested in people's private lives? It doesn't always have to be about celebrities."

"I'm not particularly interested," said Rick. "Sorry." She kept walking.

Thea had to move fast to keep up with her. "I couldn't help ... I mean, there was no one else in the café, and you weren't talking especially quietly."

"It's not a secret." Rick sighed. "You're right about that."

"How do you feel?" asked Thea.

"Pardon me?" Rick stopped again. "What business is it of yours?"

"None, of course. But Melly — that's her name, isn't it? — is an exceptionally attractive woman. I can certainly imagine that an ... umm ... experience with her has its aftereffects."

"Aftereffects?" Rick grimaced. "Aftereffects," she repeated. "Yes, you could say that." She shook her head. "But I'm certainly not going to discuss them with you. Especially not in the middle of the street."

"Of course not. How about at your place?"

Rick's eyebrows shot up in surprise. "At my place?"

"You live nearby, don't you? I kind of picked that up incidentally."

Rick pursed her lips derisively. "You pick up a lot."

"A side effect of my profession," said Thea with a smile. Her smile intensified. "I have my voice recorder with me. I just need a place to set it down."

⋘⋙

"**W**hat are you doing down there?"

"What do you think?" Thea laughed, as her fingers wandered deeper between Rick's legs.

"I have to get up," said Rick. "I have to go to work. We can't keep –"

"Hmm." Thea didn't let that disturb her.

"Thea ... please ... all night we ..." Rick moaned, because Thea had nearly reached her goal.

"But nights aren't enough for me," whispered Thea.

"I haven't had a full night's sleep in a week," groaned Rick.

"In my opinion, sleep is highly overrated," said Thea.

"No." Rick tried to push Thea away, but Thea entered her, and Rick gave up.

"Now, then." Thea smiled contentedly.

Chapter 5
At Sappho

"**Y**ou're not serious!" Sabrina's eyes flew open. "She was there when you got home?"

"She's got a lot of nerve," said Carolin.

"I . . ." Anita wrung her hands and looked at the floor. "I can't just send her away."

"Why not?" Sabrina shook her head. "After all the liberties she's taken with you, I thought you'd finally come to your senses."

"She . . . she needs me," said Anita softly. "She said so."

"Is that a new song, or has it been playing for a while now?" asked Carolin with a sigh.

"One cappuccino, one latte, and one fresh-squeezed vitamin bomb," said Melly with a smile, as she brought them their order.

"Melly, what would you say?" asked Carolin. "Marlene showed up at Anita's place again. After a week's absence."

"I haven't seen her in here, either, for a few days" nodded Melly, not particularly interested.

"We have to do something," said Carolin.

"About Marlene?" Melly laughed. "She's not all that bad. You just have to tell her what's what."

Sabrina's eyebrows rose. When Melly went back to the counter, Sabrina stood up and followed her. "You once had a thing with Marlene?" she asked.

Melly shrugged. "Early on, when I first came to the café. It was a long time ago," she said.

Sabrina involuntarily eyed Melly's breasts, which jutted out prominently under her tight, sleeveless top.

Melly laughed. "Yep, that's what she's into." She looked over toward the table. "Although of course I can't compete with Anita."

"Why . . ." Sabrina frowned. "Why did you take up with her?"

"Oh, she has a certain . . . robust charm," replied Melly with a laugh.

"Charm? Marlene?" Sabrina looked dumbfounded.

"I think she just wasn't as unhappy then as she is now," said Melly. "She was still working as a truck driver back then; she only came in here once in a while."

"Yes, I remember. Chris told me she drove trucks," said Sabrina.

"It was her dream job," said Melly, "but since they revoked her driver's license, she has to work behind a desk. That's what makes her so short-tempered."

"Why did they take away her driver's license?" asked Sabrina.

"Why do you think?" Melly rolled her eyes.

"Alcohol?"

"Of course. She drinks way too much." Melly took a couple of bottles out of the refrigerator and began to mix a cocktail. "I told her so, too, but she won't discuss it with anyone."

"I don't think anyone can talk to her about much of anything," said Sabrina. She glanced over at Anita, who was chatting away with Carolin.

"I wouldn't say that." Melly filled the cocktail shaker with ice. "You just have to find the right place to start with her."

Sabrina laughed skeptically. "And how do you find that? Then maybe I could give Anita a tip or two."

"Anita ..." Melly looked over at the table. "There's no sense in that. Women like Anita are toxic for Marlene. They bring out the worst in her."

Sabrina stared at her, speechless. "You're telling me it's Anita's fault?" she asked.

"It's not anyone's fault," said Melly. "That's not what I said."

Melly poured and decorated the cocktail and took it to a table. Sabrina returned to Carolin and Anita.

"Get your key back from her," she heard Carolin say.

"I can't do that." Anita's forehead was furrowed with worry.

"You have to." Carolin appeared outraged. "She can't just come and go as she pleases. It's *your* apartment."

"Don't get yourself all worked up, Carolin," said Sabrina. "It's Anita's decision to make."

Carolin looked at her, aghast.

"What do you see in Marlene, anyway?" Sabrina asked Anita. "Carolin and I obviously can't comprehend it, but something about her must appeal to you."

"She's so ..." a ready smile spread across Anita's face, "strong."

"Does she hit you?" asked Carolin, before Sabrina could prevent her.

Anita's eyes flew open. "No," she said. "She never hit me."

"But others have?" asked Sabrina. "Other women you were with?"

Anita lowered her gaze.

"Is that a yes?" Carolin pressed.

"No." Anita's voice was barely a breath.

Carolin looked at Sabrina. Sabrina shook her head. "Did you hear that there's a reading coming up at the alternative bookstore?" she asked, emphatically relaxed. "I'd love to go. Rumor has it that the author is going to be Rita Mae Brown, with her newest book."

"I hate Rita Mae Brown," said Carolin. "You couldn't pay me to read her books!"

"I'll have to manage without you, then," sighed Sabrina. "What about you, Anita?"

Anita looked up, smiling shyly. "I'd love to go," she said.

"Are you all having fun?" Chris came in, greeted Sabrina with a kiss, and sat down. "I just ran into Rick. They ought to be here any second."

"They?" Carolin looked at her in surprise.

At that moment, the door opened and Rick and Thea came in.

Chris grinned. "Yes, they."

Carolin raised her eyebrows with interest and checked Thea out, thoroughly.

"Hello people," said Rick. She pulled up a chair and sat down at the table across from Chris.

"Aren't you going to offer your girlfriend a seat?" asked Sabrina, smiling.

Rick looked up and stood again. "Oh, pardon me," she said to Thea. "Please, have a seat."

Thea smiled at her and sat down. Rick pulled up another chair for herself.

"And you don't want to introduce your girlfriend to us, either," Carolin added with a grin.

"My name is Thea," said Thea, smiling. Rick looked exhausted. "I'm a journalist."

"And in that capacity, you . . . interviewed Rick?" asked Carolin.

"Y-yes. Yes, you could call it that," replied Thea with an even wider smile.

Carolin and Sabrina grinned. "How was your day, honey?" Sabrina asked Chris, stroking her leg. "Tiring?"

"It was okay." Chris leaned back, smiling at Sabrina's attentions.

Melly came to their table, glanced briefly at Rick, and then nodded at Chris. "What would you like to drink?"

"Champagne cocktails!" Chris laughed. "No, bring me a Proud
Mary, please."

"Coffee," said Thea. "I'm totally beat. A quadruple espresso or
something." She reattached herself to Rick and cuddled up close to
her.

"I could offer you two doubles," said Melly.

"Ricky, don't you want anything?" Thea caressed Rick's cheek.

"A beer," said Rick quickly.

"I think coffee would be a better choice," said Thea. "Beer makes
you tired, and I'd like it better if you stayed a little frisky." She nib-
bled tenderly on Rick's earlobe and looked up at Melly. "Bring her
the same as me. You can cancel the beer."

Melly seemed to want to raise her eyebrows, but she refrained.
"All right," she said, and went back to the counter.

"Thea," said Sabrina thoughtfully. "Thea Funk?" Thea nodded. "I
know your show," Sabrina continued. "I listen to it sometimes."

"And? Do you like it?" asked Thea, briefly releasing Rick.

"It's very amusing," said Sabrina.

"Does that mean you don't like it?" asked Thea.

"When you're interviewing guests in the studio, it's often very
interesting," said Sabrina. "I like the live atmosphere."

"Yeah, that's the most exciting part," said Thea. "Usually I edit
the interviews together before the broadcast and just play them
back, which means the show is going to be just a little boring for
me. But when I have live guests, something unexpected could happen, anytime." She let her hand glide across Rick's shirt, opened a
button, and slid it inside. Rick didn't seem to feel very well, but
said nothing.

"Have you known Rick for long?" Chris asked, in feigned inno-
cence. She knew the answer, since she'd spoken to Rick a week
ago, and there hadn't been any mention of Thea.

"Forever!" Thea laughed. "It seems like it, anyway. Isn't that so,
darling?" She stroked Rick's breast under her shirt, as everyone
could clearly see.

"A week," Rick said laboriously.

Chris could barely suppress a grin. "And you're just now introducing her to us?"

"We were ... busy," said Rick, who sat up, causing Thea's hand to slide out from under her shirt, which she buttoned back up.

"Oh, yes ..." Thea confirmed, smiling. "Rick has qualities that people don't see at first glance."

Rick gave her a chastising look. "Would you please stop that?"

"But darling," Thea snuggled up to Rick's back, since she'd leaned forward. "We've been having so much fun. Aren't your friends allowed to know that?"

Melly brought two large coffee cups filled to the brim with their pitch black liquid. "Quadruple," she said, putting the cups down and handing Chris her cocktail.

Rick suddenly embraced Thea and kissed her deeply and passionately, while her hands ran up and down along Thea's body.

Melly turned around and walked quickly toward the kitchen.

Sabrina put her lips to Chris's ear. "Oh, man, here we go," she whispered merrily. "Who do you think is going to win?"

Chapter 6
Carolin

Carolin had been on the go for the entire morning, making purchase after purchase: food, candles, new bed linens, and a wonderfully fragrant bath oil.

Exhausted from such extreme consumerism, she came into Sappho and dropped onto a chair, letting her bags fall to the floor around her.

"Did you rob a department store?" Melly came over to her, smiling.

"Several," sighed Carolin. "I've been out since six-thirty this morning."

Melly gave the bags a casual glance. "Oh, bed sheets. A new love?"

Carolin's cheeks colored slightly. "I'm having a visitor."

"A special visitor, obviously." Melly grinned. "But if you don't want to talk about it . . ."

"Bring me a large chocolate milkshake," said Carolin. "Then I'll be more talkative."

Melly brought Carolin's treat over and sat down next to her. "I didn't know you'd met someone. Lately you've been coming here alone. I mean, with the group, but not with a –"

"Yes." Carolin sighed. "We met six months ago."

"Six months ago?" Melly stared at her in surprise. "And she's never been in here?"

"She doesn't live around here," said Carolin. "We met on the internet."

"The internet?" Melly gaped. "Isn't the selection here big enough?"

"Meh, the selection." Carolin laughed softly. "It's always the same ones. Women I've known for years. And they're all just out of the question."

"Well, yeah, but sometimes someone new comes by," said Melly.

"Who then immediately gets reeled in by one of the womanpoachers," said Carolin. "I'm not that type."

"Melly, bring me the special right away, please. I'm in a hurry!" Sabrina came rushing in as if she were on the lam. She stopped just short of Carolin's table. "Ah, Carolin. Nice that you're here, too. Now I don't have to eat by myself." She saw the bags, and just like Melly, automatically peeked inside. "Bed linens? What's her name?"

"Is there no other reason for buying bed linens?" asked Carolin peevishly.

"The special is lasagna," said Melly. "Is that all right?"

"Yes, fine." Sabrina sat down. "And a salad. But fast. My boss is breathing down my neck."

Melly went into the kitchen.

"Good grief, what a day!" groaned Sabrina. "First thing this morning, my boss was already going ninety miles an hour. An order went wrong, so the shipment has to go out again, and everything is late."

"You'll manage," said Carolin with a smile. "You're a born office manager."

"Yes, the title sounds good," said Sabrina. "I used to be the secretary, then the assistant, and now I'm the office manager. But the work hasn't changed."

"But you like it," said Carolin. "No matter what they call it."

"That's true," said Sabrina. "I love it when things are busy."

Melly brought the lasagna. "Careful, hot," she said.

Sabrina started with the salad. "So?" she asked after a bite. "Who's going to sleep on the new sheets?"

"Her new love," said Melly. "Who she met six months ago and has been keeping from us. Or did you know something about it?" She looked inquiringly at Sabrina.

Sabrina shook her head. "No." She glanced at Carolin before applying herself to the lasagna. "Why didn't you say anything about her?"

"We've only been e-mailing each other," replied Carolin, somewhat embarrassed.

"You still could have told us," complained Sabrina. "Why just e-mail?"

"She lives in Kassel," said Carolin.

"Have you visited her?"

"No." Carolin drank the last of her milkshake and gazed into the glass as though its emptiness were extremely interesting.

"You mean, not in the whole six months? You've only written to each other?" Sabrina set her fork aside in surprise.

"Yes," said Carolin. "We had to get to know each other first."

"And now she's coming to visit you," said Melly. "So you've never seen each other in person before?"

"Mm-hmm." Carolin nodded.

"Whee!" Sabrina grinned. "So this is the first time?"

Melly grinned, too. "And fresh sheets right away!"

"You two are so dumb." Carolin gathered up her bags. "Truly nice friends."

"Please, Carolin." Sabrina picked up her fork again. "What else is she coming for? A cup of coffee?"

"We don't know ... I don't know yet," said Carolin. "Things sometimes go differently from the way you expect."

"Can they?" Melly and Sabrina both looked at her very doubtingly.

"Of course they can," insisted Carolin.

"But that's not why you bought the sheets," grinned Melly. "So when is she coming?"

"Today," said Carolin softly.

℘℘

Carolin stood at the train station. She'd bought a rose, which she was hanging on to for dear life. She never thought she could get so carried away with the whole thing. Ina wasn't the first woman she'd ever been interested in, after all. But her e-mails had a very special tone to them, something that made Carolin feel vulnerable, and a bit anxious.

She stared down the tracks and tried to tell whether the train was coming yet. She'd already been standing there for half an hour. Because she didn't want to risk being late, she'd set out much too early.

The station's loudspeaker came on at the same time as the display changed on the platform. Twenty-minute delay. *Oh, my God!* Carolin was already on her last nerve.

She sat on a bench and put the rose down next to her. Should she go get something to drink in the station concourse? That might help pass the time a little faster.

A shadow fell over her and stretched itself over the rose. The next moment, someone was sitting on it.

"Oh, excuse me." The young woman stood and picked up the rose she'd sat on. "I beg your pardon, please, I didn't see this." She attempted to straighten out the petals, which now hung tenuously from the stem, squashed, broken, crushed. "I'm so sorry." She smiled. "I'll buy you a new one. There's time – the train's been delayed, anyway."

"That ... that's not necessary," stammered Carolin. The young woman's smile had hit her like lightning in her belly.

"Of course it's necessary," the woman said. "You're picking up your sweetheart; you can't present him with such a squashed love token. What will he think of you?" She turned around and quickly disappeared.

Carolin remained behind, bewildered. What was this about? She came to pick up Ina, and here she was, drooling over another woman? And she hadn't even seen Ina yet.

She shook her head at herself. Nothing like this had ever happened to her before. But it would surely straighten itself out.

⋘⋙

"I've been yearning for you." Ina's voice was soft, and her lips felt their way tenderly across Carolin's cheek on the way to her mouth.

"It's good that you're here." Carolin swallowed. "So good."

Ina smiled. "Are you disappointed?"

"Because you sent me a fake picture?" Carolin laughed lightly. "No. But why did you do it?"

"I'm sorry," said Ina. "But I ... well, I've had some bad experiences."

"If you hadn't spoken to me, I would never have recognized you," smiled Carolin. "I was already thinking you weren't on the train."

"Yes, I know." Ina caressed Carolin's cheek with her mouth again. "But you had the rose. I knew you'd have one."

"You knew?" Carolin was astounded.

"Actually, it's always like that," said Ina.

"Always?" Carolin leaned back a bit and withdrew her cheek from Ina's caresses. "How often do you do this?"

"Not often." Ina laughed. "But it's not the first time, either, and it's just to be expected – the bit with the rose."

"If you sent an actual picture of *yourself*, you'd probably get an entire bouquet," said Carolin.

"Why?" asked Ina.

Carolin grinned. "Pardon me if I'm shocking you excessively, but you are beautiful. More beautiful than any woman I've ever seen."

"That's the problem," sighed Ina. "That's why I send my best friend's picture instead of my own."

"Your best friend looks quite nice, too," said Carolin. "But compared to you –" She looked tenderly at Ina. "You are gorgeous, and I'm glad that you're finally here."

"Me too," whispered Ina, hugging Carolin even tighter. "During the whole long ride, I imagined how it would be when I arrived, when we met."

"And? Do I meet your expectations?" Carolin quivered slightly as she embraced Ina.

"Absolutely and completely," said Ina. Her hands wandered across Carolin's back. "I imagined you exactly like this, so soft . . . and warm . . ." Her voice dropped lower still. "I want to sleep with you," she whispered. "Please . . ."

Carolin took a deep breath. "I want that, too," she whispered back. "I've wanted that from the very first moment." She laughed lightly. "They were right about that."

"Who?" Ina seemed irritated.

"Melly and Sabrina," said Carolin. "They said things would go that way."

"Go that way?" Ina appeared even more irritated and leaned away.

"Well, you know . . . that we'd immediately . . ." Carolin felt the embarrassment rising in her cheeks.

"We don't have to," said Ina, disentangling herself from Carolin. "I just thought we . . . were in agreement about that."

"We are." Carolin smiled. "This has nothing to do with the two of them. It was stupid of me to mention it."

"Your friends?" asked Ina. "You told them about me?"

"Not until today," said Carolin, "but then . . . I was at Sappho, and it just sort of slipped out."

"At Sappho?" Ina's eyebrows rose.

"That's our favorite café," said Carolin. "We always meet there."

"Ah, yes," said Ina. "I think you've mentioned it."

"Yes, it's . . . I think they're expecting me to show up with you tonight," said Carolin, a bit bashfully. "Of course you don't have to. But they're curious to meet you, of course."

Ina smiled. "Are you sure we're going to have time for that?" She took Carolin into her arms again and kissed her, tenderly at first, then more passionately, until Carolin moaned.

"Probably not," she whispered with effort.

"Come," breathed Ina throatily. "I want you." She pulled Carolin down onto the living room couch.

What did I bother to buy bed linens for? thought Carolin, but Ina's kisses were diminishing her ability to think. Now, she could only feel.

Ina unfastened Carolin's pants and slipped her hand inside, gliding underneath her panties. Carolin moaned as Ina's fingers touched her center, explored her wetness, and pressed in deeper.

Carolin groped for Ina's waistband, undid the button, pulled down the zipper, pressed her hand between cloth and skin. Ina sighed against her mouth. Carolin found the entrance; the labia almost spread themselves, they were so swollen and wet. Ina was moaning now, too; they moaned together.

Ina came quickly, as if she'd just been waiting to be touched. "I'm sorry," she said. "I was thinking about you for the entire ride, and so —"

Carolin smiled. "I know," she said. She caressed Ina's face. "That's quite all right."

Ina's fingers began to move again between Carolin's legs. "That doesn't mean you're off the hook, though," she said, grinning.

Carolin closed her eyes because she was overwhelmed with sensation. "I didn't think I was," she whispered weakly.

Chapter 7

Chris and Sabrina

"What do you mean, you wonder if they're coming this evening?" Sabrina gave Melly a questioning look.

"You two are such old gossips," laughed Chris. "Don't you think the two of them have anything better to do?"

"What could they possibly have to do?" asked Sabrina, as her hand stroked the length of Chris's thigh. "I can't imagine a thing."

"I think I'd better leave the two of you alone." Melly laughed and left.

Sabrina bent down to Chris and kissed her. "Does that give you ideas, perhaps?"

"What kind of ideas?" asked Chris with a smile.

"We could go home," said Sabrina.

"Oof." Chris ran her hand over her eyes. "I had an awfully hard week."

Sabrina ran her lips softly along Chris's cheek. "You can relax," she whispered. "You don't have to do anything at all."

Chris laughed easily. "It's not really that simple."

"I'll spoil you," whispered Sabrina. "Then you'll forget about your hard week." Her hand slid gently over Chris's breast.

Chris reached for her hand and held it tight. "I can't, Sabsi. Really, I can't. I'm too tired. When we go home, I just want to sleep, preferably through the entire weekend."

Sabrina pulled back. "Do you know how long it's been?"

"I know." Chris grimaced. "When the project is finally finished, when I have room to breathe again –"

"You always say that," replied Sabrina. "And then a new project comes along . . . and another one . . ."

"You're right." Chris tenderly caressed Sabrina's cheek. "I love you. You know that."

"Yes." Sabrina examined Chris's face. "I know."

⋯

"I'm sorry, Sabsi." Chris came into the bathroom and hugged Sabrina from behind. "I just really couldn't."

Sabrina looked into the mirror, in which she could see her own and Chris's faces at the same time. "Did you get enough sleep?"

"So-so." Chris kissed Sabrina on her bare shoulder. "Breakfast?" She left the bathroom without waiting for an answer.

"Yes. Breakfast." Sabrina called to her. She sighed and ran the brush through her hair once more. It was glossy from the new conditioner she'd just used, and it smelled like an enchanted forest. But Chris hadn't even noticed.

Chris was rattling dishes in the kitchen. "Marmalade or honey?" she called across the hallway.

"I don't feel like anything that sweet today," said Sabrina. She put away the brush and crossed the hall to the kitchen. "I'll just have coffee."

"Just coffee?" Chris looked at her, astonished. "On Saturday morning? But this is your favorite luxury breakfast time, with everything the cellar and kitchen have to offer."

"Not today," said Sabrina. "I already ate. You slept late."

"You're still mad at me," said Chris. She came up to Sabrina and stood facing her, their bodies almost touching.

"I'm not mad at you," said Sabrina. She wanted to turn away, but Chris held her there.

"Yes, you are," she said. "Was it really that bad? I didn't know –" She cleared her throat. "I didn't know it meant so much to you."

"After four years, you should know me better," said Sabrina.

"I thought I did," Chris said quietly.

Sabrina tilted her head back and took a deep breath. She looked at Chris. "I'm a woman, Chris. I want to be desired."

Chris opened her eyes in surprise. "I do desire you."

Sabrina pursed her lips. "I haven't noticed any signs of that for a long time."

"We're both so tied to our work –" said Chris.

"We always have been," countered Sabrina. "But even so, we didn't used to go for weeks –" she laughed dryly, "or *months* without sex."

"It hasn't been months," said Chris.

"Oh, yes. It has." Sabrina looked at her from beneath furrowed brows. "If you don't count the quickies."

"I've been so tired ..." said Chris apologetically. "I thought you ... that you at least got something out of it, those times."

"Oh, sure, I did," said Sabrina ironically. "Those five minutes were great."

"Oh, God." Chris smacked herself on the forehead. "Why didn't you say something to me before?"

"I wanted to," said Sabrina. "When we had time for each other again."

Chris let her hand fall. She bent forward slightly. "Your hair smells wonderful," she said softly. She fanned out Sabrina's glossy abundance with her fingers, then laid it across the nape of Sabrina's neck and pulled her close. She buried her face in the fragrant splendor and soaked up the scent. "Hmm."

"Chris," Sabrina whispered weakly. "Please, don't do this to me."

"I'm not," breathed Chris. She caressed Sabrina's throat, her hair, her bare shoulders. "I'll take my time with you this time. All day, if you like."

"I love you, Chris. I love you so much," whispered Sabrina. She took Chris's face in her hands. "If only you knew how much."

"I love you, too. I'm so sorry," said Chris. "I'll make it all up to you." She kissed Sabrina and caressed her. Slowly, she loosened the towel that Sabrina had wrapped around herself and let it fall to the floor. "You are so beautiful," whispered Chris, overcome.

Sabrina pulled Chris's T-shirt over her head and pressed close to her. "Here in the kitchen?" she asked.

"Everywhere!" Chris laughed. "We'll make the whole house unsafe."

"I don't know if the neighbors will appreciate that much," answered Sabrina with a grin.

"We won't ask them," said Chris, lifting Sabrina up and setting her on the table. "Passion wins over reason. They must understand that." She let Sabrina sink back onto the table. "Enjoy it, darling," she whispered.

Chapter 8
Carolin

"**M**y goodness, it's busy here tonight!"

Melly shrugged. "Saturday. That's normal." She ran quickly with a couple of plates into the kitchen.

"This is really an interesting spot," said Ina, looking around.

"Yes." Carolin tried to pick out some familiar faces in the crowd. "Maybe it wasn't such a good idea to come here."

"Oh, no." Ina smiled. "We don't have anything like this in Kassel. I find it fascinating. So many women . . ."

"Uh . . ." Carolin tugged on Ina's sleeve like a small child trying to get attention. "You're here with me. I hope that's clear."

"Of course." Ina laughed. "I'm not going to be unfaithful to you on the very first night, don't worry." She wrapped an arm around Carolin's waist.

"You mean, if it weren't the first night –?"

"Oh, Caro – don't talk about things like that now. This is the wrong place for that kind of talk."

"Then maybe we'd better go back home," said Carolin, who was noticing, meanwhile, that Ina's beauty had already attracted the attention of several women.

"Am I interpreting what I see back there correctly?" Ina didn't seem to have heard her. "That looks like a dance floor."

"Yeah." Carolin sighed. "There's a live band tonight."

"Wonderful!" Ina beamed. "I love to dance."

"I'm not so famous for that," said Carolin. "But it seems like I brought you here on the right evening."

"Absolutely." Ina pressed forward to the stage that lay behind the dance floor.

Carolin had to follow her, whether she wanted to or not.

"Hey, Carolin." One of the women she was laboriously making her way past spoke to her. "Are you excited about the band?"

"Marlene." Carolin stopped, puzzled.

"We really want to dance," a voice wound its way out from behind Marlene.

"Anita." Now Carolin's puzzlement was absolute.

Anita snuggled up to Marlene. "I've been looking forward to it all week," she said with shining eyes.

Somehow I've wandered into the wrong movie, thought Carolin. *Or the last one was the wrong one.* "Yes . . . uh . . . have fun, then," she stuttered, and tried desperately to spot Ina in the crowd.

Chapter 9
Rick

"**O**h, yes, please, let's observe *The Peculiar Behavior of Sexually Mature Lesbians During Mating Season* in action!" Thea was full of enthusiasm.

"That's a hetero book you're citing," said Rick. "It has nothing to do with us."

"I meant the movie." Thea grinned. "I rarely read books."

"Even though you're a journalist?" Rick looked astonished.

"I'm a radio journalist," said Thea. "Print media isn't really my thing. I hardly ever read the newspaper either."

"You are peculiar."

"That's what I always say." Thea didn't seem bothered a bit. "And I love observing other peculiar people, like tonight at Sappho. I'm sure everyone will be there."

"Yeah, I assume so. But I'm not particularly wild about it."

"And here I thought you were a total wild thing." Thea caressed Rick's naked posterior. They still lay in bed.

Rick turned around so that Thea could no longer reach her backside, but this, of course, wasn't a very good idea, since Thea just pounced on Rick's breasts.

Rick groaned. "Okay, fine, let's go to Sappho. I agree."

"But we still have some time beforehand," said Thea, caressing Rick's breasts, her belly, her thighs.

"One would think you hadn't had sex for years, the way you seem to need to make up for it all at once," said Rick.

"I haven't been with a woman in a long time," said Thea, while her mouth wandered downwards along Rick's body. "That's true."

"I can hardly imagine that." Rick laughed. "As persuasive as you are, they still managed to say no?"

"I didn't ask them." She pushed Rick's thighs apart and laid herself between them.

"You really haven't had sex in a long time?" Rick propped herself up on her elbows, amazed, and looked down at Thea.

"I didn't say that." She licked lightly across Rick's groin with the tip of her tongue.

Rick moaned aloud, but was too irritated to give herself over to the feeling completely. "But you said –" She broke off. "You sleep with men, too?" she asked, wide-eyed.

"Sometimes," said Thea, without looking up.

Rick rolled onto her side and quickly stood up. "And you didn't tell me that?"

Thea looked at her with surprise. "Is it important?"

"Important?" Rick scrutinized her as she lay on the bed. "You don't think that that's important?"

"Not really." Thea shrugged. "For me, only the person matters, not the gender."

Rick ran her hand through her hair. She didn't look at Thea.

"You never asked me," Thea added.

"No." Rick threw a brief glance at her and turned around. She went into the bathroom.

"Rick." Thea stood up and followed her. "Does that make such a big difference?"

"To me it does. I'm going to shower." Rick pulled open the door of the shower stall.

"Please ..." Thea laid a hand on Rick's back. "I know I should have told you, but ... well, there was hardly any opportunity." She smiled a bit crookedly.

"You made sure of that," said Rick, stepping into the cubicle.

"But not because of that. That wasn't the reason. I just forgot to say anything to you, because I was so ... because I felt so attracted to you. I ... like you a lot." She acted self-conscious, which was new for her.

Rick turned around. "I like you, too. But your views might take some getting used to."

"They're not ... views," said Thea unhappily. "I'm just as bi as you are lesbian. We were both born that way."

Rick sighed. "You're right, of course, but I ... I have issues with that. I'll just have to think about it." She shut the shower door and turned the water on.

"Rick." Thea opened the door again. "I'm with you now, no one else. Isn't that enough?"

"The whole bathroom is getting wet," said Rick.

Thea hesitated for a moment, then stepped into the shower stall and closed the door behind her. "Maybe that really is why I didn't tell you. Unconsciously. Women are always so funny about it. Men think it's sexy when a woman tells them she's bi. But women . . ."

"Lesbians, you mean," said Rick dryly. "Other women are rather less interested."

"Yes." Thea looked at the floor. "Lesbians. Or straight women who think that any bi woman is going to eat them alive."

"They always assume that of us lesbians, too." Rick laughed. "They really have no sense."

"Well, they've never known any other type of behavior – from men," said Thea apologetically.

"And I'm sure you know all about that."

Thea took a step toward Rick and flung her arms around her neck. She nestled up against Rick's wet body. The water ran warmly over them, and the ripples seemed almost like oil on troubled waters. "But that doesn't have anything to do with us, Rick. Nothing at all."

"I'm not so sure about that," Rick replied. "When was your last AIDS test?" Although Thea still nuzzled her, Rick didn't hug her back.

Thea went stiff. She stepped back. "I," she swallowed, "never do it without a condom."

"From the get-go?" Rick's eyebrows rose. "Were you so savvy in your younger years?"

"No." Thea shook her head. "Back then, I was just as ignorant as everyone else. But that was a long time ago."

"Have you been tested?" Rick asked again.

"Yes, damn it!" Thea tore open the shower door and stepped out into the bathroom. "And the test was negative. Are you happy now?" She shut the door with an angry shove.

Rick stayed in the shower for longer than usual. When she came out, Thea was dressed.

"I assume you want me to leave now," Thea said.

"I would like to have my apartment to myself for a while, yes." Rick went to the closet to put some clothes on.

"Rick . . . I –" Thea closed her eyes and then quickly opened them again. "Fine. I understand." She went to the bedroom door. There she turned around once more. "I'm sorry, Rick," she said. "I didn't want this to happen."

Rick sighed. "Neither did I," she said, pulling on a T-shirt. "Maybe we should've talked about it earlier."

"Maybe we should have." Thea left.

☙❧

"**H**ello, Rick. Did Thea let you out of her clutches for once?' Chris grinned as she and Sabrina entered Sappho.

"Yes," said Rick, turning around and leaning against the bar.

Chris looked at Sabrina and raised her eyebrows questioningly. Sabrina shrugged. "I'm going to the little girls' room. Are you staying here?"

Chris looked over at Rick, who was still leaning with her back to the bar. "I think so."

Sabrina nodded and fought her way through a cluster of people to the toilets.

Chris leaned against the bar next to Rick. "Is Thea here, too?"

Rick shook her head.

Chris waved at the waitress behind the counter, Melly's backup. "A beer."

The server nodded, took a glass, and began to draw the beer.

"Did you have a fight?" asked Chris, without looking at Rick.

"Hmm." Rick's answer sounded like neither assent nor denial.

"You must have." Chris laughed. "I can't imagine Thea lasting this long without touching you."

"That's not the way things are, Chris," said Rick grimly.

"So what's going on?" Chris took a sip of her beer. "Problems?"

"Depends on how you see it."

"You don't want to talk?" Chris turned toward Rick.

"She's bi," grumbled Rick. "She told me today."

"Oh." Chris nodded understandingly. "That is a problem, indeed."

"She thought it wasn't." Rick laughed dryly. "That it wasn't important."

"Yeah, bi women have a different view of things than we do. I've noticed that myself."

"Is Sabrina –?"

"No." Chris shook her head. "No, thank God."

"Consider yourself lucky."

"I do." Chris smiled. "Very lucky."

"Oh, you two are the dream couple anyway." Rick waved her away. "What kind of problems could you have?"

If only you knew, thought Chris. "When things come up, we try to talk them through. That usually helps."

"Yeah, well. Talking things through doesn't change the facts." Rick knocked back the rest of her beer and ordered another.

"No, it doesn't, but it's better than mind reading. More reliable." She laid a hand on Rick's shoulder. "Thea won't be back?"

"I don't know." Rick shrugged. "It makes no difference to me."

"So it's final?"

"I hope so."

"Maybe everything just happened too fast between you two. You should have taken your time. Then you would've found out before things got so far along."

"I didn't want to go so fast," said Rick. "Thea wanted to."

"Yes, I noticed." Chris grinned. "You always looked a little like the poor victim."

"Yep, that's what I was."

"You could've said no."

Rick's eyes followed Melly, who was walking past them. "Yes, I could have."

Chris let her gaze wander to Melly as well. "Ohhh, I see. Thea was just a substitute."

"I didn't have time to think about it," Rick defended herself.

"That's fine. But then it wasn't love between you and Thea. That should make it easier."

Rick made a dismissive sound. "No, it had nothing to do with love. We just spent time together in bed."

Chapter 10
Dance Night

"**H**ello, Sabrina." Anita stepped out of a bathroom stall; Sabrina was washing her hands.

"Hello, Anita." Sabrina smiled. "How are you?"

"Well. Very well." Anita smiled downright blissfully. "I'm here with Marlene."

"With Marlene?" Bewilderment spread across Sabrina's face. She forgot to turn off the water.

"You knew she came back," said Anita, somewhat irritated. She held her hands under the water that was still running into the sink in front of Sabrina.

Sabrina straightened up and reached for a paper towel. "Yes," she said. "Because she needs you so much." She looked skeptical.

"She does," replied Anita. "And I need her." The blissful smile spread itself back across her face.

Sabrina cocked her head to one side. "She gave you a couple of orgasms. Your eyes are still sparkling."

Anita turned red. "So are yours," she said. She looked Sabrina defiantly in the eye.

"Yes, that's true," said Sabrina. "But Chris and I are married, and we love each other. Chris would never –" She broke off and cleared her throat. "She would never try to keep me in line that way." *She really wouldn't? What was that this morning?*

"Marlene loves me, too," said Anita obstinately. "And I love her!"

"I know that *you* do," said Sabrina, "as incomprehensible as that is, but Marlene –"

"All of you're against her," interrupted Anita. "You don't understand her. But I understand her. Because I love her."

"Do you think she's changed?" asked Sabrina. "Do you think you're suddenly going to have meaningful conversations and," she pursed her lips, "good sex, every day? Not too long ago, things sounded very different."

"I never should have told you that," said Anita, and her face closed up. "It's not like you're a friend."

"Yes, Anita, I am." Sabrina suppressed a sigh. "But face the facts.

Marlene is the way she is. She's never going to change. She's going to hurt you again, and you're going to suffer again. You have to end it. She's not good for you. You have no future together."

"You're hateful!" Anita broke down in tears.

"Anita ..." Sabrina tried to hold onto her, but Anita lunged for the door and yanked it open. In less than a second, she had vanished.

"What's up with Anita?" Carolin was looking in the direction in which Anita had just whizzed past.

"She doesn't want to let go of Marlene," explained Sabrina as she drifted over. "Unfortunately, I told her that Marlene isn't going to be any good for her." She sighed.

"But we've told her that a couple of times already," replied Carolin, bewildered. "She never reacted this way before."

"Marlene has ... umm ... convinced her that things can be nice with her," said Sabrina vaguely.

"Oh." Carolin grinned. "I never would have thought she was capable of that."

"What wouldn't you have thought she was capable of?"

"Oh, dear, pardon me," said Carolin. She looked at Ina. "This is my friend Sabrina. Sabrina, this is Ina."

"Ina?" Sabrina frowned. "Oh," she said then. "You're the ... visitor from out of town." The corners of her mouth twitched.

"Kassel," said Ina.

"Yes, Kassel. Far away from Cologne." Sabrina was still trying to keep from smirking. "How did you like the sheets?"

Carolin looked daggers at her.

"The sheets? What sheets?" Ina asked blankly.

"Oh, nothing, nothing," said Sabrina. "I just thought ..."

"It would be better if you stopped thinking," said Carolin.

"Yes. Yes, I'm sure it would." Sabrina got herself under control and looked at Ina. "It's lovely that we finally get to meet you."

"It's a pleasure to meet you, too," said Ina. "Caro has already told me a little about your gang. I remember your name. Because mine is inside it." She grinned.

"So what did you tell her about me?" Sabrina asked Carolin.

"What a great couple you are, you and Chris," said Carolin quickly. "An example to us all."

"Well, well," said Sabrina. "You've made an example of me? And what if I don't want to be one?"

"Then you should behave differently," grinned Carolin. "With you two, it's always love, peace, and harmony. I have no idea how you do it."

By not telling people about all the things that go wrong, thought Sabrina. "We love each other," she said.

"Yes." Ina linked arms with Carolin. "That's a good start." She pulled Carolin to her and kissed her so passionately that Sabrina had no choice but to leave them to it. She took herself back to the bar with a smile.

"Why are you smiling so knowingly?" asked Chris.

"I just came across Carolin ... with *Ina* ..." Sabrina was still smiling.

"Ina? Who is Ina?" asked Chris.

"Her visitor from Kassel. The one she's only exchanged e-mails with before."

"Aha," said Chris. "Why didn't you bring her over?"

"She and Carolin were," Sabrina grinned, "... occupied. I'm sure they'll come by later. Although —" She scrutinized Chris. "I don't know if I'm entirely pleased about that."

"Why?" Chris looked quizzical.

Sabrina looked out at the crowd, to see whether Carolin and Ina might already be on their way over. "Ina isn't the type you like to introduce to your wife," she said.

Anita and Marlene

"What are you bawling about? Did I do something wrong again?" Marlene rolled her eyes in irritation.

"No," sobbed Anita. "Not you. Sabrina."

"Sabrina?" Marlene looked around. "I haven't even seen her today."

"She was —" Anita continued to weep. "She was — I ran into her in the bathroom."

"You girls, always having to go to the john together . . ." grinned Marlene.

"Not together," said Anita. She fumbled a tiny handkerchief out of a miniscule purse and wiped her nose. "She was just there. And then I . . . then I –"

"Get to the point already," said Marlene impatiently. "This is taking forever."

"Yes." Anita attempted to pull herself together. "I told her I was here with you, and then she –"

"I can imagine," interrupted Marlene, sneering. "Sabrina has never liked me, although I wouldn't have minded doing – well, never mind. So that's why you're bawling? Because she gave you some more baloney about me?"

"She . . . she said you're no good for me, and that we . . . that we have no future," sobbed Anita.

"So, nothing new." Marlene shrugged. "What are you getting so worked up for?"

"But . . . but . . . we do have one, a future, don't we?" Anita looked imploringly at Marlene. "You want me." She lowered her head bashfully. "Today you said so."

"Did I?" asked Marlene. "What you don't say when the day's long enough . . ." She shook her head. "Of course I want you." She starred at Anita's breasts, which were still heaving with her sobs. "I showed you that well enough today, didn't I?" She reached for Anita and pulled her close. "I'd be glad to show you again right now," she said, kissing Anita forcefully. "Where's that bathroom again?"

"No, Marlene, please, no," whispered Anita. "Not in the restroom."

"It doesn't matter where," said Marlene. "Main thing is, it's hot." She grabbed at Anita between the legs. "Are you still wet from before?"

"I love you, Marlene," whispered Anita. "Please, tell me . . . tell me that you love me, too. Just once."

"Of course I do, honey," said Marlene. Her eyes flickered. "I'm going to love you right now, until you don't know what hit you."

"That's not what I mean," said Anita softly. "I –"

"Come on." Marlene grabbed her wrist and pulled her along behind her. "I can't wait any more."

Rick and Thea

Rick was watching Chris and Sabrina dance. Even there, you could clearly see their love on display. They looked into each other's eyes as if they'd just met, their bodies merged in their movement with the music, and they seemed to be bound together so tightly that nothing could separate them.

Rick sighed. *Why can't that happen to me for once?* she thought. *True love – but it will.* Involuntarily, her gaze swung over to the bar. Melly ... Melly? Melly and Thea? She gawked at the two women, who seemed to be enjoying a brilliant conversation with one another. Melly laughed – and Thea did, too.

What drove Thea here? Rick hadn't expected to see her again this evening. And with Melly, at that.

Thea watched Rick out of the corner of her eye. Standing at the edge of the dance floor, Rick was contemplating the dancers with a wistful look. Finally, she looked Thea's way. *Yes!* Thea wanted to cry out, but she restrained herself, and continued her conversation with Melly.

"You really get some very interesting glimpses into lesbian life at Sappho," she said. "I can make good use of them in my reporting."

"All you really have to do for that here in Cologne is walk across the street," said Melly. "There are lesbians and gays everywhere."

"The gay men at Pride – were you there this year?" asked Thea.

"No." Melly shook her head. "I was somewhere else."

"Well, that doesn't really matter. It's the same every year," said Thea. "An extra session of Carnival."

"Yes, the gay guys do like to dress up," said Melly. "Lesbians, not so much." She looked out across the dance floor, and her gaze seemed to stop there a while.

"Unfortunately," said Thea. "The gay guys are always so much fun. I sometimes wish lesbians were more like that."

"Yeah." Melly didn't seem to be listening. Her gaze still lingered at the edge of the dance floor.

"Although – what would they dress up as? Princesses?" Thea laughed.

"Yes, that's true." Melly laughed also. "That wouldn't look very good on most of them."

Thea caught some movement out of the corner of her eye. "Have you known Rick long?" she asked quickly.

"Hmm." Melly wiped the counter with a cloth. "Relatively."

"Actually, you know everyone here at Sappho pretty well, don't you?" asked Thea.

"More or less," said Melly vaguely. "That's the nature of the beast."

"Yes, of course." Thea made an effort not to be obvious about noticing Rick's approach.

"What are you doing here, Thea?" asked Rick.

"I was just saying that I enjoy the ... seeing the women here dancing," Thea replied innocently.

"I find it very irritating that you actually showed up," said Rick.

"Rick." Melly looked at her. "If you have something private to discuss, do it outside. I don't want any trouble in here."

"I'm not making any trouble," said Rick. Her jaws were clenched. "Thea is the problem."

"I don't see it that way," said Melly. "Thea and I were just having a conversation. Before you came over, everything was fine."

"Fine?" Rick stared at Melly. Then she turned her gaze to Thea. "Ah, so that's how it is."

"You don't know what you're talking about," said Melly. Thea remained silent. "I think you've had a bit too much to drink. Maybe you ought to go home."

"To clear the way for you two?" Rick looked angrily from Thea to Melly, and back again.

"Don't make a fool of yourself, Rick," said Melly. "I chat with all of my guests."

"A bit more attentively with some, right?" Rick peered directly into Melly's eyes. "Just like you did with me." She glanced at Thea. "And now – with her?"

Melly sighed. "I have nothing more to say about this." She turned around and went into the kitchen.

Rick stared after her, then turned to face Thea. "What do you want?" she asked. "Did you get what you wanted?"

"I didn't want anything." Thea lifted her hands. "Just a little conversation, maybe some dancing – that's all."

"Likely story," said Rick through gritted teeth.

"There's no way I could have known you would be here," said Thea. "This afternoon, you seemed to be saying that coming here wouldn't mean much to you."

"You knew exactly –" Rick broke off. "Fine, then. Was that it?"

"Don't put on airs, Rick," said Thea. "You're acting like it was my fault, what happened this afternoon – or didn't happen, or whatever. I really don't know what your issue is. It was your decision, that you can't deal with my bisexuality ... or don't want to. As far as I'm concerned, everything could have gone on the same as it was."

"Yes, naturally." Rick made a hollow sound.

"Yes – *naturally*," Thea repeated pointedly. "That's what it is ... for both of us."

Rick stared at her, speechless. "When you're right, you're right," she said then, suddenly. "I apologize for my behavior."

"Rick ..." Thea stroked Rick's eyebrows with one finger. "Can't we just pick up where we left off? Now that you know, everything is much simpler. We can practice safer sex, if you want. Although I can assure you –"

"It's not about that," said Rick.

"No?" Thea frowned. "So what is it?"

"Bi women are unreliable," said Rick.

"That's a cliché," said Thea. "Why should we be any more unreliable than anyone else?"

"When a man turns up, you're gone," said Rick. She sat down on the barstool next to Thea and rubbed her temples.

"Says who?" answered Thea. "And by the way: Why would that bother you? You didn't want to have anything more to do with me anyway. Actually, you didn't want to from the start."

"How astonishing that you noticed," said Rick. Her temples were buzzing more and more.

"Yes," said Thea seriously. "I did notice."

"So then why did you –?" Rick waved it away. "It's not important." She stood up. "I have to leave. My head is about to explode. I think I'm coming down with a cold."

"I'm good at rubbing salve on chests." Thea grinned.

Rick threw her a brief glance. "I bet you are. Say hello to Chris and Sabrina when they come back. You can tell them I'll call."

"Shouldn't I take you home?"

Rick shook her head. "No, Thea, really. It's over."

Thea gazed after her as Rick departed from Sappho.

"Man, things are really getting hot in here!" Ina laughed as she rubbed her hands to dry them.

"How so?" Carolin looked quizzical.

"In the stall at the back," said Ina. She was still smiling and shaking her head. "Two gals were going at it in there, good grief . . . panting and moaning just like a porno."

"Huh." Carolin grinned a bit awkwardly. "That happens once in a while."

Ina's eyebrows rose. "It's not entirely unfamiliar to you?"

"Hmm," murmured Carolin, looking vaguely off into space.

Ina encircled her waist and pulled her close. "Are you naughty like that?" She ran her lips along Carolin's cheek. "Should we try it, too?" Her hand massaged Carolin's breast, her thumb stroking the hard nipple.

Carolin stifled a moan. "Maybe we should go form a choir with the others?" she asked with an effort.

"Why not?" Ina laughed once again. "I have no objection." Her hand caressed Carolin's backside.

Carolin shut her eyes. Although they had only just gotten out of bed to come to Sappho, each touch of Ina's brought Carolin immediately back to incandescence. "Me neither," she whispered.

"Where's Rick?" asked Chris when she returned to the bar, flushed from dancing, and saw Thea.

"She left," said Thea. "She's not feeling very well. She said she might be coming down with a cold."

"Ah," said Chris. She gave an expressive look to Sabrina, whose mouth was twitching at the corners. "A beer," Chris ordered from the server behind the bar. "A large one. It's hot on that dance floor!" She laughed and gazed at Sabrina.

Sabrina smiled. "Would you order me a water?" she asked.

Chris nodded and turned back to the bartender.

"Rick said I should tell you hello. She'll call you," said Thea.

"Hmhm." Sabrina looked back toward the dance floor.

"She didn't leave because of me," said Thea. "I think she really is getting sick. She had a bad headache."

"That's none of my business," said Sabrina. "You don't have to explain anything to me."

"You're sitting on an awfully high horse," said Thea bitterly. "It's pretty easy for you – four years with the same woman."

"Pardon me." Sabrina turned toward her. "I didn't mean it that way." She examined Thea's face. "You really like Rick," she declared, astonished.

"Oh, yes." Thea took a deep breath. "That I do."

"I didn't know," said Sabrina. "I thought –"

"I know what you thought," said Thea. "Everyone thinks that."

"I'm sorry." Sabrina gave Thea a consoling pat on the arm.

Chris, handing her the glass of water she'd ordered, looked at her in amazement.

"I'll drop by Rick's in the morning sometime," said Sabrina. "Maybe she'll need medicine or something."

"Really?" asked Chris, still amazed.

"Really," confirmed Sabrina, looking at her.

Chris let her gaze rest on Thea for a few seconds.

"What are you staring at?" hissed Thea furiously. "Never seen a bi woman before?" She threw some money on the counter and stormed out.

Chris gave Sabrina a bewildered look. "What was that all about?"

"She's in love with Rick," said Sabrina. "Apparently pretty badly."

"Oh," said Chris.

"Yes." Sabrina sighed. "That's what I thought." She looked toward the dance floor. "Ooh, look who's coming," she said, grinning.

"Hello, you two." Carolin stepped up to them, smiling. "We found you after all."

Sabrina grinned even wider. "It wasn't that hard," she said.

Carolin cleared her throat self-consciously. "May I introduce you? This is –"

"Hello, Chris," said Ina.

"Hello, Ina." Chris appeared petrified.

"You know each other?" Carolin looked from one to the other.

"In passing," said Chris with an unmoving face.

"Do you still remember Rome?" asked Ina, smiling.

"Also, only in passing," said Chris, standing up and heading for the restroom.

"You met Chris in Rome?" Carolin asked Ina.

"Yes." Ina laughed. "That was years ago, an eternity. We were both hitchhiking across Europe with just our backpacks and we met in one of those mattress camps." She shook her head. "Officially, of course, it was a youth hostel, but it was just one mattress after another on the floor. And you had to watch like hell that you didn't lose your pack, or at least its contents. Turn around once and everything would be gone." She laughed again. "We were just kids then. Hardly had anything to lose."

"I didn't even know Chris had ever been to Rome," said Carolin with a questioning look at Sabrina.

"Neither did I," murmured Sabrina.

Chapter 11
Melly

"**I**s Ina gone?" Melly slid an espresso across the counter to Carolin.

"Yes." Carolin sighed. "Last night. But she's coming back next weekend." A happy smile spread across her face.

"You're not taking turns?"

"No." Carolin shook her head. "I offered, but she says she likes coming here. There's more to do here than in Kassel."

"I'll bet." Melly laughed. "And?" She tilted her head to one side. "Was it worth the wait?"

Carolin turned red. "Yes."

"She looks like a model. That's unusual."

"Yes." Carolin sighed even deeper than the first time. "When we were here the night before last, quite a few people noticed that."

"It's hard to overlook," said Melly. "Are you afraid someone is going to steal her away from you?"

"Oh, yes!" Carolin let her head fall to the counter. "I'd rather not take her anywhere at all."

"Yes, it's nice to stay in bed, too," grinned Melly.

"Hmm." Carolin turned even redder.

"That's where you were most of the time, isn't it?" Melly was amusing herself royally. She ruffled Carolin's hair. "That's completely normal at the beginning. And sometimes beautiful women are, too – completely normal, I mean. They aren't all constantly hunting for their next conquest."

"I hope so." Carolin straightened up. "I have to go. The espresso is starting to take effect; I can at least go to work." She smiled. "It's going to be a sleepy Monday today."

"You'll survive. And tonight you can get a good night's sleep," laughed Melly.

Carolin waved and left.

Melly went back to the kitchen. "Have you set the menu for today?" she asked the cook.

"Yes." Evelyn looked up. "There were fresh pumpkins at the wholesale market this morning, really nice produce. So there's cream of pumpkin soup." Melly made a face. The cook laughed. "Just because you don't like it, does that mean the guests can't have any?"

Melly shook her head. "It's your decision," she said. "You're the chef."

"There's pumpkin ravioli, too, by the way," said Evelyn. "I'm just about done with the dough."

"You're really trying to do me in today, aren't you?" Melly laughed. "Ev, Ev. Tell me again why I hired you."

"Because you couldn't find anyone better?" Evelyn winked.

"I'm very glad," said Melly. "Since you've been here, Sappho's cuisine has risen to a whole different level."

"You didn't really have a real chef before." Evelyn shrugged. "Improving on that wasn't exactly rocket science."

"Perhaps not," smiled Melly. "But then again, maybe you're just good." She stood next to Evelyn at the stove. "Looks delicious."

"Yes." Evelyn looked at her.

Melly cleared her throat and stepped back. "I'll leave you to your realm, then. You clearly don't need me in here." She left the kitchen quickly.

Evelyn watched her go. "I wouldn't exactly say that," she murmured.

Chapter 12
Sabrina

"I'm pleased to see so many of you here for our reading," said the dark-haired woman who was tugging nervously at her glasses. "Anna Lessing … the new star in the lesbian literary heavens …" she turned to the author sitting next to her at a bistro table that was barely large enough for microphone and books, "is honoring us this evening by reading from one of her books. We're very proud to have been able to get her for this reading. And now, enjoy." She withdrew, visibly relieved, and left the field to the author.

"First of all, I want to add my own warm welcome to all of you," said Anna Lessing with a smile. "I hope you'll enjoy what I have to read."

What a voice, thought Sabrina. *If her writing is just as erotic –*

Someone sat down next to her. She glanced only briefly to the side, taken by surprise. "Anita?" she whispered.

"I want to apologize to you," Anita whispered back. "Later." Her eyes motioned toward the author, who had already begun to read.

Sabrina nodded in wonderment and turned her attention back to the woman with the erotic voice.

Suddenly, there was some movement in the back rows, and a moment later, an extra chair was added to the ones already set up.

"Thea." Sabrina spoke the name aloud in her surprise.

The author stopped reading and cleared her throat. "If the three ladies in the back have something important to share with the audience, maybe they should come up to the front," she said with an easy smile.

"Pardon me." Thea rose halfway. "I'm Thea Funk, I'm a journalist. I arrived late because my broadcast was on the air and I couldn't get away earlier. Would you be so kind as to grant me an interview after the reading?" She laughed so winningly that Anna Lessing nodded.

"If I may continue reading now . . ." she said.

"Please." Thea sat down.

"When I saw her that morning, it was as though I were suddenly at one with nature, at one with life," read Anna Lessing.

Yes. Sabrina leaned back. *That's how it is when you fall in love. Why doesn't it stay that way?* She shrank back from her own thoughts and stared ahead, as if she hadn't thought them but Anna Lessing had spoken them instead.

"She was everything that I wanted, that I had ever wished for."

Of course, that's how it is. Chris is everything that I want and that I've ever wished for. Sabrina didn't want the next thought to take shape, but it forced itself forward, superimposed on the text being read in the background. *But am I that to her, also?* She bit her lip. *Sometimes I don't feel like I am. Not anymore.*

She and Chris had been a couple for so long that she could hardly imagine anything different. But she felt like part of a couple less and less often these days; on the contrary, she often felt alone, as if she were single.

Chris made an effort, indeed, a considerable one. When she thought of it and had the time. Time – that was the problem.

"I always wanted to be with her."

Yes! Yes, that captured it. Not quite every minute of the day, but at least in the evening, at least at night.

But now, almost always, Chris came home in the middle of the night, dead tired and hardly capable of conducting a conversation or even just listening. She fell into bed and fell right asleep, and the next day, she got up at an ungodly early hour and was gone before Sabrina was even awake.

She didn't want to disturb Sabrina, was what she offered as her excuse, she didn't want to tear Sabrina from her slumber so early, she wanted to be considerate.

This was of course very thoughtful of her, but sometimes ... sometimes, Sabrina wished Chris weren't so considerate – that she'd wake her up and take possession of her, and passionately, show her that she could hardly bear to be apart from her. Mornings were precisely when Sabrina was most in the mood for sex – but Chris was never there.

Or sometimes Sabrina would've liked simply to sit with Chris at the breakfast table – and not just on weekends. But even that time together was becoming rarer and rarer; Chris was working week-ends more and more often.

Sabrina had asked Chris to spend this evening with her, to come with her to the reading, to give her the gift of some time together. With every sign of genuine regret, Chris had referred to the new project for which she still had to draw the plans. By tomorrow.

Initially, Sabrina had seen Chris' architectural career as an ad-vantage. She had hoped that someday Chris would build them a house that fulfilled their every wish, a nest for the two of them.

Chris had promised that again and again, but all the other projects took precedence... of course, she had to earn the money first. But nothing was that simple, these days.

Sabrina had accepted this ... and accepted it ... and accepted it. Every time.

She loved Chris. She knew that she'd loved her since the first time she'd laid eyes on her, and nothing had changed there. And the problem wasn't about sex, either – even though there was a lack in that department, too, because Chris so rarely showed inter-est or was even awake enough for it. It was about attention; the very thing that makes a relationship a relationship. The together-ness.

She had no doubt that Chris loved her. She said it often enough, and Sabrina knew she wasn't lying. But Chris' "I love you, sweetie" and a companionable kiss before she rolled over and went to sleep, after she'd just gotten home a few minutes earlier – that wasn't quite Sabrina's idea of love.

Around her, everyone began to applaud. She startled awake, as though from a dream. She'd followed nothing at all of the last part of the reading. But then, she was planning to buy the book anyway.

"Isn't she great?" asked Anita radiantly. "Such a wonderful woman!"

"Yes." Sabrina looked toward the front and saw Thea speaking with Anna Lessing. Presumably, she was trying to secure an interview with the author for her radio program.

"Sabrina, I ... I just wanted to say that I'm sorry," continued Anita, the radiance disappearing from her face. "I want to apologize. You were absolutely right."

Sabrina frowned at her. "About what?" she asked. She felt she was missing a connection somewhere.

"About ... Marlene," Anita answered hesitantly.

"Oh. Yes. I'm sorry," said Sabrina.

"You shouldn't be." Anita sighed. "I was stupid. As always."

"That's nonsense, Anita!" Sabrina was suddenly annoyed; she didn't know why. "You are not stupid."

"No, in some ways I am, unfortunately," said Anita. "I always fall for the same men – and now, for the same kind of woman."

"Marlene is your first woman?" Sabrina gaped at her.

"Yes." Anita looked at the floor.

"Well, didn't you luck out," said Sabrina, ironically.

"I know. You're right. You tried to be my friend and warn me, but I didn't want to listen. I thought ..." Anita swallowed, "I thought it would be different with a woman. But it isn't."

Sabrina laughed dryly. "Not with that kind of woman! There are others, though."

"Yes." Anita looked at her. "You were lucky. You and Chris, you love each other, you understand each other, you're always there for each other. That's how I always imagined it would be for me, too."

Always there for each other. Sabrina wanted to groan. It might look that way from the outside, but in reality ... "So you finally broke up with her?"

"I ..." Anita dropped her gaze again. "I know I have to."

"You still haven't –?" Sabrina shook her head. "Then what did you apologize to me for? It didn't accomplish anything."

"No," said Anita. "It did accomplish something. I thought about it."

"Well, good." Sabrina sighed. "If that's enough for you ..." *And me? Is it enough for me? Aren't I behaving just like Anita?*

"It ... it ... I can't just leave her in the lurch," said Anita unhappily. "She's so helpless."

"Helpless?" Sabrina couldn't stop shaking her head. "Marlene?"

"You don't know her," said Anita. "She's ... well, she hasn't had much good happen in her life."

"And neither have you, I would assume," said Sabrina. "But is that any reason to act the way Marlene does?"

"She can't help it," said Anita.

"In any event, she should thank God or whoever else for such an understanding woman!" Sabrina erupted angrily. "Who is so supportive of her, so she can carry on as always." *I'm not mad at her, I'm mad at myself. I'm scolding her, but it's not like I do any better. I have to talk to Chris.* "I'm sorry. I didn't mean to yell. I just think you should —" She broke off. *What am I giving her advice for? I should be setting an example for her, and I can't.* "Just do what's best for you. Only you can know what that is."

"Thank you," said Anita. "You really are a good friend." She smiled shyly.

"Any time," replied Sabrina. "Call me if you need me." She stood up. "I'm going to buy the book. Maybe I'll even get an autograph."

"Oh, yes, me too." Anita beamed again. "I've never gotten to meet an author in person, before. Although I read like crazy."

"Well, then, this is a first for both of us," said Sabrina. "I've never met any authors either. Except Thea, but she's a journalist; that's not the same thing."

"Exactly." Anita followed her as Sabrina went to the table where Anna Lessing was sitting and signing her books.

A couple of women were standing there, asking questions and getting a book signed. Sabrina reached for the top book on the pile and paid for it with the bookseller who was standing nearby. When it was her turn, she laid the book on the table in front of Anna Lessing.

"What name should I put down?" asked Anna Lessing. "For . . .?"

"Sabrina," said Sabrina.

"Sabrina." Anna Lessing looked at her with interest. "That's a lovely name."

"Oh, well." Sabrina shrugged. "Not exactly uncommon."

Anna Lessing's lips curled. "The name doesn't have to be uncommon, only the woman who wears it."

Sabrina very nearly blushed. "I'll have to tell my wife that the next time she mistakes me for another Sabrina."

"Oh. I see." Anna Lessing looked at her hand. "You're married."

"Yes." Sabrina turned the wedding band around on her finger as though she were about to take it off. "For a long time."

"How nice for you," said Anna Lessing, sliding the signed book over to her. "Sabrina . . ." She drew the name out, almost to infinity.

Sabrina could tell that she was really blushing now. She picked up the book quickly and walked to the rear of the bookshop.

What was this woman thinking? Coming on to her like that? Even after she knew she was married? Were there no boundaries anymore?

A wedding ring wasn't one, anyhow. Not for Anna Lessing.

ೞೞ

"**I** reserved a table at the pizzeria," said the bookseller, after most of the reading's attendees had left. "Whoever wants to can come along."

"Shall we?" Thea looked at Sabrina and Anita. "I'm always hungry after a broadcast."

"Absolutely!" Anita beamed from ear to ear. "We definitely can't pass that up."

"I think I'll just go home," said Sabrina.

"Oh, no!" Anita seemed disappointed. "I was so looking forward to talking with you some more."

"I thought you'd rather talk to someone else," said Sabrina, grinning slightly, with a glance at Anna Lessing.

"Yes, that too." Anita's voice drifted down to a sigh. "That voice . . ." Her gaze was fixed on Anna Lessing's mouth.

"She bowls people right over with that voice." Thea laughed. "Come on, Sabrina. Why do you want to go home now?"

"Chris is there," said Sabrina. "She said she still has to prepare a couple of blueprints for tomorrow."

"Then she won't have time for you anyhow," said Thea. "Right?" She looked questioningly at Sabrina.

"No, probably not." Sabrina sighed. "I suppose it'd be better if I went with you."

CB℘

"Come, have a seat." Anna Lessing smiled at Sabrina.

Sabrina looked at the empty place the writer had just offered her, but she didn't move.

Anna's lips twitched. "Are you afraid of me?"

Sabrina raised her eyebrows. "Why should I be?" She sat down forcefully on the chair.

"I thought you were," said Anna. "You ran away pretty fast, earlier."

"There were others waiting in line for autographs." Sabrina reached for the menu and opened it.

"Mm hmm," said Anna, and the corners of her mouth twitched even more. She bent slightly toward Sabrina. "Did I embarrass you then?"

"No," said Sabrina. She tried to comprehend the descriptions of the dishes on the menu, but Anna's proximity rattled her. "Here." She snapped the menu shut and pushed it over to Anna. "I'm sure you want something to eat, too."

"I already know what I want," said Anna, looking at her very directly.

Sabrina swallowed. "I'm married, Anna." She dropped her voice low enough that others wouldn't be able to hear her, she hoped.

"Have you forgotten?"

"I wasn't planning to propose," Anna replied with a smile.

Sabrina looked at her directly for the first time since she'd entered the pizzeria. Anna's eyes twinkled mockingly. "I love my wife," said Sabrina, irritated.

Anna laughed lightly. "I hope so, otherwise you wouldn't be the woman I take you to be." Her hand settled onto Sabrina's knee.

Sabrina shoved the hand away. "Thea?" She cast a glance down to the other end of the table. "Could you switch places with me? It's a little drafty over here, and you have a shawl."

"You can have the shawl," said Thea.

"No." Sabrina stood up. "I'd rather switch."

"Okay." Thea stood up as well and came over to Sabrina.

Sabrina went past her and tried to ignore Anna Lessing's mocking smile. What was that about? Why wouldn't she leave her alone? And why was she feeling so unsettled?

Sabrina sat down next to Anita.

"Couldn't you have asked me?" whispered Anita. "You had the best seat, and you just gave it up?"

"If you think that that's the best seat, you can ask Thea if she'll switch with you," said Sabrina.

"Is the draft really that uncomfortable over there?" asked Anita, frowning.

"Yes, it is ... uncomfortable," replied Sabrina. For the second time, she reached for the menu, and this time she had no problem concentrating on it – until she looked up and into Anna's waiting eyes. Anna had apparently been watching her the entire time. Her mocking smile had become even more so – if that were possible.

Once Anna was certain that Sabrina had noticed, she turned to Thea and started a conversation with her.

Sabrina asked herself why she didn't just leave immediately. Chris might be done with the blueprints by now, and maybe she wasn't so tired tonight ...

She closed her eyes briefly. Chris was in her thoughts, smiling at her. Not mockingly like Anna Lessing, but lovingly, tenderly, the way she always did. Her smile had nothing hidden behind it; it was open and honest.

Anna, on the other hand ... Sabrina opened her eyes again. This time she was lucky, and Anna was not looking directly at her. She was still talking to Thea.

"I'm wavering between pizza and lasagna," said Anita. "What are you having?"

"Me?" Sabrina looked back at the menu. "Pizza probably," she said absently.

"Then I'll take the lasagna." Anita smiled mischievously. "In the hope that you'll share some of your pizza with me. I like to do half-and-half."

"Yes, sure." Sabrina answered automatically, without actually knowing what it was Anita had said.

The waitress came and took their orders, which took a while, since quite a few people had accepted the invitation to come to the pizzeria.

Sabrina determined with relief that Anna Lessing was no longer paying attention to her. *She just needed a little distance*, she thought. *I simply should not have sat down next to her.*

"I'm sure her book is great," said Anita. "She writes such gorgeous romances." She sighed softly. "If it weren't for books like those ..."

"Then we'd have to make more of an effort in reality," concluded Sabrina, laughing gently. "Maybe that's the problem." *Yes, maybe that's it.* She was quite taken aback by her realization. A book could never replace reality, after all. But maybe it could serve as a model.

Chris didn't like to read romance novels, and she always made fun of Sabrina for doing so. But even Sabrina found very little of what was available for sale to be any good. It seemed like the authors dealt more with problems than with their solutions – and far too little with feelings.

If the reading had given a fair preview of Anna's novel, then this book was different. It was just the way Sabrina wanted it to be. Love, feelings – and sex. Exactly the right combination.

Sabrina cast another glance in Anna's direction. Did Anna live the way she wrote? Was she really so sensitive, so romantic? Thus far, Sabrina hadn't gotten that impression.

"Yes, reality ..." said Anita. "It, unfortunately, is no novel." The corners of her mouth suddenly turned downward.

Sabrina took a deep breath. "No, it isn't. But it also depends on what we make of it." She placed a hand on Anita's arm. "It's all up to us." *Who am I trying to convince? Her, or myself?*

Anita sighed. "I know that. But I'm –" Her gaze sank to the table. "My last boyfriend said I should be happy that he'd paid any attention to me at all. After all, I was just a little shopgirl who never even went to college." She looked miserably at Sabrina. "He was a medical student."

"And a pig," said Sabrina contemptuously. "How could anyone say something like that to his girlfriend?"

"I don't know if I really was his girlfriend," said Anita. "We were together for two years, but ... but he never introduced me to his friends. I was never allowed to go with him to any of his doctor parties. He said he didn't want to make a fool of himself."

Sabrina gaped at Anita. "And you put up with that for two years?"

Anita shrugged. "What was I supposed to do?"

"Shoot him. What else?"

"But he was right. Other boys I was with told me the same thing."

"Why was he with you, if he found you so embarrassing?" Sabrina asked angrily.

Anita lowered her gaze back to the table.

Sabrina made a disdainful sound. "The sex didn't embarrass him, did it?"

"No." Anita spoke softly. "I thought that was a normal relationship. I came home from work, I cooked, we ate, and then –"

"If you were having fun ..." Sabrina thought about what it would be like if Chris came home every day and their relationship played out like that.

"Fun ... no, I wasn't having any fun," Anita replied. "I thought that was normal, too. That's what I'd heard from other women."

"Oh, good heavens," said Sabrina. "What kind of women were they?"

"Women like me," said Anita. "My coworkers."

"And you never asked yourselves –?" Sabrina shook her head. "Wasn't there a single one of you –?"

"No." Anita shook her head also. "Not a single one."

"Whoa. Tough." Sabrina looked at Anita. "And then you thought, maybe it would be better with a woman?"

"Marlene ... she came into the department store and wanted driving gloves, warm ones, for her work ... I helped her find some, and then she asked me out for coffee."

"Yeah, Marlene's a real charmer, no doubt," said Sabrina derisively.

Anita flinched. "Marlene is ... she was very nice to me. With her, for the first time, I –" Her face slowly turned red.

Sabrina stopped short. "You'd never ...?"

"No," said Anita, very faintly. "Never."

"Oh." For a moment, Sabrina didn't know what to say. "Well, then ..." she cleared her throat, "now I understand a few things better. But that's no reason to let Marlene treat you like that medical student did before. It really isn't."

"It was so nice at the beginning." Anita smiled. "She picked me some flowers in the park."

"How romantic," said Sabrina with an incredulous look. "She couldn't afford a flower shop?"

"It was the first time I'd ever gotten flowers."

"You really don't expect much, do you?" Sabrina sighed. "But now she apparently isn't stealing any more flowers for you, and sex isn't everything." *I'm saying this, of all people?* She wondered at herself.

"I'm probably ... just ... not good enough," Anita said hesitantly, ashamed.

"At what? In bed?" Sabrina stared at her. "Did Marlene say that?"

"No, she –" Anita wasn't even looking at the table now, but at the floor. "Every time, she told me I was –"

"I know how she talks." Sabrina waved her off. "You don't have to repeat it." She shook her head. "So, then, you're only staying with her because you ... because she –" She couldn't comprehend it.

"She ... she's the only one who ... who ever managed it with me," whispered Anita, red with shame. "Everyone else said I was frigid."

"Men," said Sabrina. "What do they know about it?"

"I ... I think it's my fault," said Anita quietly. "Marlene can't make it happen anymore, either."

"You can't be serious," said Sabrina.

"I'm too slow. It was always like that with the men, and now with Marlene . . . also."

"Did you ever tell her that?" asked Sabrina. "I mean, that you weren't – that she should wait for you?"

"She couldn't," said Anita. "None of them can. And it's my fault, anyway."

"No, no, Anita!" Sabrina was furious. "It's not your fault. You said it worked at the beginning. So how could it be you?" She frowned at Anita. "And Marlene doesn't say anything about it? She must notice."

"No . . . she . . . she . . . doesn't notice." Anita's shoulders drooped even more. "She's always so wrapped up in herself, and when she . . . when she wants me to . . . then I just do it."

"You do what?" Sabrina looked at her in bewilderment. Then, suddenly, her expression cleared. "You fake an orgasm for her?" She still seemed not quite able to believe it.

"Of course. That's what I've always done when they wanted it."

Probably better than being called frigid, thought Sabrina. Although she could hardly imagine such a thing. "Oh, man," she said.

"You see, it is me," said Anita with conviction. "You don't have to do that, no one has to do that, it's just me."

"It's true that I've never done it," said Sabrina, "but as you said yourself, there certainly are other women who do. Your coworkers, for instance."

"Yes, that's true," said Anita, and it seemed to put her back in a better mood.

"But that doesn't mean that it's good, that it's right," said Sabrina indignantly. "Good grief, talk to Marlene, leave her, but don't do this to yourself."

"It's not all that bad. You probably see it that way, but I . . . I've done it my whole life. That's just the way it is."

"That doesn't make it any better."

"Pizza Regina, lasagna?" A woman's questioning voice interrupted the conversation.

"Yes, here." Sabrina leaned back. "The pizza."

"And I'm the lasagna." Anita laughed. "Finally!"

Sabrina marveled at how quickly Anita's mood could change. She told the most awful stories – at least, Sabrina found them awful – and the next moment, she seemed completely untouched, on cloud nine. *You probably have to be that way when you're with Marlene*, thought Sabrina. But she just couldn't fully imagine a life like that.

But is my life any better? Of course, I don't have to fake orgasms, but I do have to beg for every single one. Isn't that six of one and half a dozen of the other?

During the meal, the talk didn't stop completely, but they did confine themselves for a time to the necessities. While the servers were clearing the table, another mocking gaze from Anna struck Sabrina.

I have to get out of here, thought Sabrina. *I can't stand this anymore.* She stood up. "Would you make sure mine gets paid for?" she asked Anita. She laid some money on the table. "I think this should cover it."

"You're leaving already?" Anita looked up at her, startled.

"Yeah, I'm tired." Sabrina didn't want to get involved in any more discussions, and most definitely not in front of Anna, who was no longer letting her out of her sight.

She went to the coatroom to get her jacket.

She pulled it on, and suddenly, soft arms were reaching around her waist from behind.

"Please don't," whispered Sabrina. She felt weak and defenseless.

"Why not?" whispered Anna's voice. The small corridor was narrow and dark; no one could see them.

"Because it's not right," Sabrina whispered back.

Anna's hands caressed her hips, her waist, wandered higher. "Who knows what's right?" Smooth fingers touched the curves of Sabrina's breasts.

"I . . . I can't." Sabrina shuddered.

Anna turned Sabrina around to face her. She said nothing more, but pulled her close and kissed her. "I've been wanting to do that all evening," she murmured. Her erotic voice sent one thrill after another through Sabrina's body.

Holding her close, Sabrina examined Anna's face. Anna's eyes still seemed to be mocking her, but even plainer to see was the desire within. "I ..." Sabrina placed her hands on Anna's face, caressed it. She was captivated by Anna's lips, feeling almost magnetically drawn to them. Reality blurred, and she bent forward and kissed Anna in return.

Anna held her tightly in her arms, stroking her along her back to her bottom, pressing her center into her. "Sabrina," she whispered huskily.

Sabrina felt the flames blazing inside — that didn't take long — but it was ... wrong. The wrong woman. Nevertheless, she took pleasure in Anna's caresses, gave herself over to them, sighing. She simply couldn't hold herself back. It felt so good, and she had missed it so much.

Anna caressed Sabrina's leg, parted her thighs, pressed herself between them. "Sabrina," she whispered again. "Come ..." Her hand began to tug Sabrina's blouse from her waistband.

"No." Sabrina tore herself away suddenly and stared at Anna. Her breath came heavily. "We can never do this again!"

She fled the pizzeria at a dead run.

What have I done? Stricken with guilt, Sabrina sat for half an hour in her car in front of the door, not daring to enter the apartment. *It was nothing. Just a kiss, a few caresses ...*

She knew it had been more than that. She had yearned to give herself to Anna, to forget everything, to know no boundaries.

But the boundaries were real. She was a married woman, and Chris had ... Chris had done nothing to deserve this. Chris loved her. Wasn't that the most important thing?

Yes, it was. Love was ... love was ... not this animalistic grunting in the corridor outside the back room. Love was much more. She and Chris ... they had everything. Others envied them.

She had no reason to complain, and that was the worst of it all.

She sighed and pushed open the car door. If Chris were still awake, she would have to talk to her, to confess everything to her ...

Confess? What? A kiss in the hall? Chris would be hurt — and for what? Because of one stupid, little, meaningless surge of emotion?

She didn't want to hurt Chris. It wasn't worth that. Chris didn't need to know. It didn't mean anything.

She entered the dark apartment, where only a tiny glimmer of light made its way out of the bedroom. *She's still awake,* thought Sabrina. *I can talk to her.*

She hesitated, then went in.

The bedside lamp gave off its diffuse light; Chris lay crosswise on the bed; blueprints were spread across her thighs. Chris was sleeping. Her head had fallen to one side, and she looked very, very tired.

Sabrina looked at her and smiled. *I love you so much, Chris.* She picked up the blueprints and set them aside. Then she undressed, turned out the light, lay down next to Chris, and snuggled close to her. *I love you. I want only you.*

She placed a hand on Chris's arm and started to caress her. She knew that Anna had called forth what she was feeling now, but she wished that Chris would wake up. Then everything would be all right. Nothing would have happened. Just the usual ... between a married couple.

As she caressed Chris, she felt her excitement rising anew. She bent over Chris and kissed her, but Chris didn't wake up.

"Chris," she whispered. "Oh, please, Chris."

But Chris was completely out of it. She registered nothing of Sabrina's presence.

Sabrina cuddled up close to Chris and tried to fall asleep. She savored Chris's warmth and tried to convince herself that she was tired.

And she was, in a way, but not enough. Not enough to fall asleep, not enough to extinguish the fire inside her. *A cold shower,* she thought, *might be the best thing.*

But she didn't want a cold shower. She wanted something entirely different. She pressed herself against Chris and began to move. "Chris, wake up," she whispered.

It was useless. Chris didn't stir. Sabrina could hardly contain herself anymore. It was simply too much. She had to do something about the tension. She opened her legs, twined them around Chris's thigh, and rubbed herself against her. That would have to wake Chris.

But it didn't. Sabrina shut her eyes. *I can't do this. I can't do this while she's lying there next to me.* And yet, she had to find a solution, somehow.

She could wake Chris by force, tear her from the sleep that she so desperately needed, or she could –

She reached between her legs and dipped into her own wetness. It was embarrassing, this wetness, since most of it was there thanks to Anna, and Anna was ... Anna was not her wife, not the woman she should desire and be desired by.

Sabrina moaned softly. "Chris," she whispered. "Chris ..." She curved herself against Chris's shoulder while her own fingers did what she wished Chris were doing. She felt ashamed, but she couldn't help it.

She felt her belly tense once, twice, three times. She suppressed a final moan, panted, gasped for air. "Chris," she whispered once more. "I love you so."

She lay there, just as she was, not touching herself anymore, and finally, a few minutes later, she fell asleep.

When she awoke the next morning, she was alone.

As usual, Chris was already gone.

CB ED

"**I**'m going now." Sabrina glanced over into her boss's office.

"Is it that time again already?" Her boss looked up as if surfacing from the depths of the ocean.

"Six o'clock," said Sabrina. She sighed internally. *I love working overtime, especially when no one notices.*

"Ah, yes," said Joachim Dillinger, the head of Dillinger & Co., after a glance at the clock on his desk. "Have a nice evening."

"Thank you," said Sabrina. "See you tomorrow."

"See you –" Joachim Dillinger had already submerged again.

Sometimes it's exactly the same with Chris, thought Sabrina. *His wife clearly doesn't have it easy, either.*

She shook her head. Had she ever dreamed that she would feel exactly like a straight wife who hardly ever saw her husband? Somehow, she had imagined things would be different.

She packed her bag and retrieved the purchases she'd stashed in the office refrigerator. She wanted to cook something special this evening, for Chris and herself. Chris needed to take some time for herself for once. Last night was ... Sabrina blushed. That wasn't what she had wanted. She never wanted to experience that again.

She glanced back once more at her cleared-off desk. Tomorrow morning the chaos would be waiting for her again. She took a deep breath. What was it that Carolin had said? That Sabrina wouldn't want it any other way.

She smiled and left the office.

When she stepped outside of the building, she didn't notice the enormous bunch of flowers that was coming toward her until it was practically right in front of her. The bouquet obscured the person behind it.

Chris! A radiant smile spread across Sabrina's face. Laughing, she walked up to the oversized bouquet.

The flowers lowered themselves. "Good evening, Sabrina," said Anna, with her usual mocking smile.

Sabrina stopped abruptly; the laughter vanished from her face. "What are you doing here? How do you know where I work?"

"It wasn't difficult to find out," said Anna, still smiling. She handed Sabrina the bouquet. "Do you like roses?"

"Red long-stemmed roses by the hundred?" Sabrina laughed dryly. She didn't take them. "I'm afraid that's asking too much of me. I don't have a vase that big."

"We could buy one," Anna replied.

"There's no reason to do that. Unless you're buying it for yourself." She walked past Anna.

Anna sauntered along next to her with the bunch of roses. "If you don't like roses, tell me what your favorite flowers are and I'll buy those instead."

"I like roses." Sabrina stopped and looked at her. "But they have to come from the right woman."

"Mm-hmm." Anna nodded. "I understand."

"It seems to me that you *don't* understand!" Sabrina raged. "How many times have I told you that I'm married, that I'm not interested? And what do you do? You simply ignore me." She moved on.

"You *told* me that you aren't interested," purred Anna, "but you *showed* me something else entirely."

"I showed you nothing!" Sabrina stopped abruptly. "You . . . you caught me unawares. I was too . . . weak to resist. But that's not going to happen a second time."

"You're beautiful when you're angry," said Anna with a smile.

"That is . . ." Sabrina gasped for air. "That is probably the most trite line I've ever heard. I thought you were a writer. Don't you have anything better?"

"Yes, I do. If you let me." Anna's mocking smile deepened.

"Get that thought right out of your head." Sabrina continued toward the bus stop. "You will never get more from me than you already have. Never, do you hear me? Frame that and hang it on your wall."

"I already have," said Anna. She seemed to be enjoying herself immensely.

The bus came the moment Sabrina reached the stop. She boarded quickly, and although the bus was already overfull, she was expecting Anna to squeeze inside with her.

But she didn't. As the bus drove off, Sabrina watched Anna's face through the large back window, still smiling with amusement as it grew ever smaller.

"I'm sorry that dinner's overcooked," said Chris guiltily. "I had no way of knowing that you —"

"I tried to call you on your cell," said Sabrina. She had a hard time concealing her disappointment.

"Yes, I know. I had it turned off because I couldn't concentrate on work," said Chris. "It kept ringing the whole time."

"I . . ." Sabrina brushed her hair out of her face. "I need to talk to you, Chris."

"I know, darling." Chris raised her eyebrows even more guiltily. "I have too little time for you — for us, but that's going to change, definitely."

"When, Chris?" asked Sabrina, sighing.

"Come here." Chris pushed back her chair and patted her thigh.

Sabrina hesitated, but then stood up, went over to Chris and sat on her lap.

Chris hugged her and pulled her close. "After this project," she said, gazing tenderly at Sabrina's face. "This one project. It's the most important of all. Once it's done, we'll have lots of time for each other."

Sabrina sighed once more.

"I know," said Chris. "You've heard that before. But this time it's true. This time it's really true." She caressed Sabrina's breast. "Come on," she whispered. "Kiss me."

Sabrina was ablaze before Chris even finished speaking. Chris only had to touch her to open all the floodgates inside. "Chris," she whispered. Her lips searched for and found Chris's mouth and kissed her.

"Love," whispered Chris. Her hand fumbled its way under Sabrina's skirt and sought her panties, then slid inside.

"Let's go to bed," breathed Sabrina with difficulty. "Please . . ."

"Soon." Chris thrust her hand between Sabrina's legs, opened them, explored her wetness.

"Oh, my God, Chris . . ." gasped Sabrina.

"I love you," whispered Chris. "You're so wonderful." Her hand pressed farther in; Sabrina felt fingers entering her and moaned aloud. "I love you," repeated Chris. Her fingers began to move in and out, and her thumb lay on Sabrina's pearl, rubbing it, pressing it.

Sabrina cried out. "Chris!"

Chris rubbed faster, thrust into her, held back, then began anew.

Sabrina gasped, clinging to Chris's shoulders, sliding back and forth on her lap. Chris kissed her throat, whispered sweet nothings, driving her to the very edge with knowing fingers.

Sabrina could no longer breathe. She sensed that her nether regions had taken control of her, that she wanted nothing more than to be near Chris, to give her everything, everything she had to give, everything she desired.

Her head felt ready to explode; the tension became unbearable; she dug her nails into Chris's shoulders, moaned, gasped, came.

Her head sank heavily onto Chris's shoulder; she nestled into her, gasping for breath.

"Again?" asked Chris, smiling.

"Yes," whispered Sabrina, "but not here – in bed. It's so uncomfortable here."

Chris didn't answer.

An uneasy feeling crept over Sabrina. She lifted her head and looked at Chris. "Oh, no."

"I ... I'm sorry," said Chris with a dreadfully unhappy expression, "but I don't have time. I have to go back to the office." She sought Sabrina's eyes. "Come," she whispered. Her fingers began caressing Sabrina again.

"No, thank you!" Sabrina rose angrily from Chris's lap. "I don't need your charity, I really don't. I told you that already."

"I know. And I didn't want to ... please understand ..."

"I understand. I understand everything. I'm the most understanding wife of all. You won't find better." Sabrina was boiling with rage.

"Sabsi ..." Chris stood up and tried to take her in her arms.

Sabrina turned away. "That's it for Sabsi. At least for today. Just go to the office. And give my regards to your drawing boards. You're apparently married to them." She went to the bedroom and shut the door behind her.

Shortly thereafter, she heard the front door close as Chris left the apartment.

She tossed and turned in bed, staring at the blanket, then out the window, then rolling back and reaching for a pillow. She hugged it, pressed it to her body, cooled her hot cheeks on the smooth linens. Suddenly, she noticed that the pillow was wet. She was crying. Truly – she was crying.

She hadn't cried in a long time. It wasn't something she wished for. And it wasn't something she wanted to get used to. Vigorously, she wiped away the tears. "No, not like this," she said aloud.

She went into the bathroom and splashed some cold water on her face. It wasn't Chris's fault. Chris was ... just plain busy. She couldn't help it. Chris wanted to live up to Sabrina's expectations, just as much as she wanted to be great as an architect. That's why she'd done . . . what she'd done earlier.

Sabrina leaned back against the bathroom wall. She reached for a towel and dried her face.

She couldn't blame Chris.

And hadn't she done worse than Chris had today? She knew that Chris was at the office now and not with someone else, she knew that for certain, but Chris – could Chris be sure of the same with Sabrina?

Of course! She flung the towel furiously into the corner. *Why am I thinking these thoughts? Just because stupid Anna Lessing showed up, chasing after me?*

Stupid Anna Lessing. Damned novels. This drivel about love and friendship and eternal faith – and no problems. No, never. The books always end just as the love affair first begins, before the difficulties start.

Yes, when you're freshly in love, there are no problems. Everything is rosy. But what happens after a couple of years? By then the daily grind has settled in. The everyday monotony. The boredom of familiarity.

Not even Romeo and Juliet could have withstood that.

Sabrina went back into the living room. She began putting away the leftovers, because she couldn't come up with a better idea to help herself calm down. She knew that if she'd left the plates sitting there, Chris would have cleared them away when she came home, no matter how tired she was.

Chris was simply . . . the perfect husband. Sabrina laughed. The perfect wife, obviously, but many heterosexual women would probably wish for a husband like that. They wouldn't be dissatisfied the way she was now.

Sabrina set the dishes down in the kitchen sink. Dissatisfied, that's what she was. This dissatisfaction had been building up in her over the past few months, maybe even years.

She was a woman full of dreams and ideas, and Chris was, too. So she had thought, if the two of them got together, there would have to be fireworks all the time.

But there weren't.

It was nice, yes. Sometimes it was tender and romantic, sometimes bland and monotonous, but she always knew that Chris was there for her. Chris was as solid as a rock. She never left her in the lurch. She didn't have much time, because she worked so many hours, but if Sabrina called her right now, if there were an emergency, Chris would come immediately. She would drop everything to take care of Sabrina.

If there were an emergency . . . Sabrina sighed. Wasn't this some kind of emergency, this longing for love?

No, it wasn't. And anyway – Chris had turned off her cell phone.

She loaded everything into the dishwasher and turned it on. Then she took a shower, went into the bedroom, and lay down on the bed. Chris wouldn't come home for a long time, she knew that. She would have to fall asleep alone – as she so often did.

A dream caught her by surprise, before she was quite aware of it. Anna Lessing was smiling at her. It wasn't the usual mocking smile; instead, it was . . . Chris's smile! But it was definitely Anna Lessing. Anna Lessing with Chris's smile, with Chris's warm eyes. A peculiar mix. Nothing fit.

Anna Lessing came up to her and said "I love you" – with Chris's voice. Anna Lessing took Sabrina in her arms and kissed her, let her go, examined her face until Sabrina yearned to be kissed yet again.

Anna Lessing's voice said "You're everything that I want, that I've ever wished for."

It was a quote from the reading – no, not exactly. The "you" hadn't been in the original text. Sabrina had added it.

"Are you Anna?" Sabrina asked the phantom. "Or Chris?"

"I'm everything," said the voice. "Everything you've been wishing for."

"Then everything's fine," Sabrina murmured in her sleep.

She ran over a meadow toward the phantom and threw herself joyously into its arms. Hadn't she just lain in those arms? How did she suddenly wind up on the other side of a meadow?

But dreams were like that.

"Then everything's fine," she murmured again. "Everything's fine."

And the dream carried her away until she no longer knew that she was dreaming.

Chapter 13

Carolin

Carolin hung up the phone and smiled. Ina . . .

She was so happy to have found this woman – the woman of her dreams. Hours-long phone conversations, romantic moments, great sex – she blushed, although she was home alone – and the prospect of seeing her again the next weekend . . . she felt intoxicated.

Of course, there was also the longing . . . the longing between the weekends, every day, every hour, every minute, but she'd have to live with that. There was no woman in Cologne for her, so it had to be one from Kassel.

She looked out the window. A gorgeous spring day. She'd been on the phone with Ina half the night, and now it was morning; the birds were chirping, the sun was gradually dawning. There wasn't really any sense in going to bed now.

That is, she was in fact still in bed, but she'd hardly slept at all. She laughed. Who needed sleep? She swung her legs over the edge of the bed and walked to the bathroom. In the shower, she switched the water back and forth between cold and warm several times, as she always did. To finish up, she showered in cold water and felt refreshed, as if she'd just slept a full eight hours.

I'll go for a walk, she thought. *It's too early for anything else.*

She dressed and went out. It was still a bit cold, but when she encountered a ray of sunlight, she could feel the power that springtime was already starting to bring.

She wandered through empty streets and looked into windows behind which no lights burned. Again and again, she thought about Ina. About how nice it would be to have her here now. She laughed softly. Then, of course, she wouldn't be going for a walk. Ina had hardly seen anything of Cologne and its surroundings, except for Sappho. She liked it best at Carolin's home, where they could devote themselves to one another, undisturbed.

At least at home she can't be seduced away from me by anyone else, thought Carolin. *That is a definite advantage.*

She smiled again. Since she'd known Ina, she was almost always smiling, a pleasant feeling of being in love that held her captive from morning to night. She was drifting on cloud nine, over a land of milk and honey.

She arrived at the small park a few streets over. By now, the sun had risen higher, the day had begun, but the paths and benches were still empty of people. Carolin turned into the park, strolled past the man-made pond, and noticed a couple of ducks sleeping at the pond's edge. They had tucked their heads down into their plumage and looked completely peaceful, as though no one could possibly wake them.

Was Ina sleeping now? Carolin smiled again, imagining Ina lying in bed fast asleep, her beautiful face framed by the pillow.

"It was worth it to buy those new bed linens." Carolin said to herself and laughed. She circled the pond and sat down on a bench on the other side, watching the birds flying dutifully from tree to tree, collecting nest materials. "Spring," she said. Yes, that's what it was: spring. And spring fever.

The male birds were starting to build nests, and trying to convince the females to move into those nests and start families.

Are there lesbian bird couples, too? thought Carolin. *Where one builds a nest for the other and then they raise the children together?* She couldn't imagine it, but anything was possible.

"Did the rose last for a while?" a voice asked suddenly.

Carolin started out of her daydreams and looked up. At first she couldn't place the woman now standing in front of her and smiling down at her, but then she remembered. "Oh, yes . . . yes, I think it did," she replied, surprised.

"Are you always out and about this early?" asked the woman from the train station.

"No, I —" Carolin broke off and smiled. "No, not always. But I was already awake, so I thought I'd take a walk before I went to work. Do you live nearby, too?"

"Yes."

That smile. Carolin glanced away. What was it, then? She had been thinking glorious thoughts about Ina, and all of a sudden this woman's smile was shining brighter than the sun, outshining Ina's face in Carolin's mind's eye. "I live just a couple of streets down, that way," she said, pointing in the direction from which she'd come.

"I live nearby too, but in the other direction. May I?" The woman indicated the empty spot on the bench next to Carolin.

Carolin scooted over a bit, to give her more room. "Of course."

The woman sat down next to her, and her scent wafted across to Carolin. Carolin shut her eyes. Was this necessary?

"I feed the ducks sometimes," said the woman, "but today they're not awake yet." She laughed gently.

"Yes, they look very sleepy." Carolin laughed as well. "I walked past earlier on the other side, very close to them, but it didn't disturb them a bit."

"They're used to people."

"Sure, here in the park."

They sat next to each other and looked out at the undisturbed surface of the pond. Suddenly, a duck flew overhead and landed on the water, creating a substantial splash.

"Ah, they're awake." The woman from the train station stood up. "I can get rid of my bread after all." She walked over to the pond and tossed a couple of chunks in, came back. "It's not much, but they're always happy to take it."

"Do you come here often?" asked Carolin.

"Almost every day." The woman turned toward Carolin and smiled at her once again. "I'm an early riser."

Carolin swallowed. After a while, she could finally speak again. "I'm not, really," she said. "But it's lovely to be up this early once in a while. Completely different from later in the day, when everyone is rushing around like crazy, and there's no quiet anymore."

"So it is." The woman turned her gaze back to the pond. "Now they're all awake. As soon as the first one gets up, the others follow. Just like people. One minute, everything is completely empty, then suddenly the masses break loose over the city, all at once."

"Unfortunately, I'm going to have to add myself to the masses soon," sighed Carolin. "To plunge myself into the swarm on the streetcar. Where we're packed like sardines in a can and have to roll over each other to get off." She laughed softly. "Same thing every morning."

"And it's especially bad in the winter," said the other. "But even in the winter I ride my bicycle as often as possible. I only use public transportation in an emergency. And now, with the weather being so nice, I don't have to at all."

"Maybe I should think about biking to work too," said Carolin. "My bike has just been sitting in the basement forever. I don't even know if it still works. You don't have a long commute?"

"On the bike, it's forty-five minutes," said the other. "So I get my workout at the same time." She gave another friendly smile.

"Forty-five minutes." Carolin was impressed. "And the same coming home?"

"Yes, otherwise I wouldn't get home again." She grinned.

"That's an hour and a half a day." Carolin shook her head in surprised wonder.

"You hardly notice it once you're used to it," the woman said. "And I'm independent. It's just me, so it doesn't make any sense to drive a car into the city. And I don't like public transportation. So the bicycle is a very good alternative."

Carolin frowned. "I work on the Ring. It might not even be forty-five minutes to there."

"Depends where on the Ring," said the other woman. "I always cross it. If you like, we could ride together sometime."

Carolin stared at her. "Together?"

"Unless, of course, you'd rather leave your bike in mothballs," the woman smiled.

Well, yes, that's what I actually intended, thought Carolin. "No, that's a good idea. I'd probably never do it on my own."

"How about tomorrow?" the other woman asked. "We'll meet here at seven o'clock and ride out together."

Carolin had no idea what came over her when she answered, "Sure, seven o'clock. No problem."

"Shall we introduce ourselves?" the other woman asked, and her smile burned itself into Carolin's retina. "My name is Rebekka. Nice to meet you."

"Ah ... yes ... Carolin," Carolin managed with an effort.

"Good." Rebekka stood up. "Then until tomorrow, Carolin. I'm looking forward to it." She smiled at Carolin once more and took herself off down the path that led out of the park.

It seemed to Carolin as though she'd just been in a scene in a movie. When she stood up now, she would exit the movie theater, and it would all be forgotten.

She knew, though, that it wasn't so. Forgetting Rebekka's smile would have been exceptionally difficult. Her smile was … extraordinary.

Carolin stood and stared at the pond. The ducks had long since polished off Rebekka's bread crumbs and were now looking at Carolin as if she were responsible for providing seconds.

"I don't have anything for you." Carolin shrugged. "But maybe next time."

Next time – that would be tomorrow, when she met Rebekka so they could ride their bicycles into the city together.

She looked at her watch. It was still too early to go to work, but breakfast at Sappho would shorten the wait and perhaps bring some order back to her whirling thoughts. It felt like a sandstorm was blowing through her head, blurring everything. What had just happened?

CRBO

"Espresso?" asked Melly as Carolin came in.

"I'd rather have hot chocolate." Carolin sat down at the counter. "I already had coffee at home."

"You're up and about early," said Melly, turning around and taking a tall mug from the shelf.

"Yes, I … hardly slept," Carolin replied hesitantly.

"Ina?" Melly smiled and set a steaming mug in front of Carolin.

Carolin felt the smile overtaking her face with relief. "Yes, Ina," she said. "We were on the phone half the night."

"Still true love, hmm?" Melly grinned. "Yes, distance does make the heart grow fonder. Sometimes, anyway."

"Well, the love might grow," Carolin sighed, "but the distance really is a problem."

"If Ina likes Cologne and there's not much going on in Kassel, why doesn't she just move here? That would solve the problem."

"She . . . we haven't talked about it yet. Her job is in Kassel, too."

"But there are plenty of jobs in Cologne. Surely more than in Kassel."

"Probably." Carolin shrugged. "But she has her family there, her circle of friends – it's not that simple."

"Yeah, if you don't want to go to Kassel, I suppose the distance is just going to have to make your love grow for a while." Melly winked.

"I've never been to Kassel. Maybe it would be worth considering."

"From Cologne to Kassel? Well, have fun with that. But you do really seem to love each other." She smiled at Carolin. "Nonetheless, I would be sad if you moved away."

"Thank you," said Carolin, embarrassed. "That's nice of you."

The door opened.

"Morning, Sabrina," said Melly. "Coffee?"

"Yes, please." Sabrina came up to the counter and leaned against it. "Strong. I didn't sleep very well."

"You too?" Melly grinned. "Someone else sitting here has been burning the candle at both ends. For love . . ." She turned to the espresso machine.

"You couldn't sleep, either?" asked Sabrina.

"No, actually . . ." Carolin sipped at her cocoa. "I was on the phone with Ina."

"Ah," said Sabrina, but she didn't smile the way Melly did. "Your long-distance lover."

"Melly claims that distance makes the heart grow fonder," said Carolin, "but it's just . . . not easy."

"Not easy," repeated Sabrina. "That's true."

Melly set a double espresso in front of her. "Extra strength."

"Thank you." Sabrina took the cup and sat at a table.

All at once, three more people came up and stood at the counter, and it felt a little too crowded for Carolin. She nodded to Melly and took her cocoa over to where Sabrina sat. "I didn't know you came here for breakfast, too. I thought you and Chris always had breakfast together."

Sabrina looked up. "Not for a long time. These days Chris is already gone when I get up in the morning."

"That's too bad." Carolin massaged the whipped cream in her cocoa with her long coffee spoon, scooped up a little of it, and licked the spoon. "Yum. I love Melly's hot chocolate."

"Do you think a person can be in love with two people at the same time?" Sabrina asked suddenly.

Carolin almost choked on her drink. "I . . . umm . . . don't know. It's never happened to me."

"Me neither," said Sabrina thoughtfully.

"Has it happened to someone we know? Or is this more of a philosophical question?"

"Oh, just in general. I wanted to hear your opinion."

"For no reason at all?" Carolin looked at her warily. "I'm not used to that kind of question from you."

Sabrina didn't answer.

"Sabrina," said Carolin. "We've been friends long enough; I can tell something's up."

"No, there isn't!" Sabrina replied defiantly.

"Aha. I understand."

"I'm married. And that means something to me."

"It would mean something to me, too," replied Carolin, "if I were married." She looked at Sabrina.

"Chris is . . ." Sabrina propped her elbows on the table and laid her head in her hands. She didn't look at Carolin. "Chris is wonderful. She reads every wish in my eyes. I can't complain."

"Chris hasn't been to Sappho in a long time."

"She . . . she has a lot to do, her work is eating her alive," said Sabrina softly.

"And you have to play second fiddle to her work," continued Carolin.

"Yes." Sabrina lifted her head. "I . . . I understand that, of course. It's for us, after all. We're putting the money away, and —"

"And you're alone and unhappy in the meantime." Carolin sighed. "Have you talked to Chris about it?"

"Over and over," Sabrina sighed, too. "She says every time that the next project is the last one, but –"

"But it never is."

"No." Sabrina took a deep breath. "I love her, Carolin," she whispered. "I love her so much. I don't want it to end this way."

"You're planning to leave her?" Carolin's eyebrows rose in astonishment.

"No!" Sabrina cried out, appalled, then propped her head on her hands again. "No," she repeated in a whisper. "I would never want to do that. By no means. She's the love of my life."

"You two are such a great couple." Carolin smiled. "You're role models for the rest of us. And there's a reason for that, too. You simply belong together. Sabrina, I'm sure the problems can be overcome. Love overcomes everything – and you honestly love each other. That's so easy to see when you're together."

"*When* we're together," Sabrina repeated slowly. "But when *are* we anymore?"

"It's that bad?"

"Yes, it's that bad." Sabrina emptied her demitasse and stood up. "I have to go. My boss has probably been burning the midnight oil himself, and I won't even be able to see my desk under all his notes. I'll have to straighten his work out first."

"Putting things in order is always good," said Carolin, and she sensed that this wasn't just true for Sabrina.

CR&SO

"That bicycle is a bit on the old side, eh?" Rebekka laughed.

Carolin blushed. "Like I said, it's been sitting in the basement for a long time." Yesterday she had cleaned it, at least superficially, but it was still obvious that the vehicle had been severely neglected.

"Let's have a look." Rebekka walked around the cycle; her scent grazed Carolin, and Carolin considered whether she shouldn't really just ride the streetcar – without Rebekka next to her. "It'll work," said Rebekka after her inspection. "And if it doesn't, we'll call the bicycle emergency service."

"Bicycle emergency service?" Carolin frowned.

"It's sort of like AAA, but for bikes, not cars," laughed Rebekka. "They can repair just about anything."

"I could definitely use that," replied Carolin. "I've never been any good at that sort of thing."

"If you like, I can sign you up as a member," said Rebekka. "Then I get a premium." She grinned. "That's what I live on."

"Yeah, sure." Carolin laughed. "Then there must be nothing but bicycle riders in Cologne."

"There are more all the time," said Rebekka. "So – shall we go?" She swung herself onto her bike and waited for Carolin.

Carolin had already been struggling to get accustomed to riding a bike again. She'd walked halfway to the park, but now, in Rebekka's presence, she could hardly afford to appear to be having difficulties. She pushed off, and as the bicycle started to roll, Rebekka started pedaling too, and was soon out of the park.

This is ridiculous, thought Carolin, keeping her eyes on the path. *What have I gotten myself into?*

Rebekka looped back. "I'm sorry. I just started out at my habitual speed; I'll adapt myself to yours."

"You don't have to. I'll manage."

"Not on *that* bike." Rebekka laughed once more. "It's no problem; I'll just ride slower."

Ωظ

"**W**hat have you been doing?" Carolin's colleague Ulrike frowned, then grinned. "Never mind, I can guess."

"It's not what you're thinking," replied Carolin, out of sorts. "I just rode a bicycle – for the first time in years."

"Yes, the first time is always the most painful," smirked Ulrike. "Should I get you another pillow?"

"No, thank you; I already feel like the princess and the pea," Carolin grumbled. She was sitting on a pile of three chair cushions like a throne high above the earth.

"Is the princess ready for a couple of manuscripts?" asked Ulrike. "Will you look through them to see if there's anything interesting there?"

"Is the editorial department overloaded again?" groaned Carolin. "I actually have plenty to do already. I'm employed as the publisher's management assistant, in case you've forgotten."

"Talk to Thomas about that. I'm just the messenger." Ulrike laid a stack of manuscripts on Carolin's desk. "He thinks you're a better judge than the editorial staff."

"All right, fine." Carolin sighed. "But this time it's going to cost him a raise."

Ulrike grinned. "If you can talk him into that, let me know, and I'll go in right behind you."

Carolin nodded. "Sure."

As soon as Ulrike left her office, Carolin grimaced in pain. On the one hand, she could hardly feel her butt anymore, but in those places where she could still feel it, she definitely *felt* it. She moaned. How on earth could she have fallen for the crazy idea of riding a bicycle for over an hour when she hadn't done it in years?

Rebekka had had a good laugh. She rode every day, and it was nothing to her, but Carolin swore to herself that this was the first and last time. This evening she was going to take the streetcar again.

Of course, she'd have to let Rebekka know. Rebekka had given Carolin her phone number so they could arrange their ride home together. Carolin picked up the receiver with a sigh and dialed.

"I'm sorry, Rebekka," she said when Rebekka answered, "but I believe certain parts of my body can't handle a return trip on the two-wheeled vehicle today. I'll take the streetcar. Please don't be mad at me."

Rebekka laughed softly. "I'm not mad at you. I expected as much. You're not the first."

"What, you regularly seduce out-of-shape women into riding bicycles?" asked Carolin a bit teasingly. She didn't know why, but all at once, her aches and pains seemed to disappear. Rebekka's voice seemed to work like a balm.

"Well, seduce might be an overstatement," replied Rebekka with the same smile in her voice as before. "I just try to convince them. And some allow themselves to be convinced."

"But most of them probably aren't in the long run," laughed Carolin. "Or are they?"

"No, unfortunately not," Rebekka responded. "Although it's just a matter of time until the body gets used to it. And bicycling is very healthy."

"I'm sure," Carolin replied. "For seat cushion manufacturers."

"Oh, come on," said Rebekka, but she obviously didn't mean it too seriously, since her voice sounded like she was grinning. "Is it that bad?"

"I think you know exactly how bad it is," Carolin muttered, "since I'm not the first. You could open a hospital and make good money from this. You'd provide all your own patients."

"That's mean," said Rebekka. "I'm only trying to help benefit humanity."

"Humanity isn't as tough as it used to be", Carolin went on. "We've become a species of wimps."

Rebekka laughed softly again, and Carolin thought: *How can a laugh sound so warm when it's only coming through telephone wires?* "I lament that everyday myself," said Rebekka. "But you're pulling my leg, right?"

"Oh, no." Carolin smiled. "The thought never crossed my mind. I'm just ashamed that I'm in no condition to ride home on my bike with you this evening, and I'm trying to put the blame on you so I can feel a little better about myself."

"You didn't tell me you were a psychologist," Rebekka teased.

"No." Carolin laughed. "I'm not a psychologist; I just work for a publisher that prints psychology books. I don't read all of them, and I hardly understand any of them. But sometimes a little armchair psychology does rub off on you. That's the extent of my expertise."

"I don't believe you," said Rebekka, somewhat cryptically. "But I am sorry that your brief bicycling career is over already. Or do you think maybe you'd like to try again in a few days . . .?"

Astonishingly, Carolin felt torn, even though a minute ago she had intended never to ride a bicycle again, ever.

"Well, since you're not going to get your toaster – or whatever it was you were going to get from the bicycle club for bringing in a new member – I'll gladly make it up to you by taking you out to eat. In a few days. As soon as I can sit on a regular chair again," Carolin qualified.

"That sounds like a no," said Rebekka with a sigh. "My last hopes dashed ..."

"Oh, no, Rebekka – you're not taking this bike thing that seriously, are you?" asked Carolin, now a bit worried.

Rebekka's low, warm laugh tickled her softly through the receiver. "No. But if we go out to eat together, I will use the opportunity to work on convincing you again. I'm not going to leave the subject at the door, you know."

"You can certainly try," said Carolin, "but you won't have much success, I promise you."

"We'll see," said Rebekka. "Call me whenever you think you're up to a long enough stay on a restaurant chair."

"Sounds good. Talk to you later, then." Carolin hung up.

Why, did she feel, Carolin wondered, after just those few minutes talking to Rebekka, the same way she did after she'd been on the phone with Ina for hours? She shook herself slightly. This couldn't be good.

She leaned back in her chair and grimaced. Now that Rebekka's voice was no longer having its soothing effect on her, the aches and pains announced themselves once more. And what Sabrina had said at Sappho yesterday came back to her: Can a person be in love with two people at the same time?

Was she in love with Ina *and* Rebekka?

If it weren't for Ina, she could more easily have made sense of her feelings for Rebekka. Yes, that was it – since their first encounter at the train station, that had been it. But since Rebekka had disappeared immediately after that first brief encounter, she hadn't given it any thought. Then Ina had come along, and ... well, then she hadn't thought about anything at all – or, to be honest, she'd been thinking about *one* thing only.

Until she saw Rebekka again ...

Carolin chewed at her lower lip. Perhaps she shouldn't make

dinner plans with Rebekka; that would be best. Rebekka's presence made her uneasy even when they were just riding their bicycles next to each other. How was she going to feel during a romantic dinner for two?

Well, it didn't have to be dinner. She could invite her to lunch, in broad daylight, not in the dim romantic illumination of flickering candles. Carolin's lunch breaks were limited to an hour; that was sure to be the case for Rebekka as well. Most employers didn't want their employees staying out too long at lunchtime.

Yes, lunch. That could work. Carolin smiled, relieved. Exactly. Lunch. That was the solution.

A moment later, she frowned. What had Sabrina meant about being in love with two people at once? She couldn't have known about Rebekka, so she must've posed the question out of her own interest.

But Sabrina – in love with a woman other than Chris?

Carolin shook her head. She really couldn't imagine that. Since she'd known Chris and Sabrina, they'd always been together, had eyes only for each other. It had been that way for years.

And even if there had been something going on there, she would sooner have thought that Chris –

But Sabrina? The faithful spouse? The proper, morally impeccable wife, beyond fault or reproach? Even when Chris wasn't there, Sabrina never so much as looked at another woman. Although plenty of people looked at her. Sabrina *was* exceptionally attractive.

To Carolin, Sabrina had always been just a good friend – her best friend, actually, when she really thought about it – except for Rick, whom she'd known forever and a day. Everyone could always rely on Sabrina; she invariably had a piece of good advice or a pragmatic solution to offer. And she always seemed happy. Level-headed and calm. She only had eyes for Chris. They belonged together, fit together like a pot and its lid. And with those two, no one could really tell who was the pot and who was the lid.

Carolin smiled. She must've heard Sabrina wrong. Maybe Sabrina really had asked the question on a purely hypothetical basis. Still... the idea that Sabrina might suddenly be questioning her marriage ...

However much she wanted to vehemently deny it, Carolin would have to talk with Sabrina again. True, Chris took too little time for Sabrina and paid too much attention to her work, but that kind of thing happened all the time. A phase like this would pass. It was certainly no reason . . .

Carolin shook her head once more. No, she must have misunderstood. Or maybe Sabrina had simply been in a bad mood that day. The next time she saw Carolin she'd reassure her with a laugh that she needn't worry anymore, that everything was fine. Yes, surely, that was it.

At last, Carolin reached for a manuscript and gave herself over to her work. She hated reading manuscripts, but if Thomas insisted, it had to be done. He was the boss. She would take care of this first and get it over with. Then she could turn her attention back to her usual work, which she liked.

⊰⊱

"**R**ebekka? Is that you?"

"I'm afraid so." Rebekka smiled down at Carolin, who was already sitting at their table in the restaurant. "Shall I go, so you can recover from the shock in peace?"

"No . . . I —" Carolin swallowed. *Oh, my God.* "I . . . it's just —"

"I know," said Rebekka, "but I can't do my job in bike shorts." She sat down across from Carolin. "Have you ordered yet?" She reached for the menu.

"No, I . . . I wanted to wait for you," stuttered Carolin. She was slowly getting used to Rebekka's new appearance. No way was this the woman she'd ridden her bicycle with. "What kind of work do you do, anyway?"

"Oh, nothing special," said Rebekka, while she studied the menu. "I just sit in an office all day." She smiled at Carolin. "What are you having?"

"Having?" Carolin felt paralyzed by that smile. She couldn't think anymore – couldn't move anymore, in fact – she no longer even remembered why she was there.

"Aren't you hungry?" asked Rebekka. "Do I have to eat alone?"

"Oh ... ah ... no." Carolin gulped and tried to recover herself. "Not alone. I ... I just don't know yet –" She picked up her menu quickly and hid her face behind it.

Now that she could no longer see Rebekka, she started to calm down. She had taken Rebekka for more of the sporty-casual type; at least, that's how it seemed before. Jeans and a T-shirt or bike shorts – that had been her attire, and Carolin thought that it suited her. But today Rebekka was wearing an elegant business suit, with her long legs sheathed in a skirt that reached just to her knees, and she was wearing makeup. Carolin had hardly recognized her.

"I don't think we're quite ready," said Rebekka, and when Carolin peeked out from behind the menu, she saw that the waiter had arrived at their table.

"No, no – I'll take the number one lunch special," Carolin said quickly. *Whatever it is,* she thought.

"And please bring me the *salade niçoise* and a large bottle of Perrier," added Rebekka.

Carolin took a deep breath. Rebekka's choice of food, at least, fit with the previous sporty image. Maybe this wasn't such a drastic shift after all.

Carolin attempted to return Rebekka's smile, but it turned out rather crooked. "I'm glad we don't have that kind of dress code at the publishing house," she said uncertainly. "I would feel kind of funny in a suit."

"Really?" Rebecca regarded her. "It's standard at our company. I've gotten used to it. Thank God we have a shower at my office, because the office used to be an apartment. When I arrive all sweaty in the morning, I shower and change clothes first thing, and before I ride home in the evening I change again. It's pretty simple."

"Seems rather elaborate to me," said Carolin. She tried to look past Rebekka's eyes. Their radiance was highlighted even more by the makeup. And that smile ... "First a forty-five-minute bike ride, then a shower, then a change of clothes, then another change of clothes in the evening, then another forty-five minutes at the end of your work day?"

"It's habit by now," said Rebekka. "I sit all day, so I'm glad when I can add a little movement to my daily routine without having to go anywhere special to do it. The gym isn't really my thing."

"Mine either," said Carolin.

"Who would've thought?" Rebekka grinned.

"I told you, there's no sense in trying to talk me into anything athletic," remarked Carolin. "I'm a hopeless case. Which the ride with you proved once again. It took me days to recover."

"Which wouldn't have been the case if you'd ridden with me again the next day," said Rebekka. "That's exactly the mistake that most people make. They just quit. If you keep going, the muscle cramps go away pretty fast."

"Muscle cramps . . ." Carolin grimaced. "I wish that had been the only problem."

"Yeah, I know." Rebekka laughed softly, and her eyes gleamed so brightly that Carolin wished for a pair of sunglasses. "The aching butt is always the worst. But that passes, too."

"Oh, I believe you, but I don't much feel like testing your theory," said Carolin.

"Too bad." Rebecca's eyebrows rose. "We could've gone riding together every day."

That was, of course, an exceptionally tempting prospect – which was exactly why Carolin absolutely couldn't do it. It was *too* tempting. Then she would spend more time with Rebekka than she did with Ina – and on a regular basis, at that. She didn't want to be responsible for what might happen.

"It's okay, though. I won't want to torment you any longer," said Rebekka, smiling again. "So you work in a publishing house? That sounds interesting."

"Well, yes," replied Carolin, "sometimes it is. But lately . . ." She sighed. "Thomas – that's my boss, the owner – seems set on turning me into an editor, whereas I'm very happy working as a management assistant. That's exactly what I want, actually. I hate reading manuscripts."

"That's tough," said Rebekka. "And he forces you to do it anyway?"

"The slush pile gets higher all the time," said Carolin. "I've tried so many times to make clear to him that that isn't my job, that I love my spreadsheets and would rather stay focused on them, but he says I have a genuine eye for quality, and presto, another couple of manuscripts appear on my desk."

"He doesn't sound like a very sensitive boss," said Rebekka, dressing her salad with a little oil and vinegar. "But he obviously values you, and that's not a bad thing."

"If only he would express that in dollars and cents." Carolin made a face. "I would still hate the manuscripts, but at least I'd get some small compensation for it. Those old hippies ... back then, they protested against everything and declared all these grand freedoms, but today they're the worst of all."

"Your boss is an old hippie?" Carolin watched Rebekka eat her salad slowly, leaf by leaf.

"Unfortunately. He looks like a gray-haired teddy bear in jeans. He's actually very nice, and I get along with him, but on this one issue he's relentless. It's not about the money. I make enough, but you know in publishing, no one makes that much. It's just that —"

"You hate manuscripts." Rebekka laughed. She seemed exhilarated. "I've never thought about that while I was reading a book. What torture some books probably were for some employees at the publishers. It's a whole new point of view."

"Most people have absolutely no idea how publishing works," said Carolin. "We're a specialty publisher, too, and a small one at that. Thomas founded the company way back when because at the time there were hardly any serious psychology books. He was a psychology student. Really, the publishing company was born of necessity. Thomas never even wanted to be a publisher. I think he really wanted to be a child psychologist. But since it seemed the world was waiting for the books he put out, the company grew, and he ended up dropping out of school."

"How sad," said Rebekka, though she didn't look a bit sad. "Well, maybe it was better for the children. If he treated them as mercilessly as he treats you ..."

"Oh, it's not really that bad." Carolin laughed. "It's just sometimes I'd rather spare myself these manuscripts. Otherwise, I like my job. How about you? Do you like working where you are?"

Rebekka grinned slightly. "Yes, I like it very much. I have a lot of freedom to make decisions. That's the most important thing to me."

"Then you have it better than I do," sighed Carolin. "So you could refuse to, say, work on manuscripts?"

"Maybe. I don't know," said Rebekka. "We make toasters and things like that, that don't have much to do with paper."

"Toasters?" Carolin laughed and had to put a hand in front of her mouth, since she'd just taken a bite. The roulade nearly fell back onto her plate. "Then the toaster prize from the bicycle club wouldn't have done you much good at all!"

"I'm not sure whether the bicycle club even offers toasters, to be honest," said Rebekka, grinning. "But a person can always use a spare."

"That's true," replied Carolin. "When I think of the crazy things mine's been doing . . ."

"Has it?" Rebekka asked with interest. Toasters were apparently her world. "What brand is it?"

Carolin laughed. "If there's one thing I hadn't expected, it's that we'd end up talking about toasters."

"Sorry." Rebekka grimaced. "I deal with them every day is all. I probably bore people to death about them."

I doubt that, thought Carolin. When she looked into Rebekka's eyes – when that smile hit her – it didn't matter what Rebekka was talking about. She could be telling her about toasters or reading aloud from the phone book. "It's a Gellert. I don't know if you know that company."

The corners of Rebekka's mouth twitched. "I work there."

"Oh." Carolin gave an embarrassed smile. "I'm sorry. Anyway, it's really acting up."

"What did the warranty department say?" Rebekka asked.

"Warranty?" Carolin frowned. "I don't think it's under warranty. I've had it for quite a while."

"It hasn't always been performing badly, I hope?" Rebekka looked at her.

"No, no – actually, it's a good machine." *At least I can say that,* thought Carolin, internally mopping the sweat from her brow. "Just lately . . ."

"Then maybe it's just too old," said Rebekka. "Although, really, that shouldn't happen." She frowned also. "How about this: I'll get you a new one."

"That . . . no, Rebekka, you don't need to do that, that's ridiculous. I'll just buy one. It's getting to be time anyway."

"No," said Rebekka. "I want you to get a replacement. Bring the old toaster to our warranty office and I'll make sure it's taken care of."

"But I already told you, it's not under –"

"That doesn't matter," said Rebekka. "Just bring the machine." She smiled gently. "I work there. I'll take care of it."

"You work in the warranty department?" Carolin shook her head. "I'm sure that's no fun. Customers complaining all the time . . ."

"The customers don't complain all that often, actually," said Rebekka. "Our appliances are really well-made."

"Oh, that wasn't what I meant." Carolin raised her hands in apology. "My toaster held up for years. It was great." Rebekka really seemed to care about the company she worked for. Carolin did too. As much as she complained about Thomas, the publishing house was important to her. She even defended books that she, personally, didn't find all that special.

Carolin smiled. Funny how that sometimes happened, that the company a person worked for became part of their identity. "Okay, I'll bring the toaster in. I promise."

"Good." Rebekka nodded. "There'll be a new one ready for you tomorrow."

"Tomorrow? Really, Rebekka, I don't know if that's right. If the warranty is expired . . . you could lose your job. I don't want that." Carolin felt uneasy. She didn't want to refuse Rebekka's offer, but at the same time it seemed very odd to her. "I think it would be better if I just bought a new one."

Rebekka gave her a look that unsettled her even more. "I won't lose my job. It'll be fine. It's all part of the company's goodwill system. You don't have to give it a second thought. You can pick up the toaster or not. It's up to you."

If Rebekka's going to keep going on about this, maybe I'd better just pick up the toaster, thought Carolin, a bit irritably. *It seems to be awfully important to her*. "Well, fine," she said. "If it's really going to be all right. But you're sure you aren't going to do anything —?" She waggled her hand vaguely.

Rebekka laughed. "I won't. It'll be completely aboveboard."

CB℘

Carolin looked at her watch. She ought to have taken the toaster back first thing; now her lunch break was almost over. But since she was already more than halfway there, it would be stupid to turn back at this point.

She searched for the building the warranty department was supposed to be in. Rebekka had called that morning and told her where it was, but Carolin hadn't realized how long it would take to get there on the streetcar, so she'd left her car parked at work, since it was usually silly to use it in the city. She probably wouldn't have gotten there any faster if she had driven, anyway.

Finally she found the building. The name *Gellert* was displayed over the entrance in large letters; it was hard to miss. Apparently, Gellert was a bigger company than Carolin had realized. The name hadn't meant anything to her when she'd bought the toaster.

She went in. Directly behind the entrance was a small office for the building superintendent. An older, friendly-looking man looked inquiringly at Carolin.

She hesitated, and went over to speak to him through the small holes in the sheet of glass. "Good afternoon. I'd like to see —" She broke off. It had just occurred to her that she didn't know Rebekka's last name, and to just ask for *Rebekka* would be weird. "To get to the warranty department," she continued. "I have a device here —"

"Left up the stairs," the older man interrupted her amiably. "And then straight ahead. Can't miss it."

"Thank you." Carolin nodded, then turned left and took the stairs. It was an old stone staircase; the whole building seemed quite old. *And they make modern kitchen appliances here?* thought Carolin. *The company can't be that successful if they can't even afford a new building. I ought to be glad my toaster lasted as long as it did.*

She reached the landing and looked straight ahead. There it was: *Warranty Department.* An old swinging door, whose upper portion was made of cut glass, led inside. Here, too, they apparently couldn't afford to install modern doors.

Behind the swinging door, a similarly antiquated counter awaited her. Shelves with various devices on them seemed to stretch endlessly back into the room behind the counter.

Two staff members were in the room, an older woman and a younger one. She didn't see Rebekka. The older woman turned to Carolin. "Good afternoon. What can I do for you?"

"Good afternoon. I'm ... I have ... so this toaster here ..." Carolin held up the device.

"Ah." The older woman nodded. "You're the one with the toaster. The new one is already here." She indicated a box sitting on the counter. "You can take it right with you." She cast a glance at her younger colleague, who disappeared behind the shelves. "You'll just need to wait one moment; the employee responsible will be right with you."

"Ah ... so ... I'm not so sure," said Carolin. "The toaster isn't under warranty anymore, I'm sure of that. Shouldn't I just buy a new one? Without a warranty, I don't really have any claim –"

"That's all right." The older woman smiled. "Just have a seat for a moment. It might be a couple of minutes."

"Oh, I ... my lunch hour is almost over," said Carolin. "Do you think – couldn't you take care of it?" Obviously, Rebekka wasn't around just then; maybe she was at lunch herself, and she didn't want to pull her away.

"No, no, she'll be right here," replied the woman behind the counter. "It won't take long."

Carolin sat down on the small bench next to the swinging door and fidgeted nervously. She really couldn't wait; she was already late. She persevered for a couple of minutes anyhow, then stood up. "I'm sorry, I have to go," she said. "Please tell –"

The door swung open. "Ah, so nice that you're here," said Rebekka, smiling as she stepped in with the momentum of the door.

Carolin almost sank to the ground. Rebekka's smile truly made her weak. "Of course. You did say —"

"Of course." Rebekka looked at her older colleague behind the desk. "Is that the toaster?"

"Yes, that's the one," confirmed her colleague, exchanging a peculiar look with the younger staff member, who had gone out earlier and returned.

"Do you have the old one with you?" asked Rebekka. "The engineering department examines the returned machines to identify their weaknesses."

"Its weakness is definitely its age." Carolin laughed. "I think every gadget gives up the ghost at some point."

"Not a Gellert," said Rebekka confidently. "When they find the flaw, we can ... the company will take it into consideration for future production."

"Well, okay, if you say so," said Carolin, handing her the toaster. "Do I need to sign something?"

"Yes, I think so." Rebekka took the device and looked somewhat uncertainly at her colleagues.

"The exchange form," the older one said quickly.

"Of course. The exchange form," Rebekka repeated. She set Carolin's toaster down and went over to the computer behind the counter, which sat there in curious contrast to its antiquated surroundings. "Where do we keep those?"

"Under forms," said the younger woman, and again, the two exchanged an odd look.

"Right." Rebekka clicked around, but her efforts didn't seem to be rewarded with success.

"You haven't worked here long?" asked Carolin.

Rebekka looked up. "No," she said a bit hesitantly. "Not long."

Carolin bent forward and whispered. "And now you're doing things like this? This could definitely cost you your job. It doesn't look as though you do this every day. And if you haven't been with the company for long — do you have any kind of tenure here at all?"

Rebekka glanced up briefly. "Yes, I'm safe," she said. "I think I've found the right form." She clicked around some more, but it looked like the form wasn't there after all.

"We have a pre-printed version too," said the older of the two colleagues. "Here." She slid a form onto the counter in front of Carolin.

"Oh, good." Rebekka seemed relieved. "Just fill that out."

"And what do I have to fill out?" asked Carolin. "There's a whole lot of technical stuff here. I don't really know what a lot of it means."

Rebekka cast a quick glance over the form. "Name and address. That's enough. We'll fill out the rest."

Again, the other two exchanged glances that led Carolin to believe that this wasn't standard procedure. *Oh, Rebekka, Rebekka. What are you doing? You can't just risk your job like this.* "Rebekka," she whispered. "Please ... I don't want to be responsible for you becoming unemployed."

"You won't be," said Rebekka. "Just fill out those fields; I'll do the rest."

But Carolin wasn't sure if Rebekka actually knew how to do that, either. So far she had appeared quite competent, but here in the warranty department, where she supposedly worked, she didn't seem to know her way around very well at all.

Carolin sighed. "Okay." She entered her name and address. "Is that it?" She slid the form over to Rebekka.

Rebekka barely glanced at it. "Yes, everything's fine."

Carolin bent over her and whispered once more. "I don't know how long you've been working here, but aren't there people who could give you some training? They can't just let you stumble around here like this."

Rebekka leaned over to her older colleague and put an arm around her shoulder. "She's training me already. She does it very well. I just don't learn all that fast. But I'm coming along."

Her colleague gave her the strangest look yet.

Soon she won't have this job anymore. And it will be my fault that she's getting herself into serious hot water. She pushed the box with the new toaster back across the counter. "Rebekka, this isn't right. I'll buy myself a new one." She looked at the clock. "My lunch hour is almost up. I have to get back."

She gave a little wave and left the room.

Chapter 14

Sabrina

"How long are you planning to keep playing this game?" Sabrina sighed and glared angrily at Anna.

"Until you give in," Anna replied, smiling.

"Is it a new bouquet every day, or do you keep reusing the same one?" Sabrina stepped forward and plucked a leaf from the bouquet of roses. "What do you know, it's real. I thought it was plastic."

"That wouldn't be very romantic." Anna's eyebrows lifted in amusement.

"It isn't this way, either," countered Sabrina brusquely. "I hope you're finding enough takers for all those bouquets."

"Oh, there's no shortage of those," said Anna, strolling along next to Sabrina as usual. "Don't worry."

"What do I have to worry about?" Sabrina let out a disdainful noise. "That I'm going to be the talk of the town because you stand in front of my office building every evening with a bouquet of flowers big enough to reach from here to the Rhine?"

"Oh, it wouldn't reach that far," countered Anna. "Almost, but not quite."

"How nice that you're amused by all of this," Sabrina hissed. She stood at the bus stop. She couldn't forbid Anna to stand next to her, and Anna was so close that Sabrina could feel her warmth and distinctly perceive the scent of the roses. "Fine, then," sighed Sabrina. "I'll get something to eat with you or whatever else, but only if you'll leave me alone afterwards."

The corners of Anna's mouth drew back considerably. "I'd have no objection to *whatever else*."

Sabrina took a deep breath. "Food, theater, a movie for all I care, but that's it. I've told you enough already – you can kiss any other ideas goodbye."

"Do you have time this evening?" Anna asked. "I'm sure we can get a reservation for dinner with no difficulty. What do you like to eat?"

Sabrina's mouth twitched. "Just pick the most expensive restaurant in the city. Or is that too much to ask?" She looked innocently at Anna.

Anna laughed softly. "You think I've spent all my money on the flowers and can't afford any more, right?" She shook her head in amusement. "Even if I have to pay on credit, you're not getting rid of me that easily."

"What a pity," said Sabrina. "I thought I'd found a solution."

"You're a devil woman, Sabrina," Anna whispered to her, "and when you've sold your soul to the devil, the world is at your feet, didn't you know that? He gives you everything you wish for."

"You made a bad trade, then," Sabrina replied, "because you're not getting me."

Anna scrutinized her. "I'll reserve a table. Where should I pick you up?"

"I'll bet you know my address already," Sabrina sighed. "Since you also knew where I work . . ."

"True enough." Anna smiled. "At eight, then?"

Sabrina took an edgy breath. "Yes, at eight."

Chris wouldn't be home anywhere near that time, anyhow.

"Wow!" Anna stood in the doorway and gaped at Sabrina. "You look . . . *stunning* in that dress."

Sabrina smirked knowingly. "Yes, I thought it would increase the torment, since you're not allowed to touch me. Because if you touch me, it's all over. I hope that's clear to you. Are we agreed? Otherwise, I'm not going with you."

Anna's usual mocking smile returned. She stared at Sabrina's naked shoulders, shimmering in the light. "You can't forbid me to look at you."

"No, unfortunately, I can't," sighed Sabrina. "Wait, let me get my wrap, then we can go." She stepped back into the hallway, leaving the apartment door standing open.

"May I help you?" Anna reached out her hand.

Sabrina hesitated, then handed her the wrap.

Anna laid it around her shoulders and did not in fact touch her, while Sabrina shut her eyes. *This is wrong, completely wrong, totally the wrong idea. Why don't I just send her away?* But she knew why. First, because Anna wouldn't give up and would keep coming back, and second . . . Yes, there was another reason, which she preferred not to let herself figure out entirely.

She turned around and looked at Anna. "Shall we?"

The best restaurant in the city was — how could it be otherwise? — French, and it offered an expansive view over the Rhine. Anna had reserved a window table, and when they sat down, two waiters held their chairs for them.

"I didn't think you'd really do it," said Sabrina, picking up the menu. It was the "ladies" menu, with no prices listed; Anna would have the one with the prices on it.

"If this is my only chance to go out to eat with you, why not? Beautiful women have the right to be demanding." Anna's gaze took in Sabrina's shoulders, now bare again. "You are *very* beautiful," she continued softly.

"Can't you judge that just as well above my décolletage?" Sabrina asked sardonically.

"I'd rather not," said Anna. She directed her eyes toward Sabrina's face. "But the statement is just as true wherever I look."

"Yeah, well, don't invest too much," Sabrina replied coolly, studying the menu again. "Because you're not getting anything in return."

"Some investments only pay off with time," Anna remarked, "but generally, all of my investments pay off."

"Then you should become a stockbroker." Sabrina set the menu aside. "So you'll be able to afford more investments like this one, which is not going to earn you a thing."

Anna laughed softly. "You're a prize worth investing in. I'm firmly convinced of that."

"A prize?" Sabrina raised her eyebrows. "Are we holding a contest here?"

Anna grinned. "A sort of knights' tourney. I humbly ask that you place your kerchief upon my lance, as the lady of my heart, the one for whom I fight and whose favor I may have only if I win."

"I don't think I have any tissues with me," said Sabrina.

Anna laughed out loud. "Just lay down your prickles. You're going to pull them back in eventually anyhow."

"Not in *your* lifetime," Sabrina countered dryly.

The waiter came, ascertained the two women's choices for the evening, and recommended a wine to go with each: red for Anna, white for Sabrina. Then he discreetly withdrew.

"Isn't this romantic?" asked Anna, with a sweep of her hand, indicating the glittering lights of the Rhine. "You do appreciate romance, I hope. Or at least the romance in my books." She smiled.

"The books obviously only remotely have anything to do with the author," said Sabrina. "How can you write things like that when you . . . *Have* you experienced all that?"

Anna smirked. "That is – forgive me for saying so – not a very original question. I get asked that constantly."

"It's an obvious question," countered Sabrina. "Original or not, do you answer it?"

"Sometimes. It depends on who's asking."

"So you won't answer me."

"Do *you* think it's true?" asked Anna. "Do you think I've experienced all of it, that I'm only writing my autobiography?"

"I could imagine that." Sabrina examined Anna's face. "Maybe you're collecting material for your next book right now."

"You'll be in it, that's for sure," said Anna softly. "But whether or not it will reflect reality is entirely up to you."

Sabrina harrumphed dismissively. "Do you think I care about that?"

"Maybe not, but you can't prevent it, either."

"Are you trying to blackmail me now?" Sabrina gaped at her. "Are you saying, if I refuse to sleep with you, that I'll appear in your book as a bloodthirsty dominatrix or something?"

Anna laughed. "I wouldn't go that far." She reached for Sabrina's hand and kissed it so quickly that Sabrina could only pull it back afterward. "Nor do I believe I'll need to."

Sabrina covered that hand with the other one and took a deep breath. "Anna," she said, laboriously composed. "This is the end, not a beginning. You promised to leave me alone after this. That's the only reason I'm here."

Anna tilted her head to the side. "The *only* reason?" she asked.

"Yes, the *only* one," Sabrina replied harshly. She brushed her hair back with her hand. "I hate having to repeat myself, but if you must hear it again: I am married and haven't the slightest interest in an affair. When are you going to get that?"

"When it sounds believable," said Anna.

Sabrina shook her head. "I can say whatever I want; you'll never believe me. So what point is there in talking at all?"

"There are certain things that I *would* believe," said Anna.

"Oh, yes!" Sabrina leaned her head back and rolled her eyes. "I can imagine what things."

"Of course you can imagine. You think about them just as much as I do."

Sabrina's head jerked back in Anna's direction. "No. I don't. You only wish I did."

"Yes, I do – and I freely admit it. Why don't you?" Anna looked at Sabrina with a soul-searching gaze.

"Because it's not true," said Sabrina. "You project onto me the things you wish for, but I don't wish for them. I have nothing to admit." She propped her arms on the table and laid her head in her hands. "Anna," she whispered, "please, would you grant me a moment's rest? I had a difficult day . . . and now this –"

"May I serve the soup?" The waiter was standing next to their table. He had glided over like an invisible ghost.

Sabrina sat up. "Yes," she said wearily.

The waiter placed the dishes in front of them, and faded from view once more.

"I'm sorry," said Anna. "I didn't mean to – What was so difficult about your day?" She smiled. "Other than me?" She raised her glass. "To a harmonious evening. I'm prepared to do my part toward that."

Sabrina took a deep breath. She clinked glasses with Anna. "Me, too," she said.

During the soup, they didn't speak, but as the dishes were being cleared away and they waited for the next course, Anna came back to the subject of the day. "Come on, tell me," she said with a smile. "Is your boss getting on your nerves? It's usually something along those lines."

Sabrina sighed. "Yes, it is along those lines." She rolled her eyes. "Basically, it's always the same thing. He doesn't tell me what appointments he has, what's urgent and what isn't, what I should take care of and what he'd rather do himself. He constantly bombards me with these little slips of paper that he spreads all over my desk, in no order whatsoever, without telling me what I should do first. Of course, by now, I know what I should do about most things, but sometimes new customers come along that he has special arrangements with, that of course he hasn't told me about, and I end up standing there like –" She broke off. "Today felt like it was nothing but that. Nothing went smoothly, everything went wrong, and in the middle of the chaos, he showed up and wanted me to rattle off some statistic he'd never mentioned to me before. Then he told me that if I was going to work with so little focus, maybe this isn't the right job for me."

"Oof," said Anna, surprised. "Sounds like maybe you *should* change jobs."

"Maybe," Sabrina said. "But really – it's not all that bad. Usually, I have a good handle on all of it. And by tomorrow he'll forget it all, anyway. If I mentioned it, he wouldn't have any idea what I was talking about. Then he'd tell me that I'm the best secretary in the world and he wouldn't do without me for any price."

"Which is presumably closer to the truth than the statement he made today," smiled Anna. "I hope he tells you that often enough."

"You're right." Sabrina looked at her. "Today was more the exception. Despite the chaos and all, he's glad to have me, I think. Maybe he's having problems with his wife or something."

"I could certainly understand that," said Anna.

"Anna, please . . ." Sabrina glared at her censoriously. "I was hoping –"

Anna raised her hands in apology. "That wasn't directed at you at all. But . . . well, presumably we both know what straight women can be like."

"I imagine you know better than I do," Sabrina replied. "*You're* the one who has a thing for married women."

"Yeah, right." Anna leaned back and smiled at her. "I have a thing for married women."

Sabrina's eyebrows rose, but she refrained from further comment.

"The next course," said Anna.

Two waiters approached the table and served them both simultaneously. Only when the plates were placed perfectly did the waiters remove the silver domes to reveal the delicacies of the house. "Bon appétit," said the head waiter, clearly recognizable by his all-seeing gaze.

"Thank you." Anna bent slightly over the plate. "This smells delicious."

The waiters bowed and withdrew.

Sabrina inhaled deeply, relishing the aromas of her food. "Truly delicious," she said. "This place is certainly unique. You don't get this in a pizzeria."

"No, but you can find other interesting things in a pizzeria," said Anna, grinning.

"One more comment like that and I'm leaving," Sabrina threatened. "I'm completely serious. I want to relax, to eat in peace, and we can talk about anything except – I've already met you more than halfway. Don't keep trying my patience."

"I didn't intend to," Anna replied. "I'd only like to tell you how beautiful you are, how wonderful you look, how seductively your hair gleams, and how gloriously your eyes shine when you look at me. I'm very glad that I can be here with you and enjoy not only the food, but your company as well."

Sabrina poked at the plate with her fork and didn't look up. "That really belongs in the same category," she said to the table. "That's exactly what I don't want to hear."

"Sabrina ..." Anna looked at her, but Sabrina didn't return her gaze. "You are an incredibly beautiful woman. How am I supposed to ignore that? Should I put on a blindfold?"

"It doesn't matter what I look like. At least not where you're concerned." Sabrina looked up. "The bit about the blindfold, though – that might not be such a bad idea." She tried to conceal it, but a slight smile stole over the corners of her mouth.

"I'm amusing you," said Anna, smiling. "So I must be doing something right."

"What woman doesn't like to hear compliments like that?" said Sabrina. "Even when I know what you're trying to accomplish with them, I still feel utterly flattered. But that doesn't change any of the facts."

"That you're married and you aren't looking for an affair, I know," sighed Anna. "Nonetheless, to me your presence is like . . ." she paused slightly, "sweet nectar from the cup of life. A breath of the fruits of paradise."

"Oh, now you're dragging out the poet," said Sabrina, giving her amusement free rein. "You could have done that earlier."

"You wouldn't let me," said Anna. "I would've been glad to."

"All the things you would've been glad to . . ." Sabrina laughed lightly. "But you're not going to get there with poems, either."

"Do you like poetry?"

Sabrina shrugged. "Some of it is pretty, but mostly it does nothing for me. I'm not a big fan."

"So what else do you read?" asked Anna, smiling as she added, "Other than my books?"

"Who says I read your books?" Sabrina countered. "I can't even remember what it was that you read back at the bookstore."

"Should I read it to you again – privately?" Anna asked. "Perhaps then it will come back to you."

"I hardly think so," said Sabrina. "With me it'll go in one ear and out the other. Usually I read other writers."

"Ah. Which ones?" Anna looked at her with interest.

Sabrina thought about it and named a couple of names, and soon they were absorbed in an animated conversation about books.

The dinner stretched out for some time, until the last course was served and they finally drove home.

Anna stopped in front of Sabrina's door. "Thank you for this lovely evening," she said, looking at Sabrina. "*Very* much."

"I –" Sabrina suppressed a gulp. "I have to thank you, too. It really was a lovely evening."

"You didn't think it would be, did you?" Anna smiled.

"No." Sabrina looked at her solemnly. "And at first, it didn't look that way."

"I truly didn't want to get on your last nerve after such a difficult day at the office, but you . . . you simply bowl me over with your charm, and I – well, I'm only human." Anna laughed softly. "I hope you'll forgive me."

"I . . ." Sabrina smiled gently. "Yes, I do," she said softly. She looked at Anna and felt all at once how much she longed for her.

No – that was wrong, she couldn't do it … She pulled herself together. "Good night," she said, leaning across the console and brushing Anna's cheek with her lips.

At that moment, as her lips touched Anna's cheek, Sabrina knew it had been a huge mistake. She froze. She couldn't tear herself away, and her heart pounded loudly.

"Sabrina …" whispered Anna hoarsely. She turned her head, and her mouth slowly neared Sabrina's lips, which slipped across her cheek.

When their lips touched, Sabrina thought her head would explode. She closed her eyes; her breath came quickly. Anna's hand laid itself on her thigh. *No*, she thought. *No, this can't be.*

Anna turned toward her, her hand stroking upwards from Sabrina's thigh, gliding to her breast, touching it. Sabrina moaned. She felt Anna's hand as if it had a thousand fingers, everywhere on her body. "Anna …" she whispered. Her arms wrapped around Anna's neck as if they had a will of their own, pulling her close.

Anna's tongue tenderly parted Sabrina's lips, pressing in, caressing her gently. Sabrina could hardly control her breathing anymore. She felt like she was dissolving, floating above the earth, without a body. Anna's hands caressed her nonetheless, this nonexistent body. And it reacted.

Sabrina moaned in Anna's mouth, their tongues joining in a passionate dance. Anna's hand ran down Sabrina's leg, pushed her dress up. She caressed Sabrina's naked skin. Sabrina sank back into the seat of the car. She felt faint.

Anna slid easily over her. "Sabrina …" she murmured excitedly. Her hand groped upwards along Sabrina's thigh to her center, touched her panties. She placed her hand over the fabric thinly covering Sabrina's crotch and pressed gently. "Come," she whispered.

Sabrina lifted her pelvis; she couldn't think any longer, didn't want to. "Oh, God …" she breathed.

Anna's hand began to rub with gentle pressure, and Sabrina bit her lip to keep from crying out. Her body was clamoring for more, wanted to give itself completely over to Anna. Anna's fingers groped beneath the fabric, touched the wet center, stroked it, parted it gently –

"No!" Sabrina shoved Anna away, flung the car door open, and ran to the door of her building. As she fumbled in her purse for the keys, she was afraid Anna would come after her, but she didn't. At last Sabrina wrested the door open, plunged into the corridor, opened the apartment door, stumbled inside, slammed the door shut behind her, and leaned against it, breathing heavily. The apartment was dark. Chris wasn't home yet.

Sabrina ran her hand across her forehead, trying to calm herself. What had she done? That had been more than a kiss, much more. She had been about to give Anna –

She collapsed behind the door, sliding to the floor. *This can't be*, she thought desperately. *This cannot be!* What had she been thinking? It had been completely foreseeable that Anna would –

Damn! She banged her head against the door. Why couldn't she control herself? Her breathing eased slightly. She stood up and went into the living room. Her insides still burned; she knew that feeling wouldn't go away so easily. Chris wasn't home, and even if she had been . . .

No. She would not commit that indignity again. Doing that would almost be the same as doing it with Anna . . .

She undressed and got into a cold shower.

⚭

"**D**o you have the documents for the new customers with the special terms?" Sabrina's colleague stopped in her doorway and cast a questioning glance at Sabrina, who sat at her desk.

"Do we have any customers with *normal* terms?" asked Sabrina with a sigh.

Her colleague laughed softly. "As long as our boss is our boss, probably not."

Sabrina stood up. "I just printed them," she said, going over to the printer and taking out the pages. "Here." She handed them to her colleague. "But he still has to sign them."

"Of course." Her coworker shook her head. "And then there'll be a thousand more changes."

"Whatever," said Sabrina. She went back to her desk. The telephone rang. Sabrina reached for it and answered while the other hand moused around the computer screen looking for a file. The mouse pointer froze. "How can you –?" whispered Sabrina. She glanced at her colleague, still standing in the doorway and flipping through the documents, making sure everything was in order. "No, we no longer carry that product," she said and hung up.

Her colleague raised the stack of papers. "Looks like everything's here. I'll take it to him."

Sabrina nodded. Her throat felt constricted. The telephone rang again. She had to answer it; that was her job, and it might be a client. Hesitantly, she picked up the receiver.

"That's too bad," said Anna. "Because I really would like to have ordered one."

"How dare you call me here?" whispered Sabrina. "In the middle of my workday."

"Where else am I supposed to reach you?"

Sabrina laid her forehead on her hand. "This can't go on, Anna," she said quietly. "It just can't. You have to stop."

"But I don't want to," said Anna.

"What about your promise? I kept my end of the bargain." Sabrina sat up indignantly.

Anna laughed softly. "I don't think so."

"So you're not going to abide by our agreement?" Sabrina asked.

"I am," Anna replied. "I didn't order any roses today. Although I would really have loved to send some to your office today. After last night . . ."

Sabrina shut her eyes briefly. She had to face the facts. "Forget last night. Nothing happened."

"Quite a lot happened. Although you did leave me standing there in the middle of it." Anna laughed softly. "Or sitting, rather."

"What were you expecting?" whispered Sabrina. Her office door stood open; someone could come in at any time. "That I would just –? I told you, I don't do that sort of thing."

"But you started to." Anna's darkly erotic voice purred through the receiver. "I could feel how turned on you were," she murmured. "Only that silly ring on your finger held you back. I bet it won't next time."

"There isn't going to *be* a next time," said Sabrina, and hung up.

A moment later, the phone rang again.

Sabrina seized the receiver. "Leave me alone!" she snarled.

"Sabsi? What's wrong?"

Sabrina felt her heart skip a beat. "Chris," she whispered. She felt relief, and at the same time, her guilty conscience gnawing at her.

"I ... I'm sorry that we didn't see each other at all last night," Chris apologized. "I didn't get home until three, you were sleeping already, and this morning I had to leave so early that you weren't awake yet."

Sabrina sighed. "That's nothing new. Why didn't you wake me?"

"I couldn't," said Chris with a smile in her voice. "You looked so sweet."

"Ah, Chris ..." Sabrina felt so much at ease with Chris's voice in her ear, so different from Anna's. Not demanding. Tender.

"Will you have lunch with me today?" asked Chris. "We could go to Sappho if you want."

Sabrina realized she'd had enough of going out to eat for the time being. "Why are you asking me out to eat? Is there a special reason?"

"Yes, I ... need to tell you something," Chris answered hesitantly. "And we hardly ever see each other at home."

That's not my fault, thought Sabrina. "What do you have to tell me?"

"Meet me at Sappho, okay?" asked Chris in reply. "At one?"

Sabrina's eyebrows rose. What was going on? Why didn't Chris want to tell her what it was about? "All right. I'll be glad to get out of this madhouse for a while."

"Okay, see you then. I love you." Chris hung up.

"I love you, too, Chris," Sabrina whispered into the receiver, from which Chris's voice had already vanished.

CRITICAL

"**U**h-oh." Sabrina gazed down at the bouquet of small yellow roses Chris held out to her. She accepted the flowers and gave Chris a suspicious look. "It's that bad, what you have to tell me? You haven't given me flowers in ages."

"But you love yellow roses," said Chris, giving her a kiss and sitting down.

"Yes," said Sabrina. "But not if they're supposed to make up for something else."

"Let's eat first," said Chris. She turned around. "Melly?"

Melly came to their table. "Well, you two? Back again?"

"Yeah," said Chris. "Do you have anything special in the kitchen that you could offer us? But not a chateaubriand – that takes too long."

Melly nodded. "I'll ask Ev," she said. "What would you like to drink?"

"A beer and a water," said Chris. She looked at Sabrina. "Right?"

"That's fine." Sabrina nodded.

Melly left the table to go first to the counter and then to the kitchen.

"Do I really have to wait until after we eat before you tell me what's going on?" asked Sabrina. She tried to ignore the queasy feelings that were coming up.

"I –" Chris folded her hands in front of her on the table and looked down at them. "I'm going to Norway for six weeks; I've been offered a building site there. I'm going to earn triple what I could get here, plus a whole bunch of bonuses. Lodging, travel – it's all paid for." She drew a deep breath – she had spoken very quickly – and looked beseechingly at Sabrina. "It's for us, Sabsi."

Sabrina stared at her, speechless. "Six weeks?" she asked then, gulping. Then another discomforting thought occurred over her. "Or might it take even longer?" She knew Chris's projects, after all. Only a minuscule number of them were completed according to schedule.

Chris ducked her head. "Three months at the outside. After that, it's winter in Norway, so it has to be finished by then no matter what."

"Three months?" Sabrina whispered, appalled.

Melly brought the drinks. "Look at you two!" she said, astonished. "Have you seen a ghost?" She set the glasses in front of Chris and Sabrina. "Ev says she can make you a wonderful mixed grill platter with six different sauces and croquettes on the side. And to go with it, there's an exceptional salad."

"I . . ." Sabrina cleared her throat. "I'm not hungry anymore."

Melly raised her eyebrows. "But I wasn't even gone two minutes."

Chris looked up at her. "I'm sorry. I guess we won't be eating."

Melly shrugged. "You're the customer." She went over to another table to take the order.

"Sabsi . . . darling . . ." Chris reached for Sabrina's hands and enveloped them in her own. "It's only six weeks . . ."

"Or three months," whispered Sabrina.

"But only in the worst case," said Chris. "I might even be able to come down for a couple of days here and there."

"A couple of days." Sabrina looked at her. "We don't see each other now; what good are a couple of days? You probably couldn't manage it anyhow, because something will fall apart on the site. It always does."

"But afterward –"

"Afterward?" Sabrina flared. Her eyes flashed. "What happened after the last project, and after the next-to-last one? How long have you been promising me that after *this* one, things will be good, nothing else will come along that demands so much of you? And now you're going to Norway?"

"Darling . . ." Chris looked helplessly at her.

"Oh, Chris . . ." Sabrina laid her face in her hands and leaned back in her chair. "Do you have any idea how much I need you right now?"

"Sabsi . . ." Chris stood up, came over to her, and crouched down before her. "This is all for us. I know it's horrible, but I can earn more there, with this project, than I can here in a whole year. And we can use the money. When you stop working –"

Sabrina took her hands from her face and looked back at her. "That keeps slipping farther and farther into the future."

"No," said Chris. "After the job in Norway, then we'll be able to do it. As soon as you want."

"I want to have a child with *you*, Chris," Sabrina said tonelessly. "Not by myself." She bent forward and held Chris's gaze firmly with her own. "I need you, Chris. *You*. Not the money." She cupped Chris's face in her hands and kissed her passionately. "Let's go home," she whispered. "Right now. Please . . ."

"Oh, Sabsi . . ." Chris breathed heavily. "I wish so much that I could, but – I can't. I have a meeting right now with the agent for the Norwegian principal. I can't cancel it."

Sabrina examined Chris's face. "Please make love with me," she whispered. "I can't stand being without you anymore. I want to feel you. Lying on me, coming on me, loving me. I want to kiss you for hours, until our lips burn. Chris . . ." Her voice fell to barely a breath. "I miss you so."

"Beloved . . ." Chris gazed at her tenderly. "I know I –" Her eyes fell to the floor. "I can't. I'm so very sorry."

Sabrina took a deep breath and straightened up. "Do you know how painful this is for me?" She let out an embarrassed laugh. "I'm begging you to sleep with me. I never would have thought –"

"I would absolutely love to go home with you right now," said Chris softly. She brushed Sabrina's cheek. "I'll try to come home earlier tonight. I will. Without fail."

Sabrina looked despairingly at her. "You've tried that plenty of times."

"Yes." Chris looked into her eyes, smiling. "But today I'll succeed. With the reward that's waiting for me . . ." She stood up and bent over Sabrina. "Get out your prettiest negligee," she whispered in her ear. "The see-through one." She checked the time. "I have to go. The agent from Norway is waiting." She smiled at Sabrina once more and kissed her lovingly. "See you this evening."

"See you this evening." Sabrina looked pensively after her. She reached for her mineral water and drank a sip.

Carolin came through the door, looked around, and waved at her. She spoke briefly with Melly, and came over to Sabrina. "I saw

Chris outside," she said, pulling up a chair and sitting down. "Did you two have lunch together?"

Sabrina glanced at Chris's beer, which sat untouched on the other side of the table – the head had just finished dissipating. "No," she said. "We wanted to, but –" She broke off. "Have you ever completely thrown yourself at a woman, only to have her smile coolly and rebuff you ever so politely?" she asked Carolin with a tragicomic expression on her face.

"I – What?" Carolin gaped at her. She swallowed. "No . . . I don't think so."

"Be glad," said Sabrina. "It's an awful feeling."

"You and . . ." Carolin cast a glance toward the door. "Chris?" she asked, unbelieving. "But you two are –"

"Yes, we're married," Sabrina sighed. "I always used to think, every day in the same bed and every day –" She drank the rest of her mineral water and reached for Chris's beer. "I *begged* her to sleep with me just now. Can you imagine that?" She drank half the beer in one go. "And she's off to a meeting."

"You –?" Carolin was somewhat overwhelmed by the situation. She hadn't expected anything like this.

"Yeah. I never imagined it could happen, either." Sabrina finished the beer and waved at Melly. "Bring me another one."

"Don't you have to go back to work?" asked Carolin, looking somewhat worriedly at the empty beer glass.

"It doesn't matter," said Sabrina. "She's going to Norway."

"To Norway? Who?" Carolin frowned. She wasn't keeping up anymore.

"Chris," said Sabrina.

"Chris?" Carolin couldn't hide her astonishment. "You two are moving?"

"There's no *you two* about it," said Sabrina. In one gulp she drank half the beer that Melly had just brought.

Melly looked quizzically at Carolin, who shrugged. "Chris is going on vacation by herself? To Norway?" That was the only explanation she could think of. In a long-term relationship, it did happen from time to time that people got on each other's nerves and needed a little distance. Or so she'd heard. Carolin, herself, had unfortunately never had such a long relationship. But maybe with Ina . . .

"Not a vacation. Work," Sabrina interrupted Carolin's romantic musings.

"She's going to work in Norway?" asked Melly. "But she already works here day and night."

"Apparently that's not enough for her," said Sabrina, draining her glass.

"Should I bring you another?" asked Melly.

"I think you'd better not," remarked Carolin with a freshly concerned look at Sabrina.

"Yes, please. A large one," said Sabrina.

Carolin looked at her. "Sabrina . . . you don't usually drink very much – hardly at all, really. You'll be drunk in no time flat."

"Who cares?" asked Sabrina, staring dully at the table.

"I do, for one," said Carolin. "I'm your friend, and I care."

"I *want* to be drunk," said Sabrina. "Maybe then I won't feel –" She propped her elbows on the table and laid her head in her hands. "Maybe then I won't feel anything anymore."

"I'll bring you some coffee," said Melly, and went back to the counter.

Carolin pushed her chair closer to Sabrina and put an arm around her shoulders. "She's not going away forever, right?"

"Six weeks," whispered Sabrina. "Or maybe three months. Maybe longer." She let her arms fall to the table and laid her head on top, as though she wanted to sleep.

Carolin stroked her back gently. "That's no good, to be separated for so long, but it's not the end of the world. I don't see Ina all week either – just on weekends. It would really be uncomfortable if we were separated for more than a week, but I can imagine living through it – if the whole time I could look forward to seeing her again."

"You don't understand." Sabrina whispered into the crook of her arm. "You can't understand."

"You two have been together for a long time. That's certainly different than with Ina and me," admitted Carolin. "We've only known each other a little while. But I think the longing is the same."

"The longing." Sabrina sat up slowly. "That's the problem."

"You can come to me anytime," offered Carolin. "I mean, when you feel lonely or want someone to talk to. I'm always here for you. When I'm longing for Ina and you're pining away for Chris . . . we'll have a lot in common." She smiled at Sabrina.

"Do you really think so?" Sabrina raised her eyebrows, doubtfully.

"I can't do more than offer." Carolin shrugged. "If you think one week can't be just as dreadful as six or more, you're mistaken."

"That's not what I meant." Sabrina placed her hand on top of Carolin's and looked into her eyes, pleading for forgiveness. "I didn't set out to play the poor victim here."

"Your coffee." Melly set the cup in front of Sabrina. "You look a little better already. Carolin must be a born therapist." She laughed and stepped away from the table again.

Carolin made a funny face. "Everybody's making me out to be a therapist lately."

"Really?" Sabrina picked up the coffee and took a sip.

"Well, not really." Carolin laughed. "I think it's because I pick up all these technical terms at the publishing house. Then people think I'm in the profession, too but I'm not and I don't want to be. I wish my boss would just leave me out of the whole mess."

"My boss gives almost every customer incalculable special terms and then wonders afterward why there isn't enough money coming in," said Sabrina. "I'm familiar with crazy bosses."

"Hey, you like to read." Carolin grinned. "How about you take over my job and read the manuscripts, and I'll take over yours and calculate the special terms. I love spreadsheets."

Sabrina laughed easily. "If that were possible, I'd do it immediately. I'm not exactly the best at math."

"I don't believe that. Otherwise you wouldn't be so good at your job. But the thing with the manuscripts, that really annoys me. Next time, I'm just going to throw them in the trash."

"No, you won't." Sabrina smiled. "You're just as conscientious as I am. That's why our bosses can get away with being so crazy."

"I'm afraid you're right." Carolin sighed. "I actually came in here to eat," she said, smiling. "Will you eat with me? We haven't had a real conversation in a long time, and I think that's a shame."

"I agree." Sabrina smiled back at her. She looked at her wrist-watch. "Actually . . . ah, who cares, I can go over my lunch hour for once. Everyone else does it all the time. Let's eat." She waved Melly over. "Is Ev's offer still good? The mixed grill and salad?"

"Now, all of a sudden?" Melly was astounded. "I think so; I'll ask. Although I'd like to know in advance whether you're still going to want it in two minutes when I come back."

"Don't worry, I'm going to eat no matter what. I'm starting to get really hungry," said Carolin. "And I don't think that's going to change in the next two minutes."

Sabrina raised her hand as if to take an oath. "I solemnly swear that I'm hungry, too, and that my appetite will not disappear again."

"Hey, it's not *that* important," replied Melly, shaking her head. "You don't have to turn Sappho into a courtroom. So, two for the special? Have I got that right?"

Sabrina and Carolin nodded solemnly.

"Fine, then," said Melly, "but woe betide you if it's not true. Then I won't be able to look Ev in the eye ever again, and I'll lose the best cook I've ever had. And finding a good cook is harder than – well, never mind. I'll just ask her." She went into the kitchen.

"Finding a good cook is harder than what?" Carolin considered Sabrina. "What do you think she was going to say?"

Sabrina raised her eyebrows. "I think we both know."

"Yes." Carolin looked at the kitchen door, which was still swinging back and forth since Melly had gone through it. "Melly's pretty busy in that arena."

"Eh, she's single. She doesn't have any obligations," said Sabrina slowly. "She's allowed."

Carolin took a deep breath. "She broke Rick's heart. And that, as far as I'm concerned, is not allowed."

"Did Rick say that?"

"No. Rick doesn't talk about things like that. But I can tell." Carolin glanced over at the counter, where Melly now stood and drew a pint of beer. "We've been friends since we were kids. I know Rick."

"Why didn't you and Rick ever become a couple? You like each other so much."

"Yes, we like each other." Carolin smiled. "Like sisters. You wouldn't sleep with your sister, would you?"

Sabrina looked flummoxed. "With my sister? I think she'd object. She's married with two children."

"That doesn't mean anything. But her being your sister, that means something. And Rick means something to me, because she's like a sister to me."

"Sometimes I've thought, the way you two act with each other, there must have been something at some point."

Carolin grinned broadly. "Well, yeah, when we both discovered that we ... ahem ... liked women, we tried making out with each other a little; we were probably fifteen or so. But somehow – back then, Rick had her eye on another girl at school; she was always rhapsodizing about her, and after a while it was just too much for me."

Sabrina grinned also. "I can imagine. So you would've wanted to?"

Carolin frowned. "No. Friendship and sex, those never fit together for me. It always felt funny when I thought about it. And Rick –" She grinned. "Rick fell in love with someone new every other day."

"Then Melly is just one of many," said Sabrina.

"No." Carolin looked up and saw Melly coming toward them with two plates. "No, I don't think so."

"Enjoy," said Melly, serving them the fragrant dishes. "I'll be right back with the rest." She turned around quickly and disappeared.

Carolin watched her go. "Actually, Melly doesn't strike me as the type," she said thoughtfully. "The type for constantly changing relationships, I mean. She seems so down-to-earth."

Sabrina stared at her plate. Then, slowly, she picked up her silverware and began to eat.

Chapter 15
Anita

"No," said Anita.

"No?" Marlene pulled her hand away; for a second, she was stunned, then she grinned. "You're not serious." She put her hand back on Anita's breast.

"Oh, yes, I am," said Anita. "I am serious. Very serious." She grabbed Marlene's hand and pushed it aside.

"But honey ..." Marlene tried again.

"Do you actually even know my name?" Anita asked. "Or do you think I was baptized Honey or Sweetie?"

Now Marlene really was irritated. Anita had never put up so much resistance before. "Of course I know your name ... *Anita*," she replied with emphasis. "But most women like pet names, right?"

"And so would I," Anita replied. "If it were a unique pet name, especially for me. I'd be very happy with that."

"Especially for you?" Marlene rolled onto her back and lay, severely confused, next to Anita in bed. Then she rolled her eyes in irritation. "So it's starting already."

"What? What's starting?" Anita asked. "I'm not even allowed to ask you a question?"

"Yeah, of course you can." Marlene sighed. She glanced to the side. "But can't you do it afterwards?"

"When you're asleep?" Anita pursed her lips. "I don't want to just be talking to myself."

"I'm tired, Anita." Marlene propped herself up on one arm and looked at Anita. "I just wanted to have a little sex for relaxation and then get some rest. Tomorrow's going to be another hard day."

"Just a little sex," repeated Anita slowly, "which does nothing for me."

"What?" Marlene gaped at her.

"I should have said something a long time ago, I know," sighed Anita, "but ... well, first I had to think about it for a while. When Sabrina said —"

"Sabrina! I'll kill that bitch!" Marlene snarled like an angry dog.

"But only after you sleep with her, right? That's what you've wanted all along. Did you think I hadn't noticed?"

"She doesn't have your qualities," said Marlene, staring at Anita's breasts.

"But she turns you on because she doesn't want you," replied Anita, pulling the bedspread up over her breasts. "I said yes to you much too quickly, it seems."

"She doesn't turn me on; she's a piece of shit," muttered Marlene. "I feel sorry for Chris every day."

"Well, Chris is happy with her, because they can talk to each other."

"Talk! What good does talking do?" Marlene made a disgusted face.

"If people are interested in each other? Quite a bit."

"Can't you tell how interested I am in you?" Marlene grinned, and her hand wandered under the blanket to Anita's breasts. "What we have doesn't require a lot of pointless chit-chat."

Anita scooted to the side. "Maybe you think so. But it's not all just about sex, however much you wish it were."

"Sex is the greatest thing in the world," said Marlene. "I don't know what you have against it."

"*Love* is the greatest thing in the world," countered Anita. "And sex is part of love. I have nothing against it. But when –" She looked diffidently at Marlene. "But when only one person ever gets anything out of it, it's not so great."

"But . . . but you did –"

"Yes." Anita sighed. "In the beginning, that was true, but lately . . ."

"Then just think about the beginning." Marlene slid under the blanket over to Anita, almost on top of her.

"Marlene!" Anita pushed her away and leapt out of bed. "I should have known it would be impossible to talk to you in bed. But where else can I talk to you?"

"You're just like the other chicks," sulked Marlene, offended. "They're enthusiastic at first, but then –"

"But then they notice you're just looking for a housewife. Cleaning, laundry, cooking, and sex every day, that's all you want. You don't have any higher ambitions than that." Anita was clearly furious.

For Marlene, this was a completely new situation. "That ... but isn't that enough?" she asked, taken aback. "I'm happy with that."

"Yes, *you* are. What about me?" Anita's eyes flashed in a way that Marlene had never seen before.

"I thought ... well, I thought you liked doing all that," said Marlene blankly. "I never had to ask you to."

"And what happened when the food wasn't waiting promptly on the table?" Anita asked. "Then you had a fit. And dragged me off to bed or wherever else, to blow off steam."

"I was just doing that to kill time until dinner was ready," grinned Marlene.

"Marlene ..." Anita folded her hands. "You know I love you. I've told you often enough. That's the only reason I'm still with you. All the rest —"

Marlene furrowed her brow. "I'm not holding you back. You can leave. Just like everyone else." She turned onto her side, so Anita couldn't look directly at her anymore.

"You make it so easy for yourself," said Anita bitterly. "You think someone else is just going to come along and replace me. Girls like me are a dime a dozen, right? So why should you make any effort to keep one?"

"Come to bed," Marlene replied. "Then I'll definitely make an effort."

"There are problems that sex can't solve," said Anita wearily.

Marlene turned over and stood up. She walked up to Anita. "But it can help you forget them for a while," she said softly, standing close to Anita and looking into her eyes. She wrapped an arm around Anita, pulled her close, and kissed her. "Forget what a shitty world it is out there," she whispered. "In here, there's just the two of us." She kissed Anita harder and stroked her breast. "Come on, forget what's bothering you. I'll make it up to you. You're definitely going to get something out of this." She pushed Anita to the bed and pressed her down onto it. "Just tell me what you want, sweetie, and I'll do it just the way you want it. You'll see." She slid down Anita's body and spread her legs. "You're going to scream for real, I promise you that."

Her tongue dived in between Anita's thighs, and Anita moaned. She hadn't felt that in a long time.

"Yeah, come, honey," laughed Marlene roughly between her legs. "I know you can. Come, show me." She replaced her tongue with her fingers, penetrated Anita and licked across her clit.

Anita moaned again, louder this time. "Marlene," she whispered. "I don't want this."

"Yes, you do." Marlene began to take her harder and deeper. "You're as wet as a cat in heat."

Anita had nothing to offer in reply to Marlene's thrusts. She hung onto the bed frame. Marlene's tongue danced across her clit, she couldn't defend herself against her increasing arousal; her belly contracted, her back arched, and a moan escaped her mouth.

"That was nothing," said Marlene as Anita collapsed, breathing heavily. "I want to hear you *scream*." She draped Anita's legs over her shoulders and lifted her up. "I want to hear you scream until you can't anymore." She thrust her tongue deep into Anita, slid back out, licked the satiny lips, and repeated again, faster and faster.

Anita moaned, trying to escape from the grip that held her captive, whispering, "No, no ... don't," but understanding that she had no choice. She would have had to break Marlene's nose for her to let her go. She couldn't do that. The next orgasm rolled over her, and she moaned in torment, but Marlene didn't let up; she thrust into her, licked her, granted her no respite.

Anita bit her lip; she could tell that she'd bleed if she bit down any harder, but even the pain didn't decrease her arousal. Marlene was forcing Anita to give herself, even though she didn't want to. As tightly as she pressed her lips together, she kept suppressing moans; she felt the orgasms follow quickly, one after another, with no time to recover in between.

"Come on already," whispered Marlene impatiently. "Come on. How long are you going to make me wait?" She sucked Anita's lips into her mouth, worked them forcefully with her tongue, let them go, repeated the game, pressed the tip of her tongue against Anita's pearl, spread her labia and thrust inside.

Anita felt each orgasm robbing her of more strength; she felt the weakness in her trembling legs, waving in the air. She had to open her lips in order to breathe. "Please, let me . . ." she gasped breathlessly. "Let me go."

"You know what the price is," Marlene moaned intensely. "Scream."

"I . . . can't. I'm . . . too weak," Anita whispered with great effort.

"Yes, you can. Come." Marlene redoubled her efforts.

Anita thought her head would explode. With her legs being held up in the air, the blood was rushing to her head and she could hardly breathe any longer. She felt she was about to suffocate. She felt Marlene penetrate her with all of her fingers and lick her so hard that her clit bounced back and forth like a rubber ball. The pressure inside her became so strong that she could only gasp now; she felt a powerful cramp hit her like a monsoon wave. "No!" she screamed. "No!" But it was too late. Her whole body stiffened, she no longer had control over it, and she was barely even aware that she was screaming without interruption.

"Now, then." Marlene let her legs fall and lay down on top of her. "That wasn't so hard." She grinned, and while Anita was still panting and gasping for breath, clamped one of Anita's thighs between her legs and masturbated on her. "I thought I wasn't going to make it, waiting that long," she groaned, as she pressed Anita's leg so tightly between hers that Anita would have screamed again if she'd been able to spare the breath to do so.

Marlene's orgasms followed one right after the other; she moaned several times, and when she was finished, she let herself drop onto Anita's breasts. She sank down onto them and sighed. "Only you are this soft."

Before Marlene could fall asleep on top of her, Anita rolled her off with a tremendous effort. "I want you to leave now," she said. "Now."

"What?" Marlene blinked at her through sleepy eyes. "Don't joke around. I want to sleep." She closed her eyes.

"Marlene. This is my apartment. Don't make me call the police and have them throw you out." Anita's voice sounded firm and definite.

"The police?" Marlene at least opened one eye. "What for? What do you mean by that?"

"You're leaving now, willingly or unwillingly, that's what I mean by that," replied Anita.

"Honey ..."

"Say that word *one* more time and I won't need the police," Anita said grimly. "Get dressed."

Marlene came to the gradual realization that this wasn't a game. "Anita. What's going on? We just had super-great sex, and now you're throwing me out?" She gave Anita a quizzical look. "You mean to tell me that all of that ... that you didn't ... no." She laughed. "You can't have faked all of that."

"And I didn't," said Anita. "It was all real. The whole rape."

"Rape?" Marlene sat up and stared at her in bewilderment. "Now, listen."

"I said no. Many times."

"Yes, of course you did, but that wasn't ... you didn't really mean it. You ... you had one orgasm after another. You can't call that rape."

"When a woman says no and she's forced to have sex, what would you call it?" Anita stood up and put on her bathrobe. "Plenty of times I haven't said no, so you wouldn't have known any better, but today ... today, I said no. You should have respected that."

"Anita, really ..." Marlene sat on the edge of the bed, but didn't leave it yet. "You were having fun."

"Maybe it was fun for you," Anita replied. "And I don't want to talk about it anymore. I've asked you to leave. Are you going to go, or not?"

"I just don't believe it," mumbled Marlene.

"You don't have to believe it, you just have to do it." Anita left the bedroom. "Or do I really need to call the police?"

When Marlene came out of the bedroom, dressed, Anita was standing at the window and didn't turn around. "Please give my key back," she said. "I don't want to have to spend the money to have the lock changed."

"But of course, *precious*." Marlene emphasized the last word and threw the key onto the table. "'The Moor has done his duty; the

Moor can go.' Always the same with you women."

Shortly thereafter, the door slammed shut.

Anita finally turned around, and the tears ran down her cheeks and dripped onto the floor.

ᥫ᭡ᦂ

"**I** need a pair of really thick, warm gloves, but ones you can still work in," said Chris. "Do you have anything like that?" She gave a quick glance around Anita's department in the store.

"It's not even summer yet," replied Anita, irritated. "Those don't come in until the fall collection."

"Crap," Chris swore. "Well, maybe I'll just get something up there."

"Up there?" Anita frowned.

"In Norway," Chris explained. "I have a job there."

"In Norway." Anita looked at her, nonplussed. "Is Sabrina going with you?"

"No, it's . . . it's just for a few weeks," said Chris. She didn't seem to be feeling entirely well. "Then I'm coming back. You can make really good money there in just a short time."

"I didn't know that." Anita shook her head. "Norway. I hardly even know where that is."

"Way up north." Chris grinned. "It's so cold that I'll need gloves."

"Then I'm sure they'll have some," Anita said. "We only carry what goes with the season. We're not a specialty shop; just a department store."

"Well, yeah, I just figured it couldn't hurt to ask you. As an expert," remarked Chris. She let her gaze wander again. "I need to get something else anyhow . . . for Sabrina. Maybe you could advise me on that."

Anita laughed gently. "I think you know Sabrina better than I do."

Chris frowned. "I don't really know my way around all this fashion and accessories stuff. You two have more in common there." She glanced briefly at Anita's outfit, trying to avoid looking at her breasts. "A scarf, maybe, or a nice handkerchief – something decorative, tasteful, classy. But not too expensive, or she'll box my ears. We're saving for our baby."

"Sabrina is pregnant?" Anita stared aghast at Chris.

"Oh, damn, I shouldn't have said that." Chris tore at her hair. "She doesn't want anyone to know. Please don't tell her I said anything." She took a deep breath. "No, she's not pregnant yet, but when I come back from Norway, we want to –" Her face softened completely. "We want to get started. A little Sabrina."

Anita smiled. "Sabrina might rather have a little Chris," she said. "Or at least, I could imagine she might." She looked around quickly. "I think I have something for you. A leftover from last season, actually, so it's marked down. But it's excellent quality; it was a pretty expensive piece before it went on sale." She pulled open a drawer and withdrew the scarf. She spread it out on the shop's counter in front of Chris. "Beautiful," she said, letting it glide through her fingers. "Pure silk."

"It matches her hair." Chris smiled tenderly. "I hope she'll like it."

Anita had to swallow. The tenderness in Chris's gaze brought tears to her eyes. She ducked down behind the counter again to collect herself for a moment. "You love her very much, don't you," she said softly. She laid an empty gift box for the scarf on the glass countertop.

"How could I not? She's simply loveable," said Chris. Then she looked solemnly at Anita. "Yes, I do love her very much. More than my life. I can't even imagine life without her." Her expression turned guilty. "I don't pay enough attention to her these days, I know. But it's all for her ... and our baby. She wants to stop working when the baby comes, and then we'll only have the one income, so I have to prepare for that."

"I'm sure she understands." Anita looked at Chris.

"I'm not so sure." Chris sighed. "But I can't change it, either. It's hard to live without money."

"That's true," said Anita. "But as an architect, surely you must be doing all right."

"It's okay." Chris shrugged. "I haven't been working for that long. It was a long course of study. And nowadays, there are architects from Eastern Europe and other places who'll work for half the price, or even less. It's all up for negotiation. I don't have a set salary; it varies from job to job."

"Then I suppose I'm well off with my little shopgirl salary." Anita laughed. "At least I get the same amount every month."

"Yes, everything has its advantages and disadvantages," Chris remarked. "I'm sure you were already earning money when I was still in college having to beg the financial aid office for every penny. Honestly, I've often envied people who did vocational training in high school and went to work right after they graduated."

Anita's eyebrows rose. "And I always thought, how lucky college students are, that they get to sleep in. My boyfriend –" She broke off. "I was with a college student once," she added hastily.

"You don't only like women?" Chris seemed amazed.

"Didn't Sabrina tell you that?" Anita was also amazed.

"We see each other so rarely," said Chris, "we hardly get to talk."

"Yes, I . . . Yes." Anita picked up the scarf and took it to the register.

"What does Marlene say to that?" asked Chris.

"It's none of her business anymore." Anita typed her number into the register and ran the scarf's UPC code over the scanner.

"Ah. She's done it again," said Chris, not very surprised.

"What?" Anita tried to sound innocent.

"Scared a woman off. It's not the first time." Chris frowned concernedly. "I'm sorry, but to be honest . . . I didn't really expect anything else. Even though I'd hoped for better. For you and for Marlene."

"Me, too," said Anita, handing Chris the gift-wrapped scarf.

Chris pulled her wallet from her pants pocket and held out a bill to Anita. "You really do like Marlene, don't you?"

"I –" Anita swallowed. "Yes."

"She's such a dope." Chris shook her head. "How can she let a woman like you walk away?"

"I threw her out."

"*You?*" Chris forgot to pick up her change.

"I'm sure she'll tell you when you see each other. You're her best friend, after all." Anita laughed somewhat bitterly. "And I'm sure it will sound different then than the way I'd tell it."

Concerned, Chris replied, "I actually haven't seen her for a long time. Because I work so much, I hardly have time to get together with anyone. But in case I do see her –"

"Leave it," said Anita. "This only concerns her and me."

"Yes, of course," said Chris, "but she's going to have to learn sometime. She can't just keep –" She sighed. "I don't know what this is all about. But the fact that you threw her out, that's new. Normally, she's always the one . . . But you two were together for a pretty long time."

"Is that so?" said Anita. "It didn't seem that long to me."

"It wouldn't to most people," said Chris, "but for Marlene, more than three weeks is a major achievement." She looked sympathetically at Anita. "I really am sorry."

Anita nodded. She couldn't speak anymore, because a knot was constricting her throat.

Chris patted her shoulder. "I hope the rest of your day goes well," she said gently. "And thank you." She held up the wrapped present. "I never would have found the right gift on my own." With a last, empathetic look at Anita, she turned around and almost crashed into a woman who was coming up to the register. "Excuse me," she murmured, dodging and continuing on.

"Your girlfriend?" asked Anna Lessing with a smile, when she reached Anita at the register.

Anita no longer knew where her head was. Today was apparently her day of tribulation. Everything at once. She gulped, cleared her throat, swallowed again. "Sabrina's wife," she said. "Chris."

"Oh, Chris." Anna Lessing turned around with interest, but only saw Chris disappearing out the exit. She turned back to Anita. "I didn't know you worked here. Otherwise I might've come in sooner." She smiled at Anita.

Is she flirting with me? Anita wondered. "I . . . I've been working here for two years now."

"I don't particularly like department stores," said Anna Lessing. "I prefer smaller shops. So I hardly ever come here." She let her gaze roam from Anita's eyes to her breasts and back. "I had no idea how appealing it was."

She is coming on to me. Anita couldn't comprehend it. A moment earlier, all her thoughts had been of Marlene, the pain had clawed at her heart, she could hardly think about anything else, and now this woman stood before her and gave her gooseflesh up and down her body with that erotic voice. "Hmm, yes. I ... Can I help you somehow?"

"I'm sure you can," said Anna. Again, her gaze swallowed Anita's entire figure, examining it with interest.

Anita tried to ignore her gaze. "What are you looking for?" she asked in her most neutral salesclerk tone. "Some kind of accessory?"

"You could say that." Anna Lessing smiled mockingly. "An accessory for certain hours of the day."

Anita nearly blushed. "Then I believe you're in the wrong department."

"I don't think so." Anna clearly enjoyed the dizzying effects her magnetism was having on Anita. "I believe I'm in exactly the right department." Her eyes observed Anita with amusement. "Did you like my book? Or haven't you read it yet?"

Anita swallowed. "No, I ... read it."

Anna grinned. "And if I'm interpreting things correctly, you enjoyed it, too. What did you like in particular?"

"I ... I don't remember. The whole book," said Anita quickly. "Now, if there's nothing else I can do for you —" She tried to flee back to her department.

Anna came after her. "I can think of a great many things you could do for me."

"Please ..." Anita turned around. "I work here." She folded her hands, trying to hide exactly how disquieted she felt.

"And I don't want to keep you from your work." Anna laughed softly. "I'm looking for a small gift for a very exceptional woman. Something ... well, let's just say, something special. But I don't quite know what. And I don't mind if it's expensive."

"Then I would recommend the jewelry department," said Anita, trying to dodge the gaze that sent her whole body into an uproar.

"Yes." Anna drawled her answer. "For the moment, that would probably be best." She examined Anita once more from top to bottom. "I hope the prospects there look as good as the ones here."

"My colleague will be glad to help you. She knows her area very well."

"If *you* say so . . ." Anna smiled. "I'm sure I'll come back often."

Please don't, thought Anita. "The jewelry department is upstairs. Second floor."

Anna smiled even more mockingly than before. "Then until next time," she said, turning around and heading toward the escalator.

Anita staggered into the break room and let herself drop into a chair.

"Not feeling well?" asked a colleague who had also just come in. She stood in front of the mirror and took a lipstick out of her purse, then ran it over her lips. "There's absolutely nothing going on today. I'm bored to death."

"I wish I could say the same," Anita murmured.

"What did you say?" Her coworker turned toward her with freshly painted lips.

"Oh, nothing. Yes, not much happening today." Anita stood up and smoothed her skirt. "I just wanted to take a load off my feet for a minute."

"Go ahead, go ahead." Her coworker put the lipstick back into her purse. "There aren't any customers here, anyway. I'll keep an eye on your department."

"That's nice of you." Anita sat down again. "Thanks."

"Not a problem." Her colleague left the room.

Anita considered how long she might be able to hide in here, or whether Anna would've left the store by now. She wanted to avoid another encounter. Anna discombobulated her; she was completely different from Marlene, yet she seemed to cause the same reaction in Anita.

She's shopping for a present for another woman. She only . . . well, okay, she flirted a little. She didn't really want anything from me, she tried to reassure herself. But she still wasn't entirely convinced.

She thought back to the evening of the reading. She hadn't exchanged one word with Anna, except that she'd handed her a book for an autograph. Anita had thought Anna wouldn't even have noticed her. But obviously she had.

My breasts, she thought, sighing internally. *That's what she was most interested in today, after all. Exactly like Marlene — and all the others.* She had often thought about having breast reduction surgery, but she didn't have the money. She would gladly have traded with another woman who wished for larger breasts. Small-breasted women didn't know how good they had it. They weren't constantly being evaluated only on their appearance.

Marlene hadn't seen anything in her except those breasts; Anita knew that now. Nothing else had interested her. Good thing she'd finally made up her mind to end the humiliation.

No, don't cry! She felt the tears rising inside. All morning she'd managed to suppress them. She had cried enough yesterday.

She went into the bathroom and splashed cold water on her face. The urge to cry stuck in her throat, but she held it under control. It strangled her, barely let her breathe, but she couldn't afford red, swollen eyes. What would the customers think?

She dried her face and reapplied her makeup. Thank goodness for makeup. All traces of the previous night disappeared under a bit of foundation. After a while, her face looked back at her from the mirror as though nothing had happened.

ॐ

"**M**arlene!" Chris ran down the street and grabbed Marlene by the shoulder.

Marlene, bleary-eyed, stopped and looked at her.

"I was just with Anita at the department store," said Chris, still trying to catch her breath from running.

"What do I care?" Marlene stomped off and left Chris standing there.

"Marlene." Chris caught up with her and walked along next to her. "What the hell did you do to her, to make her throw you out? Don't you ever learn?"

"Me? Do to her?" Marlene stood still and glared at Chris with a deeply furrowed brow. "I gave her the greatest sex of her life. And that was my thanks."

"I don't believe it. That can't have been everything."

"You talked to her. She must've told you what happened," Marlene growled.

"No, she didn't. She said it only concerned you and her." Chris examined Marlene's face. "Come on, let's have a beer together. We haven't seen each other for a long time."

"You just want to grill me about it," said Marlene.

"Yes." Chris nodded. "I don't have much time, unfortunately; I'm already halfway en route to Norway –"

"Norway?" Marlene looked at her, dumbfounded.

"I'll tell you about Norway if you tell me about Anita." Chris grinned.

"There's nothing to tell," grumbled Marlene.

"I'm sure there's enough for one beer. I don't have time for more than that anyway. But if you don't want to –"

"Fine, then, a beer," Marlene agreed. "What's in Norway?"

They entered a pub a few yards farther along. "Work," said Chris. "I have to earn money. For Sabrina and me."

"Madame doesn't want to break another nail at work?" asked Marlene.

"Marlene ..." Chris rolled her eyes. "I know you can't stand each other, but Sabrina doesn't think she's above any kind of work. That's not what it's about."

They sat down at the bar and ordered two beers.

"What is it about, then?" asked Marlene.

"I just want things to go well for us," said Chris. The first beers came, and she sipped at hers. "Sabrina ought to have everything she wishes for."

"Oh, man!" Marlene downed her beer practically in one swallow. "What do you see in that woman ..."

"I'm married to her. And I'm very happy about that." Chris smiled.

"Married." Marlene let out a disdainful grunt, drank the rest of the beer, and waved with the empty glass to order a new one. "What anyone gets out of marriage I don't know, either."

"Anita is a woman to marry. Maybe she could explain it to you."

"Anita? Marry? Are you nuts?" Marlene gave her an angry look.

"Where did you get an idea like that? Or did *she* put that bug in your ear? And if she did, what did she throw me out for?"

"Apparently only you two know that. But she didn't put a bug in my ear; I already had one. Sabrina and I have been married for years, after all."

"God only knows why," grumbled Marlene. "You can have sex without all that."

"If sex is the only thing you're interested in, sure," said Chris. "But that doesn't constitute a relationship. I've tried to make that clear to you a number of times."

"You and your *relationships*," Marlene replied, emptying the second glass. The third was already waiting for her. "What's so great about those? Nothing but trouble and a huge waste of time."

"Was that the reason?" Chris asked. "Why she tossed you out on your ear? Did she say she wanted more than just sex?"

"She screamed until the walls shook," said Marlene stubbornly. "She likes sex."

"How nice for you. But if that's it, then everything should be fine."

"I don't know what her deal is," said Marlene. The next beer was already nearing its end. "Who knows with women?"

Chris laughed. "We're women, too."

"Yeah, but not like *that*." Marlene stared into her glass. "They always want something, but I have no idea what it is."

"Didn't Anita tell you what she wanted?" Chris took another sip of her beer, still her first.

"She didn't say anything!" Marlene smacked the bar. "She didn't breathe a word. *Go*, she said. Nothing else."

"Hmm." Chris stared into space. "And nothing happened before that?"

Marlene drank half of her fourth beer. "She said I raped her," she muttered over the rim.

"Excuse me?" Chris gaped at her. "*What* did you do?"

"I didn't," contradicted Marlene. "I'm telling you, she screamed, she thought it was great. And afterwards —"

Chris shook her head. "Are you all right in the head? Anita wouldn't just make up something like that."

"Yes, just like that." Marlene emptied her glass once more. "They always say no at first."

"She said no, and you still –?" Chris was less and less able to believe what she was hearing.

"Oh, come on . . ." said Marlene. "You've done it, too. They play a little hard to get, but they don't really mean it. They want to be talked into it. It turns them on."

"Well, yeah . . ." Chris's eyebrows rose. "Up to a certain point, sometimes that's true. It's a game. But rape – that's not a game anymore."

"I didn't rape her!" Marlene spoke loudly, and she was lucky that no one but the bartender was in the pub. He gave her an odd look, though.

Chris clamped her hand over Marlene's mouth. "Would you be quiet? Don't broadcast it all over the neighborhood. I believe you." She took her hand away and looked at Marlene. "But still, you admit that she said 'no.' Maybe she experienced things differently than you did."

"She experienced plenty," said Marlene. Her voice did sound a bit awkward. "The whole street heard what she experienced."

"You have to apologize to her." Chris nodded. "It doesn't matter what you think – she feels like she was raped, and you two have to sort it out. Maybe it was all just a misunderstanding."

"I have to apologize?" Marlene stared at her. "What for? I took her to seventh heaven, and I'm supposed to apologize for that?"

"Maybe it was your heaven, but not hers." Chris ran her hand through her hair and sighed. "Sometimes two people just see things differently. Sabrina says, too –" She broke off. "You just have to apologize to her, that much is for sure. Whether you know what for or not. Just apologize."

"You're completely nuts." Marlene shook her head. "I'm not going to apologize when I haven't done anything."

"So she means nothing to you? Not even that much?"

Marlene stared down at the bar. "There's someone like her on every corner. I always find someone for my bed."

"That's certainly true," said Chris, "but Anita doesn't seem to me like a woman you can find on every corner. Do you even realize that she loves you?"

"She's mentioned that once or twice," grumbled Marlene.

"She did." Chris watched her, shaking her head. "So you know that and you still treat her this way?"

"What does that have to do with anything?" asked Marlene. "They're always talking about love one way or another, those females."

"Every woman you've known has said she loves you?" Chris's eyebrows rose in disbelief.

"Not all of them." Marlene's voice was indistinct.

"How many?"

"Didn't count."

"Ten, twenty, thirty?" asked Chris. "Or just one?"

Marlene regarded her from slightly hooded eyes.

"Just one." Chris nodded. "Anita."

"Yes, damn it, so she was the only one. What difference does it make?" Marlene gripped her glass tightly.

"What *difference* does it make?" Chris shook her head once more. "You find a woman like Anita, a loving, affectionate woman, who actually loves *you*, and you commit violence against her?"

"I didn't –"

Chris held Marlene's mouth shut again. "But she thinks you did," she said quietly. "And whatever actually happened, she must have a reason to think so. At least from her point of view." She glanced at her watch. "I have to go. I'm already late." She slid down from the high barstool, fished some money out of her pants pocket, and laid it on the counter. "Please, Marlene ... go to her. Tell her that you're sorry, that you didn't want this, that you regret it terribly. As your best friend, I advise you to do that. Anita is worth it. A woman like her, you're not going to find one again anytime soon – if ever." She tilted her head back. "Damn," she breathed. "If only I had a little more time." She gestured toward the glass in Marlene's hand. "And you're going to stop that right now. Drinking won't solve the problem. Instead, think about what I told you." She gave Marlene a slap on the shoulder. "I'll call you as soon as I can."

Marlene watched Chris disappear through the door of the pub. "One more," she said to the bartender, pushing her glass across to him.

Chapter 16
Carolin

Carolin threw herself onto the couch, exhausted, and put her feet up with a sigh. Finally, she was home. The streetcar operators' strike had made it extremely difficult, but she had made it.

The doorbell rang.

Oh, no! She didn't want to see anyone else today, didn't want to get up again. She just wanted to relax, and then later she'd call Ina –

It rang again. Twice.

Who could possibly want anything from her now? It was already dark out, she didn't have any social plans in the middle of the week, and no one just dropped in on her unannounced. She lived too far out.

Then she remembered her neighbor, who had recently asked to borrow a cup of sugar. Yes, it could be something like that. She swung her legs down off the sofa and went to the door.

When she opened it, a printed picture displayed itself prominently before her. Before she could recognize what it was, it slid down out of sight. "You forgot this," said Rebekka, smiling.

Carolin didn't know where to look first, at the box Rebekka was holding out to her, or at Rebekka herself, standing there in her bicycle shorts.

"Your apartment is practically right on my way home," said Rebekka. "So I just strapped the thing to my back, so I could drop it off for you."

"You really are crazy, Rebekka." Carolin laughed. "I told you I was going to buy myself a new one."

"And? Did you?" Rebekka looked inquiringly at her.

"I haven't had time yet." Carolin shook her head. "You barely know how to do your job yet, and you're already about to lose it. If you keep doing things like this."

Rebekka stepped into the hall and set the box with the toaster on the floor. "You have a right to the toaster. I cleared everything up at work."

"No person has a right to a –" Carolin sighed. "But since you're here already, should I toast something up for you?" She laughed once again.

"No, thank you," said Rebekka. "But something to drink would be nice."

Carolin nodded. "Water? Coffee? Or something stronger?"

"Water would be great," said Rebekka.

Carolin went into the kitchen, and Rebekka followed her. "Today you really had the advantage," said Carolin. "I only just got home. The strike . . ."

"Yeah, things like that don't affect me." Rebekka laughed. "I rode past all the bus stops, and there were tons of people standing at every one of them."

"They all probably would've loved to let you take them with you," said Carolin, handing Rebekka a glass of water. "Me, too."

"You only had to say," grinned Rebekka.

"You wouldn't have taken me with you, you would've talked me into riding myself," said Carolin. She grinned likewise. "And I'd rather spare myself that."

"Wimp," said Rebekka.

"Guilty as charged." Carolin indicated the door. "Should we sit down? Or do you have to get going?"

"No." Rebekka shook her head. "I'm done for the day."

Carolin wanted to walk past Rebekka, but the kitchen was small, and she brushed Rebekka's body with hers. It hit her like a blow. Rebekka seemed to freeze similarly. She set down her glass, laid a hand on Carolin's waist, turned her around, and kissed her gently on the lips.

Carolin closed her eyes. The kiss was so sweet, Rebekka was so near, she longed for her – but this was wrong. Ina was in Kassel, but something like this . . . it wasn't Carolin's way. She opened her eyes again. "Don't, Rebekka."

Rebekka let her hand fall. "I'm sorry, I . . . my fault. I'd better go." She slipped past Carolin and left the apartment in a hurry.

Carolin lifted a hand as if to stop her, then let her arm fall. What for? She went into the hallway and shut the door. Then she picked up the box. Rebekka was tenacious, that was for sure. Carolin smiled. Rebekka was altogether –

"No," she called out loud. "No, no, no!"

She brought the box into the kitchen. Rebekka's glass was on the counter. She stared at it, as if she could see Rebekka inside.

The telephone rang. She hesitated a moment, then went over and picked up.

"Now, what is my sweetheart up to?" Ina's voice sounded gleeful.

Carolin let herself sink down onto the sofa with the telephone. "Nothing. I was thinking about you."

Aren't you ashamed of yourself? A second ago, you were still thinking about Rebekka. Ina wasn't in there at all. Carolin wished she could wipe the nagging thoughts from her head.

"I thought you were going to call me," said Ina.

"The streetcars are on strike." Carolin sighed. "I only just got home a couple of minutes ago."

"Ah, I see." Ina laughed. "You and your public transportation. Couldn't you just have driven?"

"I could have, but then I would've just been sitting in traffic right next to the streetcar," explained Carolin. "Other people had the same idea. At least with a bicycle —" She bit her tongue. But Ina didn't know anything. Carolin hadn't told her anything about Rebekka. And why should she have? It was nothing. Until this evening . . .

"Bike riding is god-awful," said Ina. "Is the strike almost over?"

"Tomorrow," said Carolin. "At least, if nothing changes. They're supposed to reach an agreement by then."

"Well, then, it's all good." Ina sighed. "I wish I were there with you now."

"Yes, I wish you were, too." Carolin's voice sounded quiet. If Ina were here now, she'd be able to forget everything; nothing else would exist except Ina and her.

"Are you still dressed?" whispered Ina.

Carolin felt hot. "I told you, I just came in."

"Would you like to . . . come again?" whispered Ina.

"Ina . . ." Carolin laid her head back. "I long for you so much . . ."

"I'll undress you," breathed Ina. "Very slowly. Bit by bit . . ."

Carolin sighed aloud.

"Come on," whispered Ina. "I want you naked."

"Yes," murmured Carolin. And she began slowly to undress, while Ina whispered sexy things in her ear.

⚮

"There's a phone call for you." Ulrike called to Carolin from her office as she walked past. "It got transferred to me because you weren't at your desk."

Carolin nodded, stepped into the office, and picked up the receiver. "Yes?"

"I want to apologize," said Rebekka.

Carolin was speechless for a moment. She was standing in Ulrike's office; she couldn't talk to Rebekka there. "It's . . . all right," she said in a dither.

"No . . . I . . . I should have thought before I acted," said Rebekka. "I'm sure your boyfriend won't be thrilled when you tell him about what happened." She laughed, embarrassed. "Even if I did buy him that rose."

Good grief, she thinks –! Carolin didn't know what she ought to say to that – especially with Ulrike right next to her, ears burning with curiosity. "I'll call you back," she said. "I'm not in my office." She hung up quickly.

"Something important?" asked Ulrike sanctimoniously.

"No, nothing important. I just have to look something up in my files." Carolin tried to flee Ulrike's office without being too obvious, before she could ask any more questions. Once in her own office, she shut the door behind her and leaned against it. Her heart pounded. Then she had to laugh. Rebekka wanted to apologize because she thought Carolin was straight.

Carolin pushed away from the door and sat down at her desk. Yes, of course, she'd never mentioned who the rose was intended for. She'd told Rebekka as little about Ina as she'd told Ina about Rebekka.

She had to clear up the misunderstanding. She reached for the receiver. Then she hesitated. Why, really? If Rebekka thought she was straight, it would be much simpler. She'd simply accept it and not think about Carolin anymore.

But it was dishonest. Yes, she was taken and she couldn't start anything with Rebekka, but Rebekka at least needed to know that things weren't what she thought. She dialed Rebekka's number.

Rebekka picked up immediately. "I didn't think you were going to call back," she said.

"I said I would." Carolin considered how to best proceed, in order to avoid giving Rebekka false hope. "My colleague picked up the call for me; I was standing in her office. Now I'm back in mine."

"I thought that was just an evasive maneuver," said Rebekka, "so you wouldn't have to talk to me."

"Why wouldn't I want to talk to you?"

Rebekka laughed softly. "The reason is fairly obvious." She cleared her throat. "I'm sorry. I shouldn't have done that. Please forgive me. It won't happen again." She laughed once more, but it didn't sound cheerful. "Certainly not, since we'll probably never see each other again. You have your toaster now."

"You're really nuts about that toaster, aren't you?" Carolin laughed. "You even brought it to my house on a bicycle."

"It wasn't just about the toaster." Rebekka's voice sounded earnest.

"I know." Carolin bit her lip. She still didn't know what she should say.

"I can only apologize again. Give your boyfriend my regards – although we haven't met. Hopefully he liked the rose." There was a rustling on the line.

"Stop! Rebekka! Don't. Don't hang up." Carolin called into the receiver.

It rustled again. "I think everything has been said." Rebekka's voice came back on the line. "I don't want to bother you any longer. This must be extremely uncomfortable for you, especially after last night."

"No ... Rebekka ... I don't know how I should say this, but –" Carolin took a deep breath. "I don't have a boyfriend."

"You broke up?" Rebekka's voice sounded startled.

"No." Carolin breathed in again, all the way down to her toes. "It's a girlfriend. You bought that rose for a woman, not a man."

For a few seconds, the line was silent. "And you're still together?" asked Rebekka then.

"Yes." Carolin sighed. "She lives in Kassel and only comes on the weekends. That's why I was at the train station."

"Then it's all the same in the end," said Rebekka. "Give *her* my regards, then, and tell her ... tell her that she's very lucky." The receiver clicked. She'd hung up.

"Rebekka, damn it ..." Carolin breathed. "Damn, damn, damn." She propped her head on her hands and tried to get a grip on everything that was rushing around in there.

Why couldn't things just have stayed the way they were? Rebekka and she could be innocent friends who went out to eat together occasionally or rode their bicycles somewhere. Well, no, the bike thing she didn't necessarily want to repeat, but Rebekka ... she did want to see Rebekka again.

To see Rebekka again. She knew that was impossible. Rebekka wanted something from her, and she, Carolin ... wanted something, too.

"Oh, no!" She groaned. Why did life have to be so complicated? For so long, she'd looked for a woman without finding one, then Ina came, and she was happy. Not a hundred percent, because they were apart all week, but the weekends were delightful, she felt simply wonderful then. And when she talked on the phone with Ina ... She turned red, she couldn't help it. There were no innocent phone conversations between them; they always ended up one way. But that was all right. They were, after all, both young, and had needs. There was nothing to be ashamed of.

But what she should be ashamed of were her thoughts about Rebekka. Rebekka probably had no one, she was free and unbound, she could do what she wanted. No one could reproach her for kissing Carolin; she hadn't betrayed anyone by doing that. But Carolin betrayed Ina in her thoughts whenever she thought about Rebekka, when she remembered Rebekka's laughing eyes... and when she wanted to kiss that soft mouth again.

She closed her eyes. This couldn't be happening!

"Thomas wants to talk to you." Ulrike tugged open the door without knocking. "He keeps getting a busy signal."

Carolin looked down at the receiver, which she hadn't hung up properly. She hadn't even noticed. "Yes, all right. I'll be right there," she said quickly.

Ulrike wasn't even listening; she had already taken off somewhere else.

Carolin took a deep breath, rubbed her temples, then shook her head as though she could shake out everything that didn't belong in there. She stood up and went to see Thomas.

Chapter 17

Rick

"Your beer, Marlene," said Melly. "But that's really the last one. You're definitely drinking too much."

Marlene picked up the glass and drank. "It's my business how much I drink. I don't need your permission."

"No, you don't," said Melly, "but I'm not serving you any more."

"Hey, Rick! Did you come to work or to drink? Drink with me." Marlene picked up her glass and brandished it in the air.

Rick, who had just come in, walked up to the counter. "Why would I come here to work?"

"Oh, all that stuff standing around out back, that's jus' your thing, right?" Marlene was already starting to slur her words.

"What stuff?"

"I bought some old chairs for the place," said Melly. "For the atmosphere. But they need some work." She set a beer in front of Rick.

Rick drank. "Should I have a look at them?"

Melly considered her for a little longer than was really necessary. "I didn't want to ask."

"Restoring furniture is what I do," Rick replied. "I'm glad for every piece of business."

"Well, if you want to ..." Melly pointed in the direction of the toilets. "They're sitting in the back hallway."

Rick nodded and put her glass down. "I'll have a look." She disappeared into the back.

"Hey, Rick, leave the bathroom attendant alone!" sniggered Marlene.

"And now you leave your glass alone." Melly took the beer glass out of Marlene's hand. "I shouldn't have given it to you in the first place."

"Hey!" Marlene reached for the receding glass, but wobbled so much that she couldn't catch it. "Do you act like that with all the women you've ever banged?"

"Marlene." Melly rolled her eyes. "You'd better go home now."

"But I don't wanna." Marlene pouted like a stubborn child. "I want beer."

"No more." Melly shook her head. "You can have coffee."

"Coffee, eew!" Marlene stood up and staggered off to the toilet.

Rick came back. "Nice chairs. I'd be happy to restore them for you." She sat down at the counter.

"Great," said Melly. "Pick them up whenever you want. At the moment, they're just getting in the way around here."

"Thanks. That's nice of you. I certainly haven't earned it, the way I've acted toward you."

"Ah, Rick ..." Melly smiled. "You're not the first one who's – Maybe it was my fault, too." She laughed. "It would be nice if we could both just not hold it against each other. That would be enough for me."

Rick was about to answer, but Melly's eye was caught by the opening door.

"Can I have a cup of coffee?" asked Anita in her usual timid manner, as she walked up to the counter.

"Of course." Melly turned around and filled a coffee filter.

"Hello, Anita," said Rick, smiling. "How are you? Long time no see."

"Good. Really good." Anita slid onto a barstool. "Except my feet hurt like hell. Saleswoman's occupational hazard." She grimaced.

"Yeah, you don't have it easy." Rick raised her glass. "A toast to all saleswomen: the heroines of our nation." She drank.

"You're teasing," said Anita.

"Not at all." Rick shook her head. "I really think you have one of the most difficult jobs out there. Certainly one of the most exhausting."

Melly put the cup of coffee in front of Anita. "That's true. I'm on my feet all day, too, so I can completely sympathize."

"Well, hello! Looky who's here."

Anita froze with the coffee cup halfway to her mouth. She nearly dropped it, then set it down with a clatter; coffee splashed over the side.

"Got your eye on Rick now, huh? Do you like Rick? Of course you like her. You like everybody." Marlene staggered over to Anita.

Anita sat there stock still, as if she were paralyzed.

Marlene looked at Rick out of watery eyes. "You don't have to worry about me. She ditched me. Ice cold. But if she likes you . . . I can def'nitely recommend her. She's a great fuck. Screams like —"

Rick lunged forward and loosed a blow on Marlene's cheek that knocked her to the ground. "I'm sorry," she said. "But that's going too far." She looked at Melly. "Will you give me a hand?" Together, they carried Marlene into the back room and laid her on the couch.

"She'll have to sleep it off," said Melly, looking at Marlene's slumped form. "Then hopefully she'll be ashamed of herself."

Anita was still sitting at the counter when they came back. She seemed not to have moved an inch.

"Pardon me," said Melly. "I didn't realize you two had broken up. Otherwise I would've told you that Marlene was here."

Anita didn't react. She was a statue.

Rick went to her and wrapped an arm around her shoulders.

Anita cringed.

"She's sleeping it off now," said Rick, "and afterwards, she ought to apologize to you."

"I have to go." Anita slid down from the barstool and stumbled out of Sappho.

Rick glanced at Melly. Melly nodded. Rick ran after Anita and caught up with her on the street. "Anita . . ." She held her firmly by the arm. "Don't you want to calm down first? Come back. Melly will make you some tea –"

Anita turned around suddenly, wrapped her arms around Rick's neck, and tried to kiss her. Rick was stunned at first, but then she fended her off with a laugh. "Anita ... no ... you're confusing me with someone else."

"You don't want me?" asked Anita. "Didn't you hear what she said? I'm sure you won't regret it." She tried again to get close to Rick.

"Anita ..." Rick held her wrists firmly. "She hurt you terribly. You're in shock. Calm down."

Anita fought her, but Rick was stronger than she was. After a while, Anita gave up. She crumpled, and Rick caught her. Anita sobbed on her breast. "You don't want me," she whispered. "Nobody wants me."

Rick held her tight and gently rubbed her back. "You're a very sweet woman." She stroked her hair. "Everyone likes you."

"I'm only ... only ..." Anita's sobs turned into quiet crying.

"Shh, shh." Rick hugged her to herself. "No, you're not. No one believes what she said. She's drunk." She tried to turn Anita around and led her back into Sappho.

"No!" Anita stood as firmly as an obstinate donkey. "Not in there. I can't go in there."

"Okay, fine." Rick could understand why that might be too much for Anita, with Marlene sleeping in the back room. "Where do you live?"

Anita told her.

"That's far," said Rick. "You came over here specially?"

"I work nearby." Anita was gradually starting to act normal again. She'd felt so lonely; her apartment held only bad memories; so Sappho had seemed like a welcoming port in a storm. What irony. It had completely slipped her mind that Marlene might be there. She'd thought of Sabrina, and Carolin and the others, but not –

"Come on," said Rick. "I live right around the corner. You can get some sleep at my place." Anita sank back against her again, and Rick took her home. She laid her on the bed, took off her shoes, and pulled the blanket over her.

"Rick." Anita's voice followed her weakly as she was about to

leave the bedroom. "Please, stay here."

Rick turned around and frowned. "Anita . . ."

"Why don't you want to sleep with me? I'm here, you're here. I wouldn't mind."

"You're not yourself. Otherwise you would mind." Rick was about to turn around again.

"I don't want to be alone, Rick. Please . . ." whispered Anita. "Please . . ." She sat up and began to undress.

Rick went back to the bed, held her shoulders, and looked at her. "You don't have to sleep with me to not be alone. I'll stay with you. But only if you behave yourself." She laughed. "I can only resist your curves up to a point, you know."

Anita let herself fall back; Rick took off her pants and shirt and slipped into bed next to her.

Immediately, Anita turned around and started to kiss and caress her.

"Don't." Rick held her wrists again. "I'll tie you up if you don't stop that. I'm warning you."

"Go ahead."

"That wasn't a sexual offer," Rick went on. "And I don't really believe you want that anyway. Be sensible, or I can't sleep here."

Anita looked at her curiously. "You really mean that."

"Of course I really mean it." Rick sighed. "Please, Anita. You're an extremely desirable woman, but I don't want to take advantage of you. Sleep first, and tomorrow we'll see."

Anita lay next to her, and Rick waited for her to fall asleep.

"May I . . . may I come closer to you?" whispered Anita's voice after a couple of minutes. "I won't do anything, I promise."

Rick took a deep breath. "If you want."

Anita scooted over and snuggled up to her. "Thank you," she whispered.

Rick wrapped an arm around her and felt Anita's breathing deepen. After a while, she was asleep.

Rick smiled. Anita's curves might be provocative, but at the moment, she felt more like she had her little sister in her arms.

It took a while, but then she fell asleep as well.

CR80

Rick woke up. Something was different The aroma of coffee was drifting through the apartment.

She cast a glance at the other side of the bed. It was empty, the pillow neatly fluffed and the blanket folded.

She heard noises. Although it was really much too early, she got up and stumbled into the kitchen.

Anita stood at the counter, carefully made up and completely dressed. She looked neat as a pin.

"I'm sorry, I didn't want to wake you," she said as Rick tottered in. "I have to go to work." She didn't look at Rick. "Do you want some coffee?" Now she glanced briefly at Rick. "I used your shower. I hope you don't mind."

"Of course not." Rick rubbed her eyes. "It's just a little early for me."

"No coffee?" Anita laughed gently. "I have to have it in the morning, no matter what."

"Me too," said Rick. "In about three hours."

"I'm really sorry, I –" Anita broke off. "I'm terribly ashamed of myself, Rick," she whispered.

Rick waved it away sleepily. "Don't worry about it. Nothing happened." She went to the kitchen table and sat down.

"I wouldn't exactly say that." Anita poured herself a cup of coffee and sat down at the table as well. "I . . . I – this is incredibly embarrassing for me. I have no idea what to say."

"Then don't say anything." Rick rubbed her eyes again and yawned. "Sorry. I'm really not used to getting up at this hour."

Anita laughed softly. "Yes, you do look a bit rumpled." She took a sip of coffee. "I'm used to it by now. I wake up automatically; I don't even need an alarm clock."

"If I didn't have an alarm clock, I'd probably sleep until afternoon. And work at night. But most people aren't too thrilled about hearing you hammer their ears off at three in the morning. Furniture restoration isn't a completely noiseless job, you know."

"You restore furniture? I didn't know that."

"I have a small workshop, nothing special. I originally trained as a carpenter, but restoring old furniture brings in more money. Nobody has new furniture made anymore. You can get mass-produced stuff way cheaper in any store."

"What kind of furniture do you restore?" asked Anita with interest.

"Everything. Whatever turns up. Chairs, armchairs, sofas, tables, cabinets – anything you can imagine."

"It must be fun to pick out the fabrics," Anita supposed.

"That's not really my thing so much," said Rick. "I'm more into the woodworking. I don't really know anything about fabrics and patterns. I leave that completely up to the customers."

"Too bad," Anita replied. "That would be the most exciting part for me."

Rick looked at her and smiled. "I believe you. If you feel like it, you can come by sometime and make a few suggestions. Some customers don't really know what it is they want; they could use a bit of advice."

"Really?" Anita looked at her in surprise.

"I don't know how much time you have outside your job. I imagine you're pretty tied up already."

"Yes. Yes, that's true, but … If it would be all right, I'd really love to try it. On my day off."

Rick stood up and took a business card out of a drawer. "Here. Telephone number and address. Call first; I'm not always in the workshop. Sometimes I'm at a customer's house."

Anita took the card and regarded it as though it were a precious gift. "Rick … you … you're unbelievable. Thank you." She stood up and gave Rick a kiss on the mouth. Then she laughed. "And now you're covered in lipstick." She took a tissue and began to clean the color from Rick's lips. Suddenly, she looked into her eyes, let the tissue drop, and kissed her again, very gently.

Rick wrapped her arms around Anita, kissed her back just as gently, and enjoyed the feeling of her pillowy breasts, nearly sinking into them. "Don't you have to go to work?" she asked softly as they separated.

"Yes, unfortunately," whispered Anita. She took a step back and looked at Rick. "I . . . May I come back? Tomorrow is my day off."

"We could set something up in the workshop. Then you can have a look at the fabrics."

"Couldn't I . . . come this evening and stay until tomorrow?" Anita looked at the floor.

"Well, yes, you could do that, too, of course," replied Rick, stunned.

"You wouldn't object? Like you did yesterday?"

"Yesterday was a special situation."

"Good. Then I'll come over this evening and cook something for you. Do you like meat and potatoes? Goulash?"

"Y-yes." Rick felt slightly caught off guard.

"Then I'll bring some." Anita stepped unwillingly away from Rick, stroked a finger across Rick's lips as if she wanted to remember them, brushed one more kiss across them, and left the kitchen.

Rick went back to bed and tried to get some more sleep, but she couldn't. She felt unsettled, but she didn't know exactly why. She tossed and turned for a while, then got up, went to her workshop, and worked until she got hungry.

It was now the hour at which she normally got up. She'd eat breakfast at Sappho and then go back to work.

"Morning." She walked up to the counter. "Coffee. A big pot," she said to Melly.

"Just coffee, or breakfast too?" asked Melly.

"Breakfast with a whole lot of coffee," nodded Rick. "I've been working for a couple of hours already."

"So early?" Melly looked at her.

"Anita had to go to work. She always gets up that early."

"She spent the night with you?" Melly slid a large cup of coffee across the countertop to her.

"Yep." Rick took a sip and set the cup down again.

"How is she?"

"Good. Considering the circumstances."

"Marlene has got to apologize to her," Melly commented angrily. "I told her so this morning when she left. Otherwise she won't be welcome to come back here again."

Rick sighed. "Unfortunately, there are plenty of other pubs she can go to. And it's not hard to get a case of beer at the supermarket, either."

"I think Sappho means something to her," said Melly. "She doesn't like to drink alone, and all the people she knows come here."

"But Marlene apologizing – you can wait until hell freezes over."

"I don't think so. She's just going to have to learn." Melly grinned. "You gave her a pretty good shiner."

"Not her first. Even if it is the first one she's gotten from me." Rick shook her head. "I get that she's taking it hard that Anita left her. But to behave like that –"

"Well, now. I seem to remember a situation with a certain Rick, who also –"

"I beg your pardon, Melly." Rick interrupted her indignantly. "I never said anything nearly as nasty about you as Marlene said about –"

"No, of course not. You would never do that. But Marlene isn't exactly Miss Manners. And she knows it's her own fault, too. I think that weighs heavily on her. She likes Anita, you know?"

"She likes her?" Rick shook her head. "Then she has a funny way of showing it."

"You know Marlene." Melly sighed. "Feelings aren't her thing. Even when she acknowledges that she has some herself. But have you ever seen her make such a fuss over a woman? Sure, she's always badmouthing them, calling them sluts and hussies, but usually she already has the next one on her arm by then. Usually all that fuss is just a tempest in a teacup. But this time . . ."

Rick frowned. "Yeah, you're right. That hadn't even occurred to me."

"When you stand here at this counter every day, things occur to you. The things I pick up about people. . ." She nodded to Rick. "I'll go back in the kitchen and tell Ev that you need a substantial breakfast."

"Yes, thank you." Rick answered absently. Again, she had the feeling that something wasn't right, but she couldn't quite put her finger on it.

CR&D

"**D**o you want some more goulash? There's still some here." Anita looked inquiringly at Rick.

"No. No, thank you." Rick smiled. "I've already eaten much too much. You're an outstanding cook."

"Thanks." Anita screwed up her mouth. "My mother wouldn't agree, though. She always told me I couldn't do anything right."

"Well, that wasn't very nice of your mother."

Anita smiled, came up close to Rick, and sat on her lap. "And now for dessert," she whispered, bending down over Rick and kissing her. "I hope it's sweet enough."

Rick shut her eyes briefly and relished Anita's tender presence. Everything about her was so soft . . . her lips, her breasts . . . "You are sweet," she whispered. Anita opened Rick's shirt and began to caress her breasts. Rick sighed. "Sweeter than the law allows."

Anita didn't answer, but slid from Rick's lap to the floor and unfastened her pants, then tried to pull them off.

Rick felt somewhat irritated. "Here in the kitchen? Wouldn't you rather go to bed instead?"

Anita looked up at her. "I thought . . . so it would go faster."

Marlene, you are such a twit. What did you do to her? "Faster?"

"Or you can –" Anita stood up. "If you want. Should I turn around?"

Marlene, next time you're getting two black eyes. Rick stood up. "I'm going to turn around now and get into bed. What you do is up to you."

Anita took a while to make her decision; Rick was already lying naked in bed when Anita she came in.

"I . . . I . . . pardon me," she said. "Did I do something wrong? I didn't want –"

"You didn't do anything wrong. I just find the bed more comfortable," said Rick. "Don't you?"

"Yes." An uncertain smile crept into the corners of Anita's mouth. "May I . . . I mean, would you like me to join you?"

"No," replied Rick. "I love to lie in bed by myself and just look at a beautiful woman standing five feet in front of me."

"I . . . I don't understand." Anita seemed confused.

Rick sighed. "Come on." She lifted the covers.

"Should I get undressed?"

"That'd probably be more practical," said Rick, raising her eyebrows.

Anita took off her clothes quickly and slipped under the blanket next to Rick. "I'm sorry. I . . . I . . ."

"Shh." Rick laid one finger on Anita's lips. "Everything's okay. Come here." She took Anita in her arms and simply held her tight. In doing so, she wondered at how little Anita's efforts had aroused her. Really, she ought to have been completely wild for her by now, but she wasn't. Even Anita's supple breasts, which had turned up in her dreams from time to time since she'd first seen her and which now pressed gently against her, didn't put any naughty ideas in her head.

Anita began to caress her again. Her hands ran over Rick's body, very gently and sweetly; soft lips brushed across Rick's throat and breasts. Rick lay back and closed her eyes. She enjoyed Anita's caresses, like the warm summer breeze that might suddenly brush her skin when she's lying on the beach. It was pleasant. But not necessarily erotic.

Anita kissed her, skimming down the length of Rick's body. All at once, Rick felt Anita's breasts brush her groin. She moaned. Okay, that was pretty erotic. She rolled Anita onto her back and lay on top of her. She kissed Anita, and slowly her kiss became deeper, no longer so gentle, but still with more tenderness than passion.

Anita's breasts pulled her magically in, and she laid her cheeks between them, sinking into their soft fullness; she wished she never had to surface from them. It was an incredible feeling. Appreciatively, she kissed the silky skin, working her way over to the left nipple, which was still sunken almost flat in its surroundings.

She sat up and looked at Anita. "Do you really want this? It doesn't look like it."

A frightened expression crossed Anita's face. She embraced Rick's cheeks, pulled her down and kissed her wildly. "No, no, I do want it," she whispered hectically. "Take me, please. I'll do anything you want."

"But that's not the point, Anita. I mean," Rick laughed, "that could be exciting under certain circumstances, but you should have a few wishes of your own."

"That's not so important." Anita looked at her. "It's nice with you, Rick. Don't worry about me. Just tell me what you want."

"I want *you* to feel good."

"I do feel good. I'm fine. You ... you're so kind to me –" Anita turned her head to the side, but Rick had already seen that her eyes were filling with tears.

"Do you always cry when you're fine?" Rick asked, slowly letting herself slide off of Anita and stroking her hair.

"I'm not crying," said Anita.

"Then look at me," said Rick.

Anita turned onto her stomach. "Please, Rick, just take me," she whispered. "You don't have to look at me for that."

"Anita, Anita ..." Rick took a deep breath. "I think we should end this experiment. It's not getting us anywhere. You're in exactly the same condition as you were yesterday, and this just doesn't make any sense. I understand how you feel; you don't have to be ashamed of it. You just need time to get through it."

"Are you sending me away?" whispered Anita.

"You can stay here if you want, but you don't have to pay for it with sex," sighed Rick. "I already told you that yesterday." She laughed. "You cooked, and you bought the food," she counted off. "I think that's enough for one night in two-star lodgings like mine."

"This would be the second night." Anita's voice sounded weak.

"I'm sure the goulash was expensive; it was very good meat. And a cook earns, per hour –"

"Don't make fun of me ... please ... Rick ..." The weakness in Anita's voice was again accompanied by a note of suppressed tears.

"I'm not making fun of you." Rick gently rubbed Anita's back, which was heaving almost undetectably. "Not in the least. I understand you very well. You don't want to be alone, and you're prepared to pay for it. There's no shame in that. People who see therapists do that every week. Or every day, if they're Woody Allen."

"You're pretty clever." Anita turned over. Her eyes were red, but dry. She wasn't crying anymore. "For a carpenter."

Rick shrugged. She bent herself to Anita's ear and whispered: "Before that, I took all college prep classes in high school. But please don't tell anyone. It could hurt my reputation." She lay back down in the bed and grinned.

Anita smiled uncertainly. "Sometimes I don't understand what you mean."

"You're not the only one. I don't understand myself, sometimes." Rick stood up. "I'm not sleepy. If you want, you can go to sleep, though. I'm going to sit on the sofa for a while and read." She pulled on underwear and a T-shirt and went to the living room.

"I'll clean up the kitchen," said Anita. "I'm not tired yet, either."

"Now that's something of a marvel," said Rick, picking up a book. "As early as you have to get up."

"I don't need a lot of sleep." Anita went into the kitchen and rattled the pots and pans. After a time, she came up to Rick in the living room. "What are you reading?"

"Nothing that would interest you. Woodworking stuff." Rick looked up. "Wow. I had no idea where that shirt was anymore. Looks good on you."

"I found it in the closet." Anita went to the shelf and browsed through the books. "I don't suppose you have any romance novels?"

Rick laughed. "No, I don't read those much. Technical books are more my speed."

Anita took out an oversize volume and sat down next to Rick. "And travel books," she said. She opened the book. "Great pictures."

"Yeah, if I had more money ... I used to hitchhike a lot. With Carolin."

"Carolin and you, you're ... good friends?" asked Anita as though she wasn't particularly interested.

Rick grinned. "Carolin and I are like sisters. Except for a couple lapses in our youth. And she is also my best friend, yes."

Anita acted as if the answer didn't interest her in the slightest, and flipped through the photography book.

"At the moment, I'm single," continued Rick. "In case that's what you wanted to know."

"I ... I – That's none of my business," said Anita. She held her head down, but nonetheless, Rick noticed a slight reddening of her cheeks.

"Anita," said Rick, closing her book. "If you want to stay here for a few days, to recuperate, I have no objection. Not permanently, but let's say, a week or so would be no problem. You don't have to pay anything for it and you don't have to offer me any quid pro quo. Is that what you want?"

"I ... Rick ..." Anita gripped the book convulsively. "I don't want to be a burden on you."

"You aren't. So, it's settled. You're staying here for the next week." Rick opened her book again and immersed herself in the finer points of specialty woods.

Anita laid the book she'd been holding on the coffee table and sank back into the sofa. "I feel so at ease with you, Rick," she sighed.

"That's nice," said Rick absently, because an exotic type of wood had just captured her attention. "I'm glad." She hardly noticed Anita moving closer to her. When Anita caressed her thigh, though, she jumped. "Anita, I told you —"

"You told me I should have a couple of wishes of my own," murmured Anita. "You've already fulfilled one of them, and the second . . ." she pushed herself onto Rick, "I'm about to show you."

Rick's book slid out of her hand, and she was lying beneath Anita on the sofa before she saw what was coming. "You just don't like the bed," she teased. "Admit it."

"Maybe." Anita brushed kisses onto her eyes, nose, and cheeks before she breezed past Rick's mouth to her ear and throat. There she began to suck.

"Oh, no, Anita! No hickey! That's always so embarrassing," groaned Rick.

"I'll get you a scarf," said Anita, taking a breath and continuing.

"Ow!" said Rick. "That hurts."

"All done," said Anita. She smiled to herself. "I'm sure it'll look good tomorrow."

"I bet you're a real artist in that area. Now let me get up."

"Why?" Anita looked down at her. "We're far from done."

"One hickey is enough. I'm not letting you do that again."

Anita bent forward and caressed Rick's lips with her own, slowly pressing into her mouth with her tongue and exploring it gently and steadily.

Rick sensed that something had changed. Anita's kiss turned her on, and to no small degree. She tried to push Anita away, but Anita was already in the better position, lying on top of her. "Anita, no, you don't have to do that," she protested, gasping, when Anita's mouth finally freed her.

"But I want to do it," whispered Anita, pushing her hands under Rick's T-shirt and rolling both nipples between her fingers.

Rick moaned loudly. "Don't ... that –" She couldn't say any more, because Anita was teasing her nipples unbearably and kissing her at the same time.

Anita's right hand abandoned Rick's breast and slid downward, pushed aside the fabric of her underpants, and thrust into her.

Rick moaned in Anita's mouth; she could hardly stand it any longer, Anita's tongue, Anita's fingers rubbing her nipple, Anita's fingers inside her, making her almost crazy. Anita placed her thumb on Rick's pearl and pressed in, gliding faster and faster over it.

Rick collected all of her strength and freed herself from Anita's kiss, because she wasn't getting enough air. She moaned, gasped, opened her legs, and tried to thrust back against Anita's fingers. Already she felt the waves approaching, whispered, "Yes," moaned once again, and tensed up. Anita's fingers still took her, but she didn't feel it anymore. The spasms swelling inside her drowned out all else.

After a while, she lay still, panting. "Stop, Anita," she whispered. "Please, stop."

Anita smiled down at her. "Was that nice?"

"Yeah." Rick was still gasping for breath. She groped beneath the oversized men's shirt Anita had dug out of her closet. "You're not wearing any panties," she whispered, surprised.

"No." Anita only breathed the answer, bent over her, and kissed Rick again. "Does that give you any ideas?"

Rick stroked Anita's naked bottom. "I'd love to lick you," she murmured, "while you sit on my face."

Anita kissed her again, sat up, and pulled her shirt off. Rick slid deeper into the couch, and Anita straddled her. Rick pushed her tongue between Anita's labia, and Anita sighed loudly above her and began to move. Rick watched her breasts whipping around above her while she licked Anita and Anita grew ever wilder. "Yes," she moaned. "Yes, oh, yes . . . yes . . ."

Rick held her hips firmly, so that Anita wouldn't keep escaping her, and licked harder.

Anita moaned louder and louder. She tried to free herself from Rick's grasp, but Rick held her there until she felt Anita's vulva twitch, felt it throb and tug, so that her tongue was nearly pulled inside.

Anita didn't scream, she only whimpered; then she collapsed, sliding backwards until she lay on the couch with her legs spread wide, as if she could no longer move.

Rick found the view exceptionally alluring. She took off her underpants and T-shirt and slid her legs like scissors over and under Anita, until their labia met.

"Oh, God . . ." Anita moaned once more. "What are you doing there?"

"Isn't it nice?" asked Rick, smiling.

"Yes, very . . . nice." Anita began to move, Rick followed her, and soon they both moaned aloud and lay entwined on the couch, multi-limbed, like an exhausted crab.

"Rick?" Anita whispered after a while.

"Hmm?" Rick felt sleepy.

"You don't think I did that as . . . payment, do you?" She sounded uncertain.

Rick slowly disentangled herself from Anita and swung her legs off the couch. She bent over Anita and grazed her lips with a gentle kiss. "No, I don't think that. But next time, we're staying in bed. I'm sore all over."

Anita smiled with relief. "You didn't want to."

"I didn't? *You* didn't!" Rick acted scandalized. She stood up and reached out a hand to Anita. "But now we're going to go to sleep."

Anita let herself be pulled up and pressed herself against Rick. "You really want to sleep? I wish this night would never end. I want to feel you, again and again, all night long." She kissed Rick ardently.

"I have to work on the chairs for Melly," said Rick, breathing hard after the kiss. "I was actually planning to do that tomorrow. And if I don't sleep –"

"I'm sure Melly won't be mad at you if it takes one day longer," said Anita. She let go of Rick, ran to the bedroom, and jumped into bed.

Rick followed her more slowly and stopped to contemplate Anita's naked body, draped very seductively across the bed. "I don't like to make Melly wait. But you're not fighting fair. Who can resist that body?"

"You have."

"That was in another world." Rick slid slowly into bed. "Tonight, anyhow, I can't resist anymore."

Chapter 18

Sabrina

"Six weeks, Sabsi, it's only six weeks." There was desperation in Chris's voice. "You'll hardly notice I'm gone."

"I notice it already," said Sabrina. "I've noticed it all along. Do you even live here anymore?"

"Yes, I know." Chris put her toiletry bag in the suitcase and tried to close it. She looked guiltily at Sabrina, who was leaning against the bedroom doorframe with folded arms. "It won't latch. Would you sit on it for me?"

"Do I even have to help you leave me?" sighed Sabrina. She went to the bed and sat on the suitcase.

"But I'm not leaving you." Chris snapped the latches shut. "How could I ever leave you? You're the woman of my dreams." She braced her hands on the suitcase, bent over, and kissed Sabrina lovingly. "The only woman there ever has been or ever will be for me. My wife."

Sabrina wrapped her arms around Chris's neck and tried to hold her there. "Kiss me," she whispered. "Kiss me again."

"I can't, I don't have time," said Chris regretfully. "My flight –"

"Please, Chris ..." Sabrina let herself slide onto the bed and pulled Chris down with her. "Please, just one more time ..."

"Sabsi ..." Chris loosed herself, laughing. "I'll miss my flight."

"You have to be there hours early anyway." Sabrina sat up and pulled Chris back down to her. "You still have lots of time."

Chris gave in and lay on top of her. "And now? Do you want to have an orgy in just these couple of minutes?"

Sabrina closed her eyes. "I just want to memorize the feeling," she whispered. "When you lie on top of me and you're so close to me."

"Oh, Sabsi." Chris kissed her tenderly. "I would rather stay here, too."

Sabrina began to move beneath her. "Chris ..." she whispered. "Chris ..."

"There's no more time for that," whispered Chris.

"I love you. I love you so much." Sabrina moaned, and her movements under Chris became ever more intense.

"You're crazy," moaned Chris, because Sabrina's movements were turning her on, and she began to follow her rhythm.

Sabrina spread her thighs; Chris sank with one leg between them and moaned aloud as Sabrina raised her own leg. She rubbed against it, and Sabrina's hips ran up and down, rubbing themselves against Chris's thigh. Their mutual rhythm grew ever wilder; Sabrina moaned without pause and threw her head from side to side, Chris squeezed her thighs together, and finally, they both stiffened almost simultaneously.

Chris fell, gasping, on top of Sabrina. "Darling, I have to go," she whispered breathlessly, picking herself up and sitting on the edge of the bed. She laughed. "Fully dressed; we haven't done that in a long time. That was more when we first got together, when we could hardly wait." She stood up. "So long, my love." She bent down and gave Sabrina a quick goodbye kiss on the lips. "I'll call you as soon as I can. I love you."

She reached for her suitcase and disappeared out the door.

Sabrina still lay on the bed; her skirt was awry, but it wasn't obvious what she had just done. She brushed the hair out of her face and breathed deeply. Chris was gone. Gone.

She closed her eyes and tried to remember one more time what she'd just experienced: Chris's weight on her, Chris's scent, her voice. She wanted to preserve the memory, because she was going to have to live on it for six weeks. At least six weeks.

CRROD

"**Y**ou're still here, Ms. Keller? I thought you'd gone home hours ago." Joachim Dillinger cast a startled glance into Sabrina's office. "It's late – even for me."

"There's just so much to catch up on," said Sabrina. "And now, in the evening, no one is here to disturb me."

"Evening?" Joachim Dillinger looked at the clock. "It's almost midnight."

"No one's waiting for me at home," Sabrina mumbled to herself.

"It can't be all that important," said Joachim Dillinger. "Come on, I'll drive you home."

"But I have to –" Sabrina looked distractedly at her desk.

"You don't have to do anything. You know how much I value you as an employee, but as a responsible boss, I also need to preserve your ability to work. And part of that is getting enough sleep, for one thing." He walked over to Sabrina's desk and pulled her upright. "I don't want to lose you; without you, the whole place would collapse."

"Even though I work with so little focus? Or so you said."

"I never said that; you must've heard wrong." Dillinger pointed at her computer screen. "Turn that thing off. We're done for today."

"Well, all right." Sabrina smiled. "But I can take the bus, there's one due in a few minutes." She shut down the PC.

"Nonsense. I'll drive you. Who knows what might happen to an attractive woman like you this late at night. There are always thugs wandering around out there." He turned around and left Sabrina's office.

Sabrina frowned. Was he driving her home now because he found her attractive and wanted something from her? Until now, he'd never actually given her that impression, but one never knew. "Mr.

Dillinger!" she called, running after him. "I'm not on your way at all."

"You're on my way now." He looked over at her while they walked to his parking spot. "Did you think I hadn't noticed you've been burning the candle at both ends over the last two weeks? You've always been very hardworking, you've put in overtime when it was necessary without a word of complaint – but that you hardly even leave the building anymore, that really won't do. I told my wife about it and she gave me an earful for taking advantage of you like that."

Ah, his wife. Sabrina smiled even more. "You told your wife about me?"

"I tell my wife everything. She asks about you all the time."

I can imagine, thought Sabrina. If he'd also told his wife that he found Sabrina attractive, then she had good reason to be asking about Sabrina. "Well, please give her my best. And tell her I'm grateful for her kind attention to my welfare."

"I'll let her know." They had arrived in the company parking lot. Dillinger's Mercedes was parked right up front, in the first space. He unlocked the car with his remote, and as he got in, he swore under his breath. "Two hundred thousand Euros and the thing wobbles from one end to the other. It's a disgrace. German quality craftsmanship, ha!"

As Mr. Dillinger continued on the decline of German craftsmanship, Sabrina lapsed back into her own thoughts. It was already two weeks that Chris had been gone, and every day, Sabrina tried to numb herself with work until she was so tired that she'd be able to fall asleep as soon as her head hit the pillow. Unfortunately, she couldn't stay asleep. She always woke up, and she always woke up thinking about Chris. She yearned for her.

Chris called every day, which only made it worse. When Sabrina heard Chris's voice, she wanted to be with her so much it hurt. She'd thought about taking some vacation time and meeting Chris in Norway, but that just wasn't possible at the moment. Dillinger had imposed a ban on taking time off while they were utterly besieged with unfulfilled orders. There was no trace of the German economic recession, at least not at Dillinger & Co.

"So, here we are," said Mr. Dillinger, pulling over to the curb. "I hope you sleep well. Don't think about work for a change."

If only I could think of nothing but work, thought Sabrina. "I'll try." She laughed softly. "Thank you very much. And don't forget to give your wife my best."

"I will, I will."

Sabrina got out and the car drove away. She opened her purse and took out her key ring. For a moment, she hesitated. The apartment would be dark as always, and there wasn't even the prospect that Chris would come home in a couple of hours. No hope of touching her and cuddling her in her sleep, or that the bed would smell like her in the morning. She wasn't there anymore.

She sighed. Four more weeks, and every day seemed like a year.

A car door slammed. Someone else was coming home late, too.

Sabrina went to the door of her building and stuck the key in the lock.

"Snazzy car your boyfriend has."

Sabrina spun around. Her heart pounded in her throat. She had never been attacked before, but at the moment she was completely alone on the street; most of her neighbors were sure to be asleep.

Then anger rose in her. "You scared me half to death," she said furiously.

Anna laughed. "I'm sorry, I didn't mean to. But I've been waiting for you for hours. I didn't realize you had an ... engagement." She looked down the street, although Dillinger's car had long since turned the corner. "He must have money, too, if he can afford wheels like that. I assume dinner was expensive. Or didn't you go out to eat at all? Did you just go directly to –"

Sabrina turned around and yanked the door open. "I don't know what business that would be of yours."

"Well, you could've told me earlier that you go for that sort of thing, then I might've laid out a little more," said Anna. "If I'd known who my competition was ..."

Sabrina slowly turned back to face her. "Are you implying that I'm for sale?" Cold fury blazed a trail through her.

Anna shrugged. "When the only option for taking you out to eat is the most expensive restaurant in the city, men usually expect some compensation for that."

Sabrina snorted contemptuously. "Not just men."

"Yes, I don't like to get zero return on my investment, either," Anna admitted.

"I think you already got more than you paid for," Sabrina replied angrily. "I need you to leave me alone. I've got to sleep."

"So do I. With you."

Sabrina frowned heavily. "And you think you're going to accomplish that by insulting me?"

"No, I –" Anna looked at the ground and suddenly seemed much less self-confident. "I was jealous, I admit it. When I saw you getting out of that car . . . at this hour. Who's the guy?"

Sabrina sighed. "My boss. And I'm not having an affair with him. We both worked late and he drove me home; that's all."

Anna appeared relieved. "I've been to your office building," she admitted. "Several days in a row now. But you didn't come out. And then I came here, and you weren't here, either. I was worried."

"Oh no." Sabrina grimaced mockingly. "Did you lose my phone number? You practically had it memorized."

"I *do* have it memorized," Anna nodded. "I dialed it umpteen times and hung up again. I knew you didn't want to talk to me."

"Not on the phone, but in the middle of the night on the street?" whispered Sabrina. She felt like their conversation was echoing through the entire city.

"No . . . of course . . . of course you don't want to talk to me anywhere. I know." Anna looked at the ground again. "I've done everything wrong from the start."

"You can say that again." Sabrina turned back to the door once again. "I'm tired, I've been working half the night for two weeks straight, and I really don't feel like discussing this with you now."

"Sabrina." Anna hugged her from behind. "I did everything wrong because this is a completely new situation for me. You're the first woman who's ever meant something to me. I don't have a routine for that. You mean so much to me, you have no idea . . ." She breathed a kiss onto the back of Sabrina's neck.

Sabrina stood there, stiff and unmoving. Anna's lips caressed her throat, and her hands wandered up to Sabrina's breasts. "Sabrina . . ." she whispered. "Sabrina . . ."

Sabrina closed her eyes. She had longed every day for Chris to caress her, for Chris to be with her, longer than these two weeks, much longer. If she could imagine that this was Chris . . .

"Anna," she said softly. "Let me go."

"Sorry." Anna's hands fell, and she stepped back.

Sabrina turned to face her. "I can't, Anna, and you know why. Don't make it so hard for me."

"I –" Anna lifted her arms helplessly and let them fall again. "I don't know what to do. I've never felt this way about another woman."

"You've never felt this way? But in your books –"

Anna smirked. "So you do read them." She became serious again and shook her head. "My books are pure fantasy; I've never experienced what's in them. They're wishes. Dreams. My dreams . . . and obviously, they match up with the dreams of a lot of readers. But they have nothing to do with my life." She looked Sabrina in the eye. "I've never encountered a woman like you before."

Sabrina took a deep breath. "What am I supposed to say to that? That we coincidentally met each other doesn't change anything about the situation. I'm not available. And even if I were . . ."

"I would still be out of the question for you." Anna sighed. "I know that's how it is, I just didn't want to accept it. The married women I've met before have . . . the word 'fidelity' wasn't in their vocabularies."

"Well, it *is* in mine." Sabrina regarded Anna thoughtfully. "I like you, Anna. Although I never thought I'd say so, I really like you. You're intelligent, charming," she smiled, "and by no means boring. I've felt very comfortable in your presence, except for –"

"Yes." Anna cleared her throat. "I know what you mean. Except for the one thing. I . . . sometimes I couldn't think about anything else, I admit it. You're simply . . . hmm . . . too attractive. I would really have to be blind to ignore that."

"What if you were blind? Would it work then?"

Anna made a face. "No. I'd still have your picture in my head. But –" She shrugged. "There's no point, anyway." She turned away and took a few steps.

"No point to what?"

Anna turned back to Sabrina. "Even if I offered to be the platonic friend you'd like to have, you wouldn't allow it now."

Sabrina smiled. "I find it difficult to believe that you know the meaning of the word 'platonic'."

"Oh, I know it." Anna laughed softly. "Yes, even I do." She raised a hand. "I don't want to keep you from your well-earned sleep any longer. I've done that for much too long already." She walked to her car, which she had parked on the street.

"Anna?" Sabrina called softly after her.

Anna turned around.

Sabrina took a couple of steps toward her. "I ... I – wouldn't have any objection to a walk." She laughed gently. "In broad daylight. Not in the dark."

Anna began to smile incredulously. "Really?"

"Yes, I – I have a ton of overtime to use up. So I could take an afternoon off." Sabrina didn't know why she was saying this; she just felt less lonely when Anna was there, and after all, there was nothing anyone could object to about going for a walk. "But –" She looked sternly at Anna. "This only involves a walk, nothing further. We can have a conversation, study nature ... whatever ... but under no circumstances –"

"Yes, yes, yes!" Anna laughed. "That ... that's ... thank you." She looked at Sabrina. "You ... you're giving me such a gift. And I'm going to prove myself worthy of it." She bowed like a gentleman of the old school. "You'll see."

"Yes, I will," said Sabrina. "Because if I don't see that, the walk and everything else will be over. Forever."

Anna smiled. "When? Tomorrow?"

Sabrina considered. "Sure, why not? I've worked so much lately, there's nothing urgent to do that I can't take care of in half a day. Anyhow, my boss scolded me today for working too late. I'll remind him of that tomorrow."

"That ... that gives me great pleasure." Anna seemed overwhelmed. She stepped forward, took Sabrina's hand, and breathed a barely perceptible kiss on it. "You have no idea how happy you've made me."

Sabrina looked at the hand that Anna had just kissed and felt very strange. "Just a walk. No more than that."

"I know." Anna smiled at her. "Until tomorrow. I'll call you, and we'll set up a time that I can pick you up." She got into her car and looked up at Sabrina. "Sleep well," she said softly.

She started the car and drove off.

Sabrina watched her go, and went slowly back to the house. She didn't feel entirely at ease with this, but still, she felt a sense of relief. Nothing had happened, and Anna seemed . . . to have finally become reasonable.

When she entered the apartment, she saw the answering machine blinking. She went over and pressed the button.

"I couldn't reach you, you're probably still at the office, but I didn't want to call you there," said Chris's warm voice. She sighed. "It's so wonderful here . . . the landscape, the sea . . . I wish you were here. Even though I'm working practically nonstop, I think of you all the time. And when I think about you, I remember why I'm slaving away like this. I see you . . . I see you and our little daughter, who looks just like you . . ." Chris laughed softly. "She has to look like you, otherwise I won't take her." Then she sighed again. "I love you, Sabsi. I just wanted to tell you that. Sleep well, and sweet dreams . . . my sweet, sweet angel." The sound of a kiss followed, and the message was over.

Sabrina listened to the message again and almost cried. She would've liked to listen to it over and over, in an infinite loop. Chris's voice, saying *I love you* and sounding so tender. As if she could be there with her any minute.

But that would only increase the torment. She sighed and went into the bedroom.

CR&

The next few days passed amazingly without incident. After Anna and Sabrina had spent an afternoon together in an open meadow — it turned out that Anna knew a thing or two about birds, which Sabrina would never have guessed – Anna picked Sabrina up after work on the next several evenings, and they explored the hiking paths just outside the city.

Sabrina sometimes wondered at Anna's reticence. She had to get used to it at first. "Why were you so aggressive with me at the beginning?" asked Sabrina as they strolled together on one of their walks. The forest path was overshadowed by green foliage that let dappled sunlight shimmer onto the ground. "Why couldn't we just have done something like this? It would've saved us both a lot of stress."

Anna laughed. "To be honest, the idea never occurred to me. I've never approached things this way."

"Why not?" asked Sabrina. "Don't you think it's a more promising route?"

Anna frowned. "Not necessarily. As you might imagine, most of the married women I mentioned before were straight, and subtlety tends not to get you very far with them. They're used to something else from men, so they don't even notice you want something from them if you don't beat them over the head with it from the get-go."

"Seriously?" Sabrina raised her eyebrows.

"Seriously. At least that's been my experience. For a lot of them, it's also their first time with a woman –" Anna broke off. "I'm sorry, I didn't want to go into so much detail."

"Go ahead. I'm interested."

"You are?"

"Anna." Sabrina shook her head.

"Okay. So what interests you about it?"

"What does a marriage mean to these women?" asked Sabrina, to herself as well as to Anna. "I mean, why did they get married in the first place? Chris and I got married because we love each other, because we always wanted to be there for each other, in good times and in bad. That obviously doesn't hold true for the women you're talking about."

"For many of them it probably did hold true once. Most of them did marry for love, I think." Anna knitted her brow, pondering. "I think something just happens over the course of the years . . . something that destroys love or slowly lets it fade. The love, and the hope for improvement. Men often settle into a marriage as though it were some kind of utility company. Most women probably have something different in mind when they think about love."

"So they're just disappointed and frustrated? Nothing else?"

Anna sighed. "Well, yeah, and the sex, of course. Men aren't particularly imaginative or inclined to fantasy in that respect, especially when it comes to a woman's needs."

Fantasy, thought Sabrina. *I don't even require that. The act itself would've been plenty for me.* "So they're just out for sex?"

"Women? No. They're looking for tenderness, for understanding, for the feeling of finally being desired again, noticed, paid attention to. For someone to listen."

"Sounds like the advice column in a women's magazine."

"Those magazines reflect reality. They wouldn't be so popular otherwise."

"Hmm." Sabrina considered. She definitely had something in common with these women. Given her experience, Anna had probably recognized that right away, and that's why she'd come onto her. But she refused to admit that she was one of those "desperate housewives," as Anna described them. First, she wasn't a housewife, and second ... how desperate would one have to be to jeopardize a marriage for a little sex? "Didn't you ever have ... I mean, didn't you ever want a girlfriend who ... well, who was completely there for you? Who isn't married?"

"Oh, I've had them. I don't go for a woman just because she's married." Anna smiled at Sabrina. "When I first saw you, I didn't know you were married. It wasn't until later that I noticed the ring. And even before then, I wanted ... I liked you a lot."

"But the fact that I'm married does seem to increase the allure for you," Sabrina replied.

"In a certain way." Anna grinned. "Maybe it's that a woman who's married has already convinced someone of her advantages, so much so that a suitor would enter that kind of commitment. So she must have something that others don't have."

Sabrina laughed out loud in surprise. "Like a quality stamp, you mean? A seal of approval? Goods that have passed inspection?"

"I wouldn't put it that way." Anna threw her head back and

laughed. "No, I really wouldn't!"

"But that's exactly what it is. That fits your description."

Anna's eyebrows rose. "I never really gave it much thought. The idea just came to me. But you're right; it does tend to point in that direction. I'm sorry, I didn't want to say that. I just talk too much."

"It's very good that you said it." Sabrina tilted her head to one side and looked at Anna. "At least now I know where I stand."

"But those women have nothing to do with you."

"I'm married," countered Sabrina. "A married woman, like all the others before."

"Not like all the others," said Anna softly. "You're something special."

"I'm nothing special." Sabrina shook her head. "I go to the office every day like millions of others; I lead an extremely average life. I don't see how that's special."

"Chris recognized your specialness," Anna replied. "Just as I did. Or do you think that you're just like everyone else to Chris?"

Sabrina grimaced. "Chris isn't up for discussion. I'd prefer it if you didn't mention her. You don't even know her."

"Actually, I did see her briefly, disappearing out of a department store," said Anna.

Sabrina stopped in surprise. "What?"

"I was with Anita in the department store, to get a present . . . to buy something. And Chris also happened to be there then . . . I mean, ahead of me; I didn't know who she was. She bought something from Anita –"

"The scarf," said Sabrina softly. "She gave me a beautiful scarf as a gift. She said she'd gotten Anita's advice about it."

"Yes. Anyhow, we almost walked right into each other, but we didn't recognize each other. Anita told me later that it was Chris."

"Still, you don't know her, and I don't want to talk about her with you."

"The topic of Chris is taboo. I understand." Anna seemed thoughtful.

"There are things that you don't understand," said Sabrina. "You write about them, but you don't understand them."

"Love, you mean?" Anna looked at Sabrina with raised eyebrows.

"Yes, that is what I mean." Sabrina's pace quickened. "Love on paper is different from love in reality. They have nothing to do with each other."

"Now, that's not true, either," protested Anna. "The things I write about do exist. The positive as well as the negative."

"Yes, but –" Sabrina stopped. "In life, love affects real people. Paper doesn't blush. People are … vulnerable. They often don't act like they should, usually because they're trying to avoid hurting another person."

"That's true. Paper wounds heal quickly … and as a writer, I can make them heal quickly, if I want to. Or I can amplify them. Exactly as required. But in reality –"

"In reality, we have to consider … a lot of things," said Sabrina. She walked on.

"Of course we do." Anna walked in silence next to Sabrina. "You don't want to hurt Chris, and that weighs on you," she continued after a while.

"I'm not talking about Chris."

"All right, we'll treat the case hypothetically, then." Anna nodded. "A couple, married for years … happily?" She looked at Sabrina, but Sabrina didn't react. "Yes, happily, I think," continued Anna, "up to a certain point. That point always exists, for everyone. The point at which the marriage is put to an endurance test. Sometimes work interferes, sometimes it's about other people. Something penetrates the idyll and destroys it, or at least makes it wobble."

"Are you writing a novel right now? Because that sounds like one."

"Yes, maybe it does sound like a novel, but it's very realistic," Anna insisted. "I've determined that over and over. The marriages, the years, the tests – it's a pattern that always repeats."

"A marriage is an obligation, a promise," said Sabrina quietly. "And whoever breaks that promise –"

"Some promises are made under false assumptions," Anna pointed out. "Or the assumptions have changed. I actually think that the politician who suggested that marriages should expire after seven years had a very good idea. People should be allowed to reassess their relationships, and if their needs are no longer being met, they should get a divorce."

"What?" Sabrina stood still once more and stared at her.

"Don't you remember that discussion from the news?" asked Anna. "With the politician from Bavaria, that hot Ms. Pauli? The one who overthrew Stoiber?" She grinned.

"No, I followed it. Who didn't? It was all over the news."

"That's right," nodded Anna. "And, I think, rightly so. Relationships aren't meant to last forever. For a certain period of time, they're all right, but a lifetime?" She shook her head. "I think that's asking too much of anyone."

"So you think." Sabrina smiled scornfully. "You've never tried it."

"For exactly that reason," said Anna. "Because I don't believe in the permanence of relationships. Why should I launch myself into that labyrinth? I might never find my way out."

"Is that what you're worried about?" Sabrina still looked scornful. "That a woman could shackle you like that? What nicer thing could one wish for?"

"Meh. I could think of a few things," said Anna, running a hand through her hair.

"I'm telling you, you don't understand what you're talking about . . . or writing about," Sabrina replied. "Who are you to judge what a relationship amounts to when you've never had one?"

"So what does a relationship amount to?"

"As if you really wanted to know . . . For you, only one thing counts. But that's not what it's about."

"It's not?" Anna raised her eyebrows skeptically.

"Not primarily," said Sabrina.

"Ah, not *primarily*. That sounds rather different."

"There's no point in us talking about this." Sabrina was starting to feel awkward. "You'd have to know what love is before you could begin to understand what I'm saying."

"Yes, love. Isn't love just another one of those L-words? Love, lust, lasciviousness, lies . . ."

"A curious collection," said Sabrina. "Why lies?"

"It seems to me that they're part and parcel of this so-called love business," Anna replied. "There's a poem by Rilke, in which he says: '*Take a look at the lovers, when first the confessing began, how quickly they lie.*' That applies to so many situations I know of."

"That's nonsense," Sabrina replied crossly. "You don't have to lie when you're in love. You confide, you tell the truth – that's also part of a relationship."

"You tell Chris everything?"

Sabrina already knew what was coming, but nevertheless, she said: "Yes."

"You've told her about me, then? About our ... evening?" Anna looked at Sabrina with her head tipped to the side.

"What is this? The Inquisition?" Sabrina turned away brusquely. "Let's go back; I'm getting cold."

Anna looked up at the radiant blue sky. "Yes, there might be a snowstorm coming," she said, but Sabrina had already turned around, so she followed her through the warmth of the glorious summer evening back to the parking lot at the head of the trail.

Cʒꙶꙴ

"**S**abrina." Carolin looked with astonishment at Sabrina, who was standing at her door.

"You ... you did say that if I wanted to talk sometime, I could come by." Sabrina seemed extraordinarily timid.

"Yes, of course." Carolin stepped aside. "Come right in." She closed the door behind Sabrina. "Would you like some coffee?"

"I think chamomile tea would be better."

"Ooh, it's that bad?" Carolin's brow furrowed sympathetically. She stroked Sabrina's arm. "How long has Chris been gone now?"

"Four weeks," said Sabrina. Tears were starting to well up in her eyes.

"You miss her very much, don't you?" Carolin went into the kitchen. "Tea may not be such a bad idea. I miss Ina, too. More all the time."

"Yes. It adds up."

Carolin tried to smile confidently. "But you're almost there. Only two more weeks. The worst is behind you." She put the tea water on.

"No."

Carolin looked questioningly at her.

"Exactly what I was afraid of has happened: the project is being extended."

"Oh, no. I'm so sorry." Carolin looked at Sabrina with concern. "Is Chris at least coming home in two weeks, for a couple of days?"

"She's going to try, but I already know what that means. It means she's not coming." Sabrina leaned against the kitchen wall and let her head fall back onto it. "I don't know how I'm supposed to survive this long," she whispered.

"One day at a time," Carolin replied. "That's what I always tell myself. On Monday I only have to make it until Tuesday, on Tuesday it's just until Wednesday ... and so on. Then it doesn't seem quite so long."

"Another six weeks? I'm not going to make it through that," breathed Sabrina. "It's so hard."

"Sabrina ..." Carolin went over to her and held her comfortingly. "That time will pass, too. Minute by minute, hour by hour."

"The hours are so long." Sabrina swallowed. "So endlessly long."

The water boiled, and Carolin let go of Sabrina to pour two cups of tea. "I never would have thought that you ... that this would bother you so much," she said, dividing the hot water carefully between the two cups. "You've always been so strong. You give advice to other people ..."

"I need to stop doing that." Sabrina pushed away from the wall and rubbed her eyes. "Giving advice to others when I don't even know how to help myself."

"That's what you have me for." Carolin smiled and handed Sabrina a cup. "Let's go sit down."

Once they'd settled onto the couch in the living room, Carolin asked, "You talk to Chris on the phone every day?"

"Yes." Sabrina sighed. "Sometimes I think I shouldn't. I long for her so much, and when I hear her voice –"

Carolin sighed as well. "I'm familiar with that feeling. It can be bad."

"But ... but when I don't get to hear her voice –" Sabrina set her cup down on the table and put her head in her hands. "I don't know what's worse."

Carolin rubbed her back gently. "I know. It's like a piece of you is missing, and you can't locate it. Like one of those dreams where you're running through a dark fog and you can't find what you're looking for. You reach out your hand, and it's empty when you pull it back." She sighed once more. "I hate that feeling."

"Oh, yes." Sabrina took her hands from her face and sat up. "If there's anything I hate, it's that." She picked up her cup and drank. "It's good for me to talk about this with you. I should've done this a long time ago."

"I offered."

"Yes. I was just so busy ... I've been working a lot." *And there's the whole Anna thing*, she added in her thoughts. In the last week they hadn't gone on any more walks, but because of that, Sabrina's loneliness had grown even more palpable. Even though being with Anna was always a risk, by now Sabrina longed for her almost as much as she did for Chris. She was ashamed to admit it, but it was true. Anna was entertaining; she saw life from a completely different angle than most people did, and she didn't agonize over things. "What have *you* been up to? I haven't been to Sappho lately, since I've been working so late."

"Oh, I ... me neither," said Carolin. "I did get together with Rick once. Rick and ... Anita."

Sabrina stopped short and stared at her. "Rick and Anita?"

Carolin shrugged. "Anita broke up with Marlene –"

"Finally!" Sabrina let out a deep sigh. Then she frowned. "And now she's with Rick –?"

"Yes." Carolin took a deep breath. "Somehow, she's with Rick now."

"Somehow?" Sabrina looked confused. "What's that supposed to mean?"

"Rick is ... well, under her supposedly hard shell beats a pretty soft heart, and I think she took Anita in out of sympathy. There was apparently a pretty ugly scene with Marlene at Sappho. Melly told me. Afterward, Anita spent the night at Rick's. And since then –"

"They've been together," finished Sabrina.

"I wouldn't say *together*, exactly." Carolin sighed. "Rick's letting her stay with her; it's not much more than that."

"That's nice of Rick."

"Rick's apartment has probably never sparkled and gleamed so much," said Carolin, smirking. "Anita is the born housewife." She grinned. "And she does have other qualities, too."

"So they *are* together."

"They're sleeping together, I would assume," said Carolin. "But that hardly means they're in a relationship."

Sabrina was reminded of her conversation with Anna. "No, that doesn't constitute a relationship," she agreed thoughtfully. "But Rick must know what she's getting into. And Anita —"

"Anita is like a leaf in the wind," sighed Carolin. "You never know quite where you stand with her. She's nice; I like her — but I think . . . she and Rick . . . it's not what I'd wish for. I've known Rick for so long. She needs someone else. But Rick has always had a weakness for helpless women. No one can break her of it."

"I wouldn't say that Melly is helpless, or Thea either," Sabrina objected.

"And that's why she isn't with either of them." Carolin shook her head. "But I'm not going to get involved. If Rick doesn't get there on her own . . ."

"You're right. It's her business," said Sabrina, and her voice sounded thoughtful once more. "Marlene . . . Anita claimed that she loved Marlene, and I had the impression it was true, as incomprehensible as that seemed. But now . . . she's with Rick?"

"After what Marlene did to her, she could hardly do anything else. Rick KO'd Marlene." Carolin grinned. "The winner gets the woman as the prize." She shook her head. "No, it wasn't actually like that, but Marlene must have acted like . . . well, Rick wouldn't normally just haul off and hit someone. She's not the violent type."

"Of course not. I've known her for a while myself. I'm amazed at the idea that she hit her at all."

"Me too," said Carolin. "Marlene must have insulted Anita badly. Melly didn't want to tell me exactly what happened, but apparently it was pretty awful."

"What else could it have been, from Marlene?" said Sabrina.

"Yeah, she's —" Carolin broke off thoughtfully. "I've asked myself from time to time why she's like that. Was she always that way? No one is born like that."

Sabrina shrugged. "To be honest, the *why* of Marlene doesn't particularly interest me."

"I feel sorry for her. I'm convinced she could've been happy with Anita. But she totally ran roughshod over her own good luck."

Sabrina put her head back and leaned against the couch. "Doesn't everyone?"

"What do you mean by that?" Carolin frowned. "You're yearning for Chris, I know, and that's awful, but actually . . . you *are* happy, aren't you?

"Happy." Sabrina took a deep breath. She closed her eyes. "What does that mean? I was happy when I met Chris; I was happy when we got married. I was happy when we started talking about having a baby —"

"A baby? You two want to have a baby?" Carolin sat up on the sofa, amazed. "You've never said a word about that."

"I . . . I – It keeps receding farther into the distance," said Sabrina quietly, turning her head along the back of the couch toward Carolin. "It's hardly even worth talking about anymore. Chris always says we can't raise a child if we don't have any money. The child ought to have everything it needs, including for the future. And I want to be there for our child, to stop working for a while. Chris would have to be the sole breadwinner for a long time."

"You . . . might not work anymore?" Carolin gaped at her in surprise. "But you love your work. I can't imagine you just being a housewife and mother."

"That's work, too. A lot of work."

"Yes, sure." Carolin stared thoughtfully ahead. "But if you won't have enough money, wouldn't it be better if you at least kept working half days? Lots of mothers do that."

"And run themselves ragged. Themselves and their children. No, we have enough money. It would stretch, but Chris thinks . . . sometimes I think she sees me as a queen. And so our child – our daughter, Chris absolutely wants a daughter – would probably be the princess."

"Have you told her that your standards aren't as high?" Carolin asked.

"So many times . . ." Sabrina let out a sigh of resignation. "Neither of us comes from a rich family. We know it's possible to grow up happily without a lot of money. But Chris . . . Chris seems to believe that she has to prove her love with as much money as possible, so I can live worry-free while she works herself into the grave. She doesn't understand —" She broke off.

"That you want her, not the money," said Carolin tenderly.

"Yes, I want her." Sabrina sat up. "As long as she's with me, nothing else matters. Money, things, work — none of that interests me when she's holding me in her arms. It all becomes so unimportant."

"But she doesn't hold you in her arms much anymore, does she? You've already . . . implied that."

"Implied." Sabrina laughed dryly. "Yes, I've implied that. We haven't slept together in months, if you want to know. We were barely seeing each other. It was almost like it is now that she's really gone. I would come home to a dark, lonely apartment and eat dinner alone, just hoping that Chris might come home and join me. At some point, I would go to bed and fell asleep alone. And then when Chris finally did get home, she would make every effort not to wake me — as if I wouldn't have been glad just to see her — and in the morning, she would get up so early that I didn't even know it. The only way I could tell that she'd been there at all was because the other side of the bed was a little rumpled. Great married life, huh?"

"Yeah, that doesn't sound very . . . appealing," said Carolin sympathetically. "But it's only temporary. And sex isn't everything."

Sabrina rubbed her forehead as if it hurt. "No, sex isn't everything, but this is about much more than that." She took a deep breath. "I'm not going to have the baby. Not under these circumstances."

"Have you told Chris that?"

"I'm going to tell her when she comes back. Maybe then she'll be able to get it that —" Sabrina shook her head. "I don't know whether or not she'll get it." She looked at Carolin. "Have you ever imagined yourself sleeping with someone out of desperation? Out of pure desperation?"

"Uh ... Sabrina ..." Carolin raised her hands. "I'm not available. I mean, you're my friend and I'm glad to help you, but –"

"No." Sabrina laughed softly. "That's not what I meant. Our friendship is worth too much for me to jeopardize it like that. But ... but I feel like I'm desperate for a little ... tenderness. Just that, do you know what I mean? Not sex, not great passion, not even love. Just tenderness. That safe-and-protected feeling of not being alone anymore."

Carolin nodded. "That I understand very well. I've never had a really long-term relationship, myself. And I'm not the type for one-night stands either. So I spent most of my nights alone."

"I'm sorry. This must all sound extremely silly to you."

"No, it doesn't." Carolin shook her head. "I don't find it the least bit silly." She opened her arms. "Do you want to come here? I can hold you. Maybe it'll help a little."

Sabrina looked doubtful, but then she slipped into Carolin's arms and snuggled up to her. She was stiff and tense, but after a while she was able to relax. She sighed.

Carolin held her tight; they sat that way for a while, and then Sabrina got up. "I need to go think about all of this some more. I'm going to go home." She smiled down at Carolin. "I'm glad you're my friend." She bent over Carolin's cheek and kissed it gently. "I really don't know who else I could've turned to." She went to the door and turned around once more. "If you ever have a problem ... I'm ready to reciprocate anytime. You know I'm unbeatable at giving advice to other people." She laughed softly.

Carolin smiled. "I'll definitely take you up on that."

Sabrina nodded and left.

Cʒᔖꙶ

The mailbox was overflowing. Sabrina hadn't emptied it for several days, but today she was going to have to. When she opened it, a large pile of papers and envelopes spilled out.

"Ads, ads, ads," she railed. Superfluous junk for which any number of trees had lost their lives. That always annoyed her.

She sorted the colorful sheets and letters out immediately and dumped them in the trash can by the door. There was very little left: a catalog she'd requested, a tax bill from the city, and — what was this?

She turned the letter over in her hand. There was no return address. But it was clearly a private letter; her name was handwritten on it in a sweeping script.

Sabrina's eyebrows rose. Who would write her a letter like that? She used her key as a letter opener. Inside was only one sheet of paper. She took it out and unfolded it. It was handwritten as well.

You are the sweetness of my life, I've missed so long.

Sabrina glanced at the bottom of the page. Of course. Anna.

There's no light in the darkness when you're not with me.

"Oh, man," thought Sabrina. "She's bringing out the big guns." But she smiled. She couldn't escape the magic of the words.

Your smile alone makes my life worth living.

Sabrina leaned her head back and closed her eyes. How could she do something like this? How could Anna write these things to her? Hadn't they agreed —? She opened her eyes again and read the rest of the poem. Then she shook her head and went back inside.

The answering machine was blinking. Two messages. Chris had apparently tried more than once to reach her. She pressed the button, set the letters down on the hall table, and went into the kitchen. She could hear the answering machine from there as well.

"I'll call you again later." Chris's voice. "Don't work too much. I love you."

Sabrina mixed herself a Campari Orange. She'd go sit on the balcony for a bit and enjoy the sunset.

"I hope you got my letter." Anna's husky voice. Sabrina nearly dropped her Campari glass. "And read it." Anna laughed. "I'm guessing you did." A small pause. "I don't want to be accused of bothering you again, but if you're interested in going for another walk, call me." She gave her number. "It's been a while now," she continued. "I figure we should enjoy these last pretty days." The message fell silent.

Sabrina took a large swallow of the Campari and set the glass down. She hadn't heard anything from Anna for a while. She'd almost forgotten her – and she'd been happy about that. And now, all of a sudden, Anna was forcing her way back into her consciousness. That was outrageous.

But that's just how Anna was. Outrageous. True, at the end she hadn't been that way anymore, but Sabrina had stopped meeting her for walks because she felt that, despite the platonic veneer, the whole thing was anything but platonic. On both sides. Even though she preferred to believe that Anna alone was the guilty party. But Sabrina tried to be honest with herself, and in admitting her own interest, Sabrina was forced to consider her own unmet needs.

Still, she had to acknowledge that those needs were there, even without Anna. Anna had drawn them forcefully to the surface again by offering the promise of their fulfillment.

Fulfillment! What fulfillment? Anna only wanted sex. She always had and always would, no matter how she packaged it. The *platonic friend* guise – that was just one more fantasy to reassure Sabrina.

Chris had been in Norway for two months already, and there was still no telling when she'd return. It seemed that despite winter and all other external circumstances, the Norwegians didn't want to let her go. And no wonder: she was an outstanding architect, and in Norway they were building on every corner, as Chris had told her over the phone. Norway was in the midst of an economic miracle like the one Germany had had after the last war. Now they needed architects, craftsmen, salespeople – everyone they could get.

In fact, it seemed to Sabrina that Chris was seriously considering staying in Norway forever. She raved about its natural beauty, the wooden houses with their warmth and charm that left any stone building in the dust, the fjords, the sea, the clear, clean air. Chris had denied it when Sabrina asked her, but Sabrina had known Chris long enough to know that, had she been alone, she probably would've had no difficulty making the decision. She knew that tone in Chris's voice all too well – the one Chris got when she was keen on something and absolutely wanted to have it.

She hadn't asked Sabrina, probably because she knew Sabrina wasn't crazy about cold climates – but that day would come, Sabrina was sure of it. And then? What was she supposed to do then? Have a child in a country she didn't know and whose language she couldn't speak? Sit alone at home, with no friends, and wait for Chris to maybe, possibly come home from work – at some point?

She didn't want to think about it anymore; it was too depressing. She went to the answering machine, listened to it again, and wrote down Anna's number. Then she picked up the phone and her Campari, went to sit out on the balcony, and dialed.

"How nice that you called," said Anna, her smile audible in her voice.

"You're right about these last pretty days," Sabrina said. "You never know when they'll be over."

"Exactly. And you have to admit, I've exercised considerable restraint lately. I hope you're convinced that my request is serious."

"Serious?" Sabrina laughed. "This poem is anything but serious. It's sort of ... oh, well."

"It's sort of *oh well*? What's that supposed to mean? Do you know how long I slaved over it?"

"When?" asked Sabrina, smirking. "Ten years ago? How many women have you sent it to already?"

Anna laughed. "You're heartless."

"I am?" Sabrina raised her eyebrows, even though Anna couldn't see.

"Yes, you are. I could bleed to death right in front of you and it wouldn't bother you."

"What are you expecting to bleed to death from? Did you have an accident?"

"Like I said, you're heartless; you're not even interested." Anna laughed. "No, I didn't have an accident; I'm still completely whole, but I'm certain my heart can't endure this strain much longer. Soon it will simply burst with longing, and then I'll bleed to death."

"Then I'd better not go for a walk with you. I have no talent whatsoever for nursing," Sabrina replied.

"Because you're heartless. Nurses are compassionate, caring creatures – so that really is not the profession for you."

"You're unbelievably brazen," said Sabrina. "However compassionate and caring your nurse might be, you'd expect her first and foremost to assuage your suffering by sleeping with you. And that –"

"That's off the table for us, I know," said Anna. "So will you go for a walk with me? I do have a couple more poems I could send you, if you want me to keep working on convincing you."

"This one is plenty, thanks." Sabrina laughed. "What if someone found your poems in the attic after my death? That happens all the time. And then I'd be mentioned in your biography as one of your many lovers. No, I'd rather not."

"You could become famous that way."

"After my death? What good would that do me?" Sabrina shook her head. Since she'd called Anna, she felt so lively, so energetic, even though she'd worked such a hard day and had actually been tired. She didn't know where all the new energy was coming from. "Let's go for a walk instead. That will be better for both of us."

"I could pick you up tomorrow. Say, around four? Or are you working later than that?"

"Let's say five." Sabrina thought about it. "Or make it five-thirty. It's still plenty light out then."

"That's fine. Five-thirty then," Anna confirmed. "Your taxi will be waiting at your door, Madame."

"You can skip the uniform. And you're not getting a tip, either."

Anna laughed. "I wasn't expecting one. What are you doing now?"

"I'm sitting on the balcony drinking Campari Orange." Sabrina sipped at her glass. "The sunset is wonderful."

"Yes, it is. I'm watching it, too. Red and orange … the colors must be just like your Campari."

Sabrina glanced at her glass. "Indeed. I hadn't even noticed."

"A Campari sunset. I'll have to make note of that; I might be able to use it in a book," said Anna.

"Do you think about anything other than your books? Do you exploit everything for them?" Sabrina frowned.

"Not everything, but a lot. If you aren't a good observer, you can't be a good writer," Anna stated.

"I guess not," said Sabrina. "Until tomorrow then. Five-thirty. Chris is about to call; I don't want to miss her." She hung up.

Why had she just said that? She didn't want to talk about Chris with Anna, but just now, she'd wanted to show Anna that she shouldn't forget what Sabrina was: a married woman.

C3ᴇᴏ

"Like back home in the Sauerland," said Anna.

"In the Sauerland? You're from the Sauerland?" Sabrina was disconcerted.

"Yes, the great, wicked writer started out small once, too." Anna laughed. "In a tiny village in the Sauerland. It's gorgeous there. I enjoyed my childhood very much. We cavorted in the woods, sledded down all the hills in the winter . . . no kid could have had it better."

"The Sauerland," repeated Sabrina.

"Now you're thinking of all the jokes you've ever heard about Sauerlanders," laughed Anna. "I hope I don't conform to any of the stereotypes."

"No, you don't." Sabrina looked at her as they strolled across a clearing together.

"How do you think I know so much about birds? And all the other animals? My grandfather told me all of it. He used to be a hunter, but then later, he decided it was more sensible to care for the animals rather than shoot them."

"How nice of him," said Sabrina mockingly.

"Oh, it was. Especially considering he was an avid hunter. He actually loved animals and he wanted to create optimal habitats for them. Part of that is that there can't be too many animals or the overcrowding will cause them either to starve or catch diseases. He was no Sunday hunter – the kind who just shoots at anything that wanders in front of their shotgun, then misses the mark so that the animal has to suffer. My grandfather never missed a shot."

"You went with him, when he ... was shooting?" Sabrina looked horrified.

"He taught me, so if I needed to shoot an animal that was suffering, I could do it."

"I could never do that," said Sabrina, turning away with a shudder.

"You'd rather let the animal suffer?" Anna asked. "You'd let it die right in front of you without doing anything about it? You think that's more humane?"

"No." Sabrina spoke quietly. "I know it isn't, but –"

"What are we talking about, here, anyway?" Anna laughed. "Are we on the hunt, or are we here to observe animals – without shooting them, of course?" She pointed toward the back of the clearing. "They'll come out soon, when the sun goes down."

"Who?" Sabrina was confused.

"Deer. I saw their tracks."

"You can read tracks?"

"It's as easy as reading a license plate, when you learn it as a child." Anna looked around. "Let's go up on that deer stand and wait." She pointed up the path a ways.

"Are we allowed?" Sabrina remembered having seen a 'keep out' sign up there.

"That's only for the dolts who have no idea how to behave on a deer stand, or who'd fall right off it," said Anna. "It doesn't apply to us."

"I've never been on a deer stand."

"Are you okay with heights?"

"Yes, I'm fine." Sabrina nodded. She looked ahead. "And it's not that high, either."

"No, it's not. But it's big enough for us."

They walked slowly over to the deer stand and climbed up.

"Isn't this wonderful?" whispered Anna. "It's like having our own little house in the clouds – like Tarzan and Jane in the trees."

"But we aren't Tarzan and Jane," said Sabrina. "Don't start imagining that."

"You're right. I don't have enough muscles to be Tarzan," laughed Anna, "and you're not naked enough to be Jane."

"Well, thank heaven."

They watched from the deer stand for a while as the sun went down. "No Campari sunset today," Anna said with regret. "The weather's going to change."

"Are you applying to be a trapper or what?" Sabrina looked at her irritably. "You're acting like you've never been in a city before."

Anna laughed softly. "I usually feel that way out in nature."

Sabrina leaned back against the deer stand's low wooden wall. "You're odd. I sometimes don't know what to think about you."

"Is that a good thing or a bad thing?"

"I don't know that, either." Sabrina regarded her a while. "I really don't know."

"Look!" Anna whispered, but she was pointing excitedly. "The first one!"

Sabrina bent carefully in the direction of Anna's arm. "You weren't kidding."

The deer were stepping out of the forest, one after the other – sniffing and looking right and left, then slowly and ever more boldly populating the clearing. There were larger and smaller ones, but most seemed to be about the same size.

"Aw, no fawns," whispered Sabrina, disappointed.

"Now?" Anna laughed softly. "The young are born in the spring; they need to be mature by the time winter comes."

"Oh, that's true. I didn't even think about that."

"Animals aren't as dumb as human women, whelping at any old time of year."

"Whelping?"

"Well, yeah." Anna shrugged. "There's not that big of a difference between humans and animals."

"You think so?" Sabrina's brows knit.

"From the biological standpoint, it's the same for all mammals."

"From the biological standpoint." Sabrina shook her head. "From the biological standpoint, you should be a man. Or I should ... one or the other of us."

"More likely me." Anna laughed. "You would be much too pretty as a man. And then you'd be gay, and I'd still get nothing out of it."

"You don't get anything out of it now."

"Shh, they can hear us." Anna put a finger to her lips.

The deer pricked up their ears and looked attentively in the direction of the deer stand.

"No one shoots at them from this deer stand," whispered Anna. "Otherwise they wouldn't be so calm."

Sabrina found it fascinating, how much Anna got into observing the animals. She seemed almost to have forgotten Sabrina.

"Crap," said Anna suddenly. "There's a thunderstorm coming."

"Where?" Sabrina saw nothing but a couple of harmless clouds.

"Back there, to the west." Anna obviously saw something that Sabrina couldn't. "We have to get down from here. It's not safe in a thunderstorm." She climbed down and waited at the bottom of the ladder for Sabrina.

Sabrina didn't quite comprehend everything that Anna was talking about, but she followed her. When they were both standing on the solid forest floor again, Anna was eager to get going. "Come on. We have to hurry. The storm is almost here."

Suddenly, a bolt of lightning crossed the sky.

"Too late," said Anna.

A fat drop fell on Sabrina's nose. She looked up. The clouds had massed into grim faces that seemed to want to devour them.

"I saw a feed shed up there," called Anna, taking off at a run as the rain began to pour. "We can take shelter underneath."

Sabrina hadn't seen anything, but she ran after Anna. A bit farther on, Anna turned off the path, and moments later yanked open the door of what looked like a hay barn.

They slipped inside and shook themselves. They were both completely soaked. Sabrina looked at Anna and started to laugh. "You look like a drenched poodle!"

Anna laughed likewise. "You too. Or more like a drenched afghan. You're prettier."

Sabrina shook her head. "Who'd have thought it. That it could start raining so fast . . ."

"That happens a lot in the summer. As long as it's warm, it's not so bad."

Sabrina wrapped her arms around herself. "You think it's warm?"

Anna looked at the gooseflesh coming out on Sabrina's bare arms. "You're freezing." She glanced around the hut. "Take your clothes off. I'll dry you off with the hay. If you stand there freezing in your wet things, you'll catch a cold."

"I think I'd rather keep my clothes on," said Sabrina.

"Don't be silly." Anna picked up a bundle of hay. "Or do you like being sick?"

"I hate it."

"So?"

Sabrina was still hesitating, so Anna went around behind her and opened the zipper of her dress. Sabrina was so surprised, she stood there motionless while Anna took off her dress. She unfastened Sabrina's bra and let it drop.

"Your panties don't seem to be too wet. You can keep those on." Anna began rubbing Sabrina's back with the hay.

"That prickles," said Sabrina.

"Of course. It's not a towel." Anna rubbed some more. "But it helps. At least you won't be freezing anymore." She stepped around to the front and rubbed Sabrina's shoulders, almost touching Sabrina's breasts. Suddenly, she looked into Sabrina's eyes. "You are so beautiful," she said softly.

Sabrina closed her eyes. She knew that it was outrageous of Anna to look at her naked. She knew she shouldn't have allowed it. She knew she was longing for Chris and not – "Please ... please don't ..." she breathed.

"I can't help it," whispered Anna, letting the bundle of hay fall, taking Sabrina into her arms, and kissing her.

Sabrina wanted to fight back, wanted to shove Anna away, wanted Anna not to touch her. She wanted all that, and yet, she just stood there and let herself be kissed. *Chris*, she thought. *Chris*.

It was Chris, not Anna. She was kissing Chris, not Anna. Chris's hands caressed her, Chris whispered tender words in her ear, Chris touched her where only she was allowed to touch her.

She kept her eyes closed; she didn't want to see what was happening, she only wanted to feel. Feel Chris with her.

Anna pushed Sabrina gently down onto the haystack, kissing her, stroking her. "Sweet Sabrina," she whispered. Her lips ran from Sabrina's mouth to her throat, caressing the hollow of her shoulder. They wandered lower, and the tip of Anna's tongue sought Sabrina's nipple, teasing it with short strokes.

Sabrina sighed.

Anna's mouth roamed to the other side and took Sabrina's nipple between her lips, licking it, letting it grow. Sabrina's nipples stood tall; they crowned her breasts like small, glistening hard candy.

"You are so beautiful," Anna whispered again. Her hand slid down Sabrina's body to her belly, then her fingers felt their way cautiously into her panties. "So beautiful ..." Anna's voice sounded rough. She kissed Sabrina again; her tongue explored Sabrina's mouth into its deepest depths. Her fingers glided between Sabrina's thighs, opened the wetness, pushed in a little.

Sabrina moaned. She thought about Chris, saw Chris before her, over her. "Come ..." she whispered. "Oh, please, come ..."

"Yes, my sweet." Anna pushed deeper inside.

Sabrina's hips rose; she wanted Chris to penetrate her deeply, to take her so deeply. "Yes," she moaned. "Yes ..."

Anna pushed her panties down over her hips, spread her legs, and knelt between them. The hay jabbed hard into her knees. She bent down and licked across Sabrina's pearl.

Sabrina thrust her hips even higher. She moaned loudly. "Take me," she whispered breathlessly. "I need you so."

Anna slid all the way in between her legs, thrust her tongue in between her labia, then replaced her tongue with her fingers.

Sabrina moaned steadily; she tossed her head from side to side; she felt her entire lower belly was on fire and about to consume her with its brutal demands. The motion of her hips became faster and faster, like a steam engine gathering speed. She no longer noticed how hard Anna had to work to hold her tight, because Sabrina was bucking like a wild colt.

"Yes ..." she moaned. "Yes ... yes ... oh, yes ... please ... please ..." Her labia throbbed intensely, because Anna was deep inside her, trying to match Sabrina's rhythm. She thrust into Sabrina while Sabrina thrust violently back against her. It was no gentle affair. More like a desperate struggle for supremacy.

Anna took Sabrina's clit between her lips and let the tip of her tongue run over it, faster and faster.

"Oh, God . . . yes . . . yes . . ." Sabrina's moans became incomprehensible. "Oh, yes!" Sabrina tensed. She fell back onto the pile of hay, panting heavily.

Anna glided up next to her and kissed her. "Was that nice?" she asked, smiling.

Sabrina gasped for breath, keeping her eyes closed. Slowly, she came back to awareness – and slowly, too, to an awareness of what she had done. She didn't want to open her eyes, but she had to.

Anna's face still looked at her, smiling.

Sabrina stood up without a word, threw on her dress, and left the hut.

"Sabrina!" Anna came running after her and held her back. "What's wrong?"

"Take me home, please," said Sabrina. She didn't look at Anna.

Anna regarded her from the side. "You're regretting this?"

Sabrina didn't answer.

They walked back to the car in silence and got in.

"Sabrina . . ." Anna watched Sabrina's stony face, which stared fixedly out the window. "You have nothing to blame yourself for. If you want to, blame it on me. It's my fault. I'm always at fault anyway. I can live with it."

"Please, take me home," said Sabrina tonelessly. "Or I'll walk."

"Ten miles?" Anna laughed softly. "I'll take you home – of course." She started the car.

The drive passed in deathly silence except for one or two attempts by Anna to get a conversation going. When they arrived in front of Sabrina's apartment, Sabrina opened the door before the car had stopped completely. She got out quickly and ran to the front door.

A minute later, she was in the apartment. She threw herself onto the couch. Slowly, the rigidity that had kept her upright, with superhuman effort, melted away.

The telephone rang. Sabrina clamped her hands over her ears. She didn't want to hear anything.

After several rings, the answering machine picked up. "I know you don't want to talk to me right now," said Anna. "But maybe you'll at least hear this message." She cleared her throat. "Please don't blame yourself. It was all my fault, mine alone. I was simply so overwhelmed by you. I shouldn't have done that. But you weren't responsible. Please, accept my apologies." She hung up.

Sabrina took her hands away from her ears. She had turned the answering machine up loud, so she could hear it in the bedroom in case Chris called after she had gone to bed. So covering her ears hadn't accomplished anything. She'd understood every word.

Anna was taking responsibility. Yeah, great. Now she felt much better.

No; of course, that had accomplished nothing whatsoever. She felt horrible. Yes, Anna had seduced her in a way, but Sabrina wasn't seventeen years old anymore. She was a grown woman, and she had to bear the responsibility for what she had done, no matter what Anna said.

She wanted to stand up, but she fell back onto the couch. All at once, an inexpressible weakness overcame her. Her eyes burned. She felt the tears forcing their way up, her eyes becoming moist, the first salty drops running down her cheeks. She didn't want to cry – it made no sense whatsoever to cry – but she cried. She couldn't do anything to stop it.

She threw her hands over her face, sobbing; her whole body shook, defending itself against the inner emptiness that had remained since her experience in the woods. She had felt nothing since then, behaved like a robot, just wanted to get home. Home. To safety.

But that kind of safety was no longer available. It had happened. The thing she most wanted to prevent had happened.

Had she really wanted to prevent it? She'd only needed to not meet with Anna – that would've been the best prevention strategy. But it was just as reliable as the strategy of recommending to a straight woman that she just should stop having sex if she didn't want any more children. It would never work. And it hadn't worked with Anna, either.

What could she do? What on earth could she do? She couldn't turn back the clock, couldn't simply strike those hours, those few minutes, from her consciousness. From her consciousness and from her life.

When straight people do this kind of thing, they wind up with unwanted children, she thought. Lucky that at least that wasn't a problem. When she imagined being pregnant now, not by Chris, but by Anna . . . Oh, my God!

She shut her eyes. Gradually, the flow of tears that had flooded her face diminished. How happy she had been . . . back then, the first time she and Chris had talked about having a child together. How unspeakably happy.

It was the greatest blessing of her life to have met Chris. They were made for each other. The first year had been like a dream. Yes, they'd fought now and then, but –

She smiled. How nice the reconciliations always were. In bed, for hours, for days. Love, tenderness, passion, sweet abandon. Again and again, until neither of them could anymore and everything was sore. Then they laughed, tried to touch each other anyway, grimaced with pain and still couldn't let go of one another. Pain and lust lay so close together. Because they were in love, none of that mattered.

The telephone rang once more. Anna. She was going to keep trying until Sabrina picked up. She'd have to turn down the volume on the answering machine. She could call Chris herself, when – as soon as she was capable of it.

Her head buzzed from crying; she got dizzy when she tried to stand up. She sat down on the arm of the couch to recover herself.

The telephone kept ringing until the answering machine switched on. "I thought you'd be home, at this hour."

Sabrina jerked up.

"I've tried calling you so many times already." Her mother's voice sighed. "And now I'm talking to this dreadful machine. You know how much I hate that."

Sabrina stood up and staggered to the phone.

"I just wanted to tell you –"

"Yes, Mama?" Sabrina had picked up and answered.

"Ah, you're there." Her mother sounded relieved. "That answering machine is driving me crazy. Every time I want to talk to you, it comes on. Where have you been all this time?"

"Working. I'm working a lot these days."

"Even more than usual? Don't you two have anything else to do with your lives, you and Chris? When I was your age –"

"When you were my age, you had two children and you were busy with us all day long. Without a break. Is that what you were going to say?"

Her mother laughed. "You're right, of course. I worked around the clock, and your father did, too. It wasn't so different. Except –"

"Except that we don't have any children." Sabrina sighed. "You wanted to tell me something?"

"Yes. Susanne tried to reach you, too, but you're never there." A faint reproach resonated in her mother's voice. "It's if you had no family at all."

"Mama ..." Sabrina rolled her eyes toward the ceiling. "When Chris gets back from Norway, I'll have more time again, but at the moment –"

"Chris is still in Norway?"

"Yes." Sabrina tried not to let the tears rise up that were collecting directly beneath her eyes.

"When is she coming back, then?"

"I don't know." Sabrina pressed against her eyes to keep them from crying. "The project has been extended, and Chris ... I think she likes Norway a lot."

"That's why she's leaving you alone for so long?"

"No, that's not why. I already told you, her work –"

"Why does she have to work abroad?" asked her mother, disgruntled. "Isn't there enough work for architects at home?"

"She gets paid better in Norway. We've talked about all this before, Mama. You know Chris isn't doing this without having some good reasons."

"The older you get, the harder it is to have your first child," said her mother. "That's also the reason I'm calling. Susanne is pregnant again." The joy in her mother's voice was unmistakable. "You're going to be an aunt for the third time."

"Lovely." Sabrina smiled. "Maybe this time it'll be a girl."

"She hopes so. And Felix hopes so, too." Her mother sighed. "Susanne will breeze right through it and keep bringing boys into the world until there's finally a girl among them. She won't give up until then."

"That's true. She will breeze through it." Sabrina laughed. "If she has to have ten of them, she won't mind."

"No, that wouldn't bother her. She's an enthusiastic mother."

"Oh, Mama ..." Sabrina took a deep breath. She knew that tone in her mother's voice. "You're getting your third grandchild now; what does it matter whether I provide you with one more?"

"It would mean a great deal to me," said her mother. "Susanne was always different from you. I knew that she ... but you –"

"I'm not the born mother, you mean?" That old theme. Sabrina brought the phone back to the couch with her.

"I didn't say that," her mother countered hesitantly. "It just maybe isn't so easy for you."

"No, it isn't. Maybe Susanne could just give me one of her ten once she's got them all." Sabrina was tired of discussing this over and over.

"Sabrina." Her mother's voice sounded reproachful.

"I'm sorry, Mama." Sabrina took another deep breath. "Chris promised me ... when she comes back ..."

"Whenever that's going to be. How long have you been waiting now? I mean, waiting for her to say yes? For her to agree."

"She does agree," Sabrina defended herself. "It's been a done deal for a long time."

"Then you should've been a mother for a year by now. Or at least pregnant."

"If Chris were a man, I probably would be. Is that what you're getting at?"

"No, that's not what I meant." Her mother sighed too. "You know how much I like Chris. And I see how happy you are with her. That's all a mother wishes for: that her own children are happy. But with a man, it would certainly be easier, you can't argue with that."

"No, I can't." Sabrina felt tired and worn down. First Anna, now her mother. Maybe her sister was about to call her, too, radiant with joy, to share the news that she was pregnant again. It was all a bit too much at once. "So I should go find myself a man, sleep with him, and get pregnant. Is that your recommendation?" She let herself sink back into the couch.

"No, child." Her mother seemed to be shaking herself. "You're married. Even though Chris is a woman – but –"

"Instead of Anna, I should've taken a man," murmured Sabrina. "Then everybody would be satisfied."

"What are you mumbling about?"

"Nothing." Sabrina spoke up again. "Nothing at all. It would be one option, wouldn't it? The simplest method for getting pregnant."

"But no, not that way. Of course, if you were in a relationship with this man –"

"That's out of the question," Sabrina interrupted her. "You know that."

"Yes, I know." Her mother sighed. "It is a little hard to understand, but I don't have to, after all. You have your reasons."

"My reasons? For what?" Sabrina felt like she'd shifted back into earlier times.

"Well, for the way you live. You could've had any boy in the entire neighborhood. All of them chased you. And one or two of them were very nice."

"Please, let's not rehash that again," Sabrina begged, irritated. She rubbed her forehead. "We've been there."

"Yes." Her mother sighed once again. "Volker still asks about you."

"Volker ought to pay attention to his wife instead."

"I think things aren't going so well in that marriage," her mother remarked ambiguously.

"That has nothing to do with me. Please, Mama . . ."

"Fine, then. I just mean, you know. He doesn't seem to be happy, and neither does she, really. She's quite the harridan, actually."

"I would be, too, if I knew my husband was still mourning his old childhood girlfriend and would rather be with her than with me. That I was only his second choice. Who knows what he's told her about me? We never actually had anything together, but men can be pretty imaginative about that kind of thing."

"You really never had anything?" asked her mother, full of hope.

"You always seemed so —"

"Volker made sure it looked that way. I never wanted any part of it."

"He has a successful business. They buy themselves new cars every year, one for her and one for him. Expensive cars."

"And for cars, I should sell myself to him? For money? Do you actually realize what you're suggesting here, Mama?"

"Ah, child, do you always have to be so negative? For a woman, it's important that her husband makes good money. That's just the way it is."

"Chris does make enough money," Sabrina said crossly. "And I earn money, too. We suffer no want. I'm well provided for, don't worry."

"Now don't fly off the handle," replied her mother, sulking a little. "Is it a crime that I only want the best for my daughter?"

"Chris *is* the best." Sabrina stood up from the sofa, agitated. "I couldn't possibly have found anything better. She loves me, and I love her. That's all that counts. The two of us —" She broke off and hung up quickly, before her mother could hear the sobs that had slipped secretly into her throat.

Yes, Chris is *the best thing that has ever happened to me. And how have I repaid her?*

CS୫∞

"**W**ill you pick me up at the airport?" asked Chris's smiling voice. "I'm looking forward to it so much. You can't possibly imagine how much I'm looking forward to it."

"I'm looking forward to it, too." Sabrina's heart beat loudly. Finally, Chris was coming back. Finally, she would see her again, not just hear her voice and long for her. Her voice failed her out of sheer happiness. "I . . ." She swallowed. "Of course I'll pick you up. What time does your flight get in?"

"Twenty past seven. That's the arrival time. By the time we're all out, then . . ."

"I'll be there. Chris?"

"Yes?"

"I love you, Chris. I love you so much."

"Ah, Sabsi ..." Chris's voice took on a yearning undertone. "We'll survive these last few hours, won't we? It's been so long ..."

"Yes. So long." Sabrina's throat constricted. She could hardly believe Chris was coming back. She'd consoled herself with that thought over and over again for so long, and now, all at once, it was coming true. "Twenty after seven," she said, as if it were an incantation. "Twenty after seven."

"Twenty after seven," Chris repeated softly. "Then I'll be there. I've been longing for you so much. I love you." She hung up.

Sabrina's hand trembled as it held the receiver. Chris ... She closed her eyes and imagined how Chris would wrap her in her arms, how she would touch her, how she would finally feel her warmth. It had been so long that she hardly remembered the feeling.

Sabrina arrived at the airport an hour early; traffic in the city center hadn't been as bad as she'd expected. Since she always took the bus to work, it had been a long time since she'd paid attention to the times that most car drivers bustled around on the streets.

She paced back and forth in the airport terminal, nervous and excited, constantly looking at the board on which the flights were announced. Chris's flight wasn't posted yet, not by a long stretch. The board was full of flights from Singapore and Bangkok, Tunisia and Mallorca. There didn't seem to be any airports at all in northern Europe.

Then, finally ... ah, no. Stockholm, not Oslo. Sabrina stared at the display as though she could transform one city's name into another. The display jumped upwards. The uppermost lines disappeared, and others appeared below. Arrived, arrived, arrived, delayed.

Delayed? No, not Chris's flight, another one from Dubai. Sabrina exhaled with relief. She'd waited months, but these last hours, these last minutes were pure torture. She felt like she was about to faint; everything swam before her eyes; her blood pressure seemed to be around two hundred, although she usually suffered from low blood pressure. The blood whooshed through her temples.

The display jumped around, and clear down at the bottom she read *Oslo*. At last. This time, Sabrina stared at it as though she had to hold onto the name so it wouldn't disappear again. The lines slid higher and higher, minute by minute. Arrived.

Sabrina ran to the security checkpoint. She couldn't go in, she wasn't a passenger; she had to wait until Chris came out. She stood on her tiptoes and craned her neck, trying to see anything. It took forever for the first passengers to emerge. There ... no, that wasn't Chris. A mother with several children came out; she was steering two luggage carts simultaneously, and the children hung from her like a cluster of grapes.

Sabrina watched her admiringly. Mothers were really phenomenal. With all that they could do.

"You're watching strange women? Didn't you miss me at all?"

Sabrina's heart nearly stopped. "Chris," she whispered.

Chris hugged her from behind, kissed her neck, turned her around, pulled her into her arms, and kissed, kissed, kissed her. "Sabsi," she whispered. "Sabsi."

Sabrina kept her eyes closed while Chris kissed her, giving herself over completely to the kisses. She opened her eyes when Chris let go of her and examined her face as though she'd never seen it before. "Chris," she whispered again. Her voice broke. She looked into Chris's adoring eyes, which smiled back at her; she still couldn't believe it. It wasn't a dream. Chris was with her, finally with her again.

Chris pulled her back into her arms and kissed her anew, this time intimately and tenderly, less hungrily than the first time. "Sabsi," she whispered again. "Oh, Sabsi. How I've longed for you."

"Chris ..." Sabrina burrowed into Chris, hugged her tightly, didn't want to let go of her. "I missed you so much."

"I missed you, too." Chris stroked her back, kissed her hair, inhaled her scent. "You smell so good," she whispered. "I should have bottled that scent and taken it with me. Maybe then it wouldn't have been so bad."

"You smell like the forest." Sabrina leaned back slightly. "Like Christmas."

"Yes, there's plenty of forests up there." Chris laughed. She looked at Sabrina with the most loving eyes Sabrina thought she'd ever seen. "But all the forests, all the nature in the world couldn't replace you." She regarded Sabrina's face, let her gaze wander over it with no end in sight.

"If we stand here any longer, we're going to take root ourselves." Sabrina laughed, too. She freed herself from Chris. "Come home. Come." Her voice became softer and softer toward the finish.

"Home. Yes." Chris picked up her suitcase. "Home with you. I thought about that during the whole flight. I'm coming home to you. As if I'd been gone for years."

"It seemed that way to me, too." Sabrina linked arms with Chris and the two of them walked together to the exit. "Many, many years. Much too long."

"Yes, much too long." Chris glanced over at her. "If I'd known it would take so long —"

"Well, it's over." Sabrina interrupted her. "You're back again. That's all that counts."

Sabrina had a hard time concentrating on the traffic as they drove from the airport back into the city.

"Should I drive?" asked Chris, laughing. "You seem nervous."

"Are you feeling up to it? I'm sure you worked right up to the very last minute."

"Well ... yes, I did." Chris shrugged. "But then I just sat the whole time on the airplane; I finally got a chance to relax."

Sabrina drove into a parking lot at the next opportunity. "Yes, please, you drive. I'd be grateful for that." She looked at Chris.

Chris bent over to her and kissed her. Her hand ran along Sabrina's side, touching her breast. "Sabsi," she whispered huskily.

Sabrina shut off the motor. "And I have everything prepared so nicely at home." She ratcheted the lever at the side of her seat down to make it recline.

Chris slid on top of her. "Is this bad?"

Sabrina smiled. "No. Why do you think I could barely drive?"

"Sabsi," whispered Chris again, "my sweet angel."

Sabrina reached down and unfastened Chris's pants, then pushed them down over her bottom. As she touched the naked skin, Chris moaned. "I'm sorry," she gasped, "I think —"

"That's fine." Sabrina slid between Chris's legs from behind, pressed into her and felt how wet she was. "Now I know how much you've been looking forward to seeing me," she laughed softly.

Chris moaned again. "Yes ... a lot ..." She thrust against Sabrina's fingers that took her from behind, moaned louder, and came with a sound like her very last breath. She lay briefly on top of Sabrina, then propped herself up. She put the other seat down, too, turned Sabrina to face her, and laid Sabrina's legs across her shoulders.

"Chris, if anyone comes into this parking lot ..." whispered Sabrina.

Chris laughed. "I just hung my naked butt up on the windshield. If somebody wants to peek, let 'em peek." She pushed Sabrina's skirt up and pulled her panties down. "Damn ..." She tore them.

"Chris!" Sabrina laughed excitedly. "I bought those special for today."

"I can't wait," Chris whispered throatily. "I have to have you."

Sabrina closed her eyes while Chris plunged between her legs. If someone did come along, at least she wouldn't see them. "Darling," she whispered. "You haven't done that in a long time, torn my underwear."

"I'm sorry," Chris breathed hoarsely. She thrust her tongue in between Sabrina's thighs.

Sabrina moaned. "Oh, yes ... I want you ... I want you so much ..."

Chris didn't leave her any time to think about it; she took her quickly and without ceremony. Twice in a row.

Sabrina moaned and gasped; she writhed on the seat, her legs spread wide over Chris's shoulders. When she came to herself again, she ardently hoped that no one had wandered by, above all, no one with a camera. "Chris ... Chris," she moaned, when Chris wanted to take her for a third time. "Please, let's drive home. I feel like I'm in a fishbowl here."

Chris seemed to hesitate, then she let her legs down. "I'm so sorry, love. I'm terrible."

Sabrina laughed. "I'm just as bad as you. There's nothing I'd rather do than keep going, but —"

"All right." Chris pulled her onto the passenger seat, did a makeshift readjustment of her own clothing, and climbed into the driver's seat. She put it up again. "But I might just break the sound barrier." She turned the car on and drove off with squealing tires.

Still lying down on the seat, Sabrina was tossed from side to side. She held on tight, pulled herself up, brought her seat upright as well, and buckled herself in. "I don't remember you being such a fast driver," she said, laughing nervously. "Did you learn that in Norway?"

"Yep." Chris grinned. "In Norway they zip through the woods at a hundred miles an hour."

"Chris, please . . . I want to get home as fast as possible, too, but —" Sabrina braced herself against the dashboard.

Chris throttled back slightly. "I . . . I just can't wait," she said roughly. "How often I've imagined holding you in my arms again, lying in your arms . . ."

"Me, too." Sabrina spoke quietly. "But not in the hospital."

Chris continued to speed, but they got home in one piece. They made no effort at all to take Chris's luggage in with them, just plunged into the apartment and fell all over each other right inside the door. After some time, they made it to the bedroom; one could easily trace their path by following the cast-off pieces of clothing.

"Chris . . . Chris . . . Chris . . ." Sabrina sighed while Chris caressed her breasts. "Oh, my God, it's so good that you're back."

"My angel." Chris let her lips glide down from Sabrina's breasts, then suddenly rushed upward and kissed her. "I wish I could divide myself up," she panted breathlessly, "above and below at the same time, and on your breasts, too. I can't go without any part of you for more than five seconds."

Sabrina laughed. "I feel the same way. I want to touch you, kiss you —" Her eyes went dark. "I want you —"

"Get the dildo," Chris whispered excitedly. "The double one."

Sabrina jumped out of bed. She returned with the rod. "I hope I can remember how this works. We haven't used it in ages."

Chris reached for her and pulled Sabrina down to her. She devoured Sabrina's mouth while she laid the dildo between them. "You don't forget something like this. It's like riding a bike."

The dildo entered Sabrina, and at the same time, she saw the other part disappear into Chris. They sat facing each other and began to thrust into one another. They moaned in the same cadence. The rhythm became quicker, they moaned louder, and finally they thrust so firmly into one another that Sabrina cried out.

Chris moaned once more and let herself fall back onto the bed. "You're wearing me out, Sabsi," she panted.

Sabrina, too, just lay there panting. "What do you mean, *I'm* doing it?"

"My angel. I love you so." Chris carefully pulled the dildo out of herself, but not out of Sabrina. She turned around and began again to take Sabrina with the dildo.

Sabrina moaned. "I don't think I can anymore, Chris."

Chris bent over her, still thrusting into her with the rod. "I think that's just a rumor," she said, smiling.

Sabrina held tight to Chris, writhing; she tried to escape the rod, then at the next moment, thrust her hips into it. She only wanted to be taken by Chris, nothing else. It should never stop, never end.

"I love you so much," Chris whispered over her again.

Sabrina felt the tears come. Maybe it was overexertion, but maybe it was also ... something else. "I love you, Chris," she sobbed. "If only you knew how much I love you."

"I know it," Chris whispered; the dildo rode into Sabrina and back out again, faster and faster.

Sabrina's hips performed a dervish dance, to follow it, escape it, follow it. She moaned; she clawed painfully at Chris's shoulders; she panted; she called out, the cries becoming ever sharper. She felt the thick rod filling her up, forcing her thighs apart. Her insides seized on the object in her center as if she wanted to crush it; she didn't let it go again. She screamed again, loud and piercing, and froze beneath the rod that had demanded her utmost surrender.

Chris ceased her movements. She pulled the dildo out, lay between Sabrina's legs, and licked her.

"No, Chris, no!" Sabrina hooked her fingers in Chris's hair. "I can't anymore, please ..."

Chris looked up. "Really?" She grinned.

"Chris . . ." Sabrina blinked down at her out of hooded eyes. "Oh, Chris . . ." She opened her legs even wider.

Chris dove into her once more, then turned herself around, so that Sabrina could dive into her simultaneously. Barely had the orgasms receded when Sabrina sat on Chris and rode her until Chris couldn't stand it anymore, turned her over and buried her beneath herself. It went on without end.

"Why did you cry, love?" asked Chris, hours later, when they were finally forced to take a break. "Did I hurt you?" She looked concerned.

"No." Sabrina stroked Chris's face and smiled. "No, you didn't hurt me. It was just so beautiful."

"So beautiful you had to cry?" Chris traced her eyebrows gently. "Or awful?"

"Awfully beautiful," said Sabrina. "Terribly beautiful. It's been so long . . ."

"Yes." Chris bent over her and kissed her. "Much too long. I'll never leave you alone that long again."

Sabrina looked at her. "Do you promise me that?" She sought Chris's face with her eyes. "You must never leave me alone again . . . please . . ." She held Chris close, nestling into her arms. "Never again."

"Well, for a week or two, maybe . . ." said Chris.

Sabrina shot up in alarm. "A week or two?"

"You can come along. Since you've worked so much lately. Then it'll be more like a vacation. It would only be once or twice a year."

"How's that supposed to work? It's never really just for a week or two. Your projects . . ."

Chris looked at her. "Sabsi, I'd really like to . . . Norway is so beautiful . . ."

Sabrina took a deep breath. "I knew it."

"What did you know?" Chris raised her eyebrows questioningly.

"That you'd want to live in Norway." Sabrina stared, sightless, into space. "You've always been partial to the north."

"And you aren't. I know." Chris sighed. "It wouldn't be forever.

Maybe for a couple of years . . .?" She gave Sabrina such an innocent look that she would've had to soften if she'd looked at Chris.

But she didn't. She kept staring in the opposite direction. "How is that supposed to work, Chris?" she asked wearily. "You're independent, you can work anywhere, but I'm an employee of a company that's here. I have a good job –"

"Which you were planning to give up anyway, when the baby comes." Chris sat up and wrapped her arm around Sabrina's bare shoulders. "So what's the difference? In Norway, it's also much easier to get pregnant. They don't have the restrictions they have here." She pressed a kiss onto Sabrina's neck.

"Is that so?" Sabrina turned her head and looked at Chris from the side. "That's a point."

"Yes, isn't it?" Chris sprang excitedly out of the bed. "Then we'd have that problem solved; you could take care of the baby, and I'd manage the construction sites –"

"And we'd never see each other. Just like it's been for so long," said Sabrina. "Am I supposed to be satisfied with that?"

"No." Chris dropped down next to her on the mattress. "In Norway, it's different. It's not as hectic as it is here. I'd need to work much less to make the same money."

"But would you?" Sabrina sighed. "I don't see that happening."

"I prom–"

"Chris." Sabrina raised her eyebrows. "How many promises like that have you already broken? I'd rather you didn't promise me anything else."

"Well, okay." Chris took a deep breath. "But about the baby . . . I mean, you could concentrate on that completely . . ."

"In an unfamiliar country, where I don't speak the language. I couldn't even take a part-time job as a secretary, no matter how good I am. When the baby is older, I mean."

"By then maybe we'd be back here," said Chris.

"Oh, Chris, what are you trying to pull? Do you think I don't see how your eyes light up?" Sabrina examined Chris's face. "How much you're looking forward to living there again? How you're longing for it?"

Chris tilted her head and wrinkled her brow. "It's so completely different," she said. "It would be a new beginning."

"For us?" Sabrina looked at her in astonishment. "What do we need that for? We're ... we're not ..." She stuttered. "I mean, everything is fine," she added quickly.

"I know I've made a lot of mistakes," Chris replied. "Far too many. I've neglected you horribly. If I come back home ... well, it'll just keep going like that. And here, you have to pay more in taxes than you earn, especially as an independent contractor. In Norway ... in Norway, we'd have much more time for ourselves, too. For us and our little Sabrina."

"There's no way I'm going to call her Sabrina, even if she looks just like me." Sabrina laughed. "I've never liked the name."

"The name is sweet," said Chris, smiling, pulling Sabrina down on top of her and kissing her. "Just as sweet as you."

ಣಲ

Sabrina awoke with the feeling that she wasn't alone. But when she opened her eyes, she was. The bed next to her was empty ... as always. Only after a moment did it become clear to her that the bed wasn't as always. The blanket was completely twisted up, and the scent – well, yes, it smelled like sex, but first and foremost, it smelled like Chris. She smiled.

"Breakfast." Chris came in with a large tray on which everything imaginable was beautifully arranged. "Just for you, my darling. You've had a hard night." She grinned.

Sabrina's eyebrows lifted. "Not just me. You, too."

Chris shrugged. "I've been hauling around trees every day." She set the tray on Sabrina's lap. "Is anything missing?"

"If you're planning to stuff an entire company of hungry mouths, no."

Chris flopped down next to her on the bed so that the coffee sloshed over.

"Chris," scolded Sabrina.

"Ah, Sabsi," Chris smiled at her, "I'm so happy."

"Me, too." Sabrina smiled. "Aren't you going to eat breakfast?"

"Yes, I –"

The doorbell shrilled.

Sabrina glanced up, and Chris looked around. "Who could that be, this early in the morning?"

"It's not early in the morning; it's almost noon," corrected Sabrina after a peek at the alarm clock. "That'll be the mailman. Maybe a certified letter from the city or something." She started to set the tray aside.

"You stay here." Chris jumped up, ran into the bathroom, and threw on Sabrina's bathrobe. "I'll go."

Sabrina heard Chris opening the door and speaking with the mail carrier. It was apparently a complicated matter, because it took some time. Sabrina drank coffee and buttered a slice of toast.

"Who's Anna?"

Sabrina's head jerked up.

Chris stood in the doorway with a bouquet of roses and a card in her hand.

Sabrina was unable to speak.

"According to the card, the roses are from her. At least two dozen." Chris looked at the bouquet in her hand.

Sabrina cleared her throat. "Yes. She likes to overdo things."

Chris stared mutely at her.

Sabrina set the tray aside and stood up. "I ... I have to tell you something, Chris," she whispered.

Chris threw the roses onto the bed and ran her hands through her hair. "Yes, I think you do."

"It ... it ... I felt so forsaken," whispered Sabrina. She looked at Chris unhappily. "So frightfully lonely and alone."

Chris looked disbelievingly at the roses, then back at Sabrina, then at the card in her hand.

"You were gone, and I longed for you so. It was horrible. Every day, I hoped I'd get used to it. I struggled with it, but ... but it got worse from day to day, not better."

"It was like that for me, too," said Chris flatly.

"Yes, but you were in Norway. You had your work, new people, a completely new environment. I tried to numb myself with work, too. I stayed in the office until midnight sometimes, but even that didn't help. I was dead tired, but I lay awake and couldn't think of anything but you. I missed you so, so awfully."

"I missed you, too. Sometimes I lay awake until I was just so exhausted that I fell asleep."

"Sometimes. But . . . don't you understand? I . . . I was here, and I didn't know . . . I didn't know when you were coming back. Or if you would call again and say the project had been pushed back again . . . into next year." Sabrina threw her hands over her face. "I felt so abandoned," she whispered in a voice that barely held back the tears.

"Who is Anna?" Chris asked once more, without any emphasis at all.

Sabrina breathed deeply and took her hands from her face. "She's a writer. You remember, I asked you to go with me to that reading? I met her there."

"I should have gone with you."

"Yes, you should have, you really should have." Sabrina went to the cupboard and began to dress.

"What are you doing?" asked Chris.

"I'll move out immediately. I know I can't expect you to let me live here any longer." Sabrina tucked her blouse into her jeans.

"You . . . you can't just . . ." Chris sank back onto the bed. "You actually did . . . with this Anna . . .?" She appeared shaken to the core.

"I won't lie," said Sabrina as she began to pack a few things into a suitcase. "I think it would be evil to lie about something like this."

"But . . . why . . . you . . .?" Chris looked up at her in disbelief.

"I'm not the saint you made me out to be. Obviously." She cast a quick glance at Chris. "I was . . . I thought – Oh, Chris, what does it matter?" She went into the bathroom to get her toothbrush and a few sundries.

"Sabrina . . ." Chris stood up and blocked her path. "You can't just leave like this. We haven't even talked about it."

"There's nothing to talk about. The facts speak for themselves."

"No." Chris held her by the shoulders. "This can't be. Not you."

"Yes, Chris." Sabrina tried to free herself, but Chris wouldn't let go of her. "I told you, I don't deny it. It happened." Sabrina gazed past Chris. She couldn't look her in the eye.

"But because of that ... you can't just call everything into question because of that. And in Norway, I could've – Things like this happen now and then, when people are separated for a long time."

"And? Did you?" Sabrina looked at Chris.

Chris furrowed her brow as if she were ashamed. "No. But I did look at another woman that way sometimes, and didn't think anything of it."

"But you didn't sleep with her. That's the difference."

Chris's hands fell feebly from Sabrina's shoulders. Apparently, it was just now dawning on her exactly what they were talking about. "Was it good?" she asked softly. "Better than ... with me?" She gazed at the floor.

"Oh, Chris." Sabrina went around Chris and put her things in the suitcase. "That's not what this is about."

"What is it about, then?" Chris turned around and looked at her. "What you weren't getting from me, she gave you. She's better than I am."

Sabrina looked at the roses lying on the bed. "She isn't better than you." She swallowed. "She could never be better than you. She was just ... there."

"She was here when I wasn't. I should have been here," said Chris, shattered.

"Yes, you should have been." Sabrina sighed. "I asked you for that so often. A little time ..."

"But now. Now everything can be different. I'll have more time for you, I prom–"

Sabrina interrupted her with a look.

"I won't just promise it. I'll *do* it," said Chris. "I ... I'll get over this. You were lonely. You needed someone. I'll get over it and forget about it."

Sabrina took a deep breath. "Even if you could forget it, I never could." She faced Chris. "And I don't believe that you can forget it, either. You don't forget about something like this. When I'm lying in your arms, you'll always be asking yourself whether I might be thinking about her. Isn't that so?"

Chris bowed her head.

"It is," said Sabrina. "I know you. We made a vow of fidelity to each other. You kept that vow, and I broke it. That vow was ... the most important thing to me. The most important thing in our marriage. If someone isn't faithful, everything else is pointless."

"Then why couldn't you –?" Chris raised her head.

"Yes, why couldn't I?" Sabrina felt her eyes burning. How many times had she asked herself that already? "Could I have? I don't know. If I could have, I probably would have." She looked around. "I don't know when I can come get the rest of my things. Is it a big imposition to keep them here for now?" She glanced at Chris.

Chris shook her head. "We both had girlfriends before we were married," she said softly. "And I've never asked myself if you were thinking about them when you were in my arms. I was able to forget that."

"That, yes, but –" Sabrina looked thoughtfully at Chris. "I've never thought about it, either."

"Well, then, you see." Chris tried to reach for the glimmer of light that had appeared on the horizon. "It's ... it's all my fault, anyway ... because I left you alone. I betrayed you with my work, one could say. You only took your revenge."

"Revenge?" A rueful smile overtook Sabrina's face. "No, I really can't claim that. Even if it were true, I had no right to vengeance."

"No, I –" Chris looked beseechingly at her. "If I can grant you that right, then why can't you accept it?"

"I can't. I just can't." Sabrina cast another wistful glance at Chris. "We both had girlfriends before our marriage ..." she repeated slowly. She hesitated, then took a deep breath. "What happened with Ina?" she asked through tightly compressed lips.

"Ina? Why Ina?" Chris seemed taken by surprise.

"You never told me about her. I didn't know anything about her until we met her at Sappho. And that time in Rome seems to have been a very pleasant one. You never even told me you'd ever been to Rome."

"There's a lot of interesting architecture in Rome. When I was in college –"

"What happened with Ina, Chris?" Sabrina asked again. "You can tell me now. After what I did, I haven't earned any further consideration. Even if what you have to say is painful."

"That was a long time before we met," Chris answered evasively.

"Yes, I know, but love . . ." Sabrina swallowed, "love doesn't just stop. Did you love her? Do you love her?" She had wondered about that so often during Chris's absence.

It was obvious that Ina was more to Chris than just a harmless ex-girlfriend. Would Chris still have taken the job in Norway if Ina were the one left behind? If she were with her? Or would she have passed up the job in order to be with Ina? Would Ina have been more important to her than Sabrina was? Before Chris had gone to Norway, she'd never dared to ask.

"Sabrina, please . . . don't torture yourself that way. Stay with me. We'll forget what was. Ina, Anna – that doesn't need to matter now. What's important is the two of us. Just the two of us."

"So you did love her," sighed Sabrina. "I thought so. And since you never told me about her, there must still be something there, otherwise you would have told me. You still love her." It hurt dreadfully, and she felt that that was the decisive reason to leave, since exactly that pain that she was feeling now was what she had caused Chris. She could never make up for that.

"I –" Chris ran a hand through her hair and turned away from Sabrina. "Yes, I did love her. But that was a long time ago. So many years . . ."

"Years can sometimes seem like hours, or like minutes. When you don't forget a person –"

Chris turned around. "When you came along, I forgot everything," she said softly.

"No, you didn't." Sabrina shut the suitcase and carried it into the hall. "Otherwise you wouldn't be reacting this way now. You still love her. Maybe you can do that – love two women at the same time. Maybe you've been doing that the whole time. Since we've been together."

"Sabrina . . . Sabsi . . ." Chris came after her, looked at her imploringly, and reached out a hand toward her.

"I have no right to blame you for anything," said Sabrina. "Because I've done worse. It was all just a big mistake. Our love, our marriage . . ."

"No!" Chris cried out. "No, it wasn't!" She stepped over to Sabrina and held her tightly in her arms. "Stay with me, please. I'll forget everything. What you did, what I did . . . it can't end this way. Please, darling . . ." She kissed Sabrina hard on the mouth, as if she were trying to convince her by force.

Sabrina let herself be kissed, but she didn't kiss back. "None of it makes any sense anymore, Chris," she said when Chris let go of her. "We betrayed each other from the start. In our thoughts, at least. I didn't know it, but that's how it was. And now I've betrayed you in more than just thoughts. That's unforgivable. I have to go."

Sabrina turned around. "I haven't earned this," she said, pulling her wedding ring from her finger, laying it on the table, and leaving the apartment.

END OF BOOK ONE

What becomes of Sabrina and Chris?
Is this the end of their great love?
And what becomes of Carolin, Anita, Rick, Marlene and the others?
Their fortunes develop in Book Two . . .

An excerpt from

Forbidden Passion

by

Ruth Gogoll

Tiny letters danced across the screen in front of Kim's eyes. Exhausted, she rubbed at her eyelids. Working at a computer for hours at a stretch wasn't exactly restful. But when she could work no more, she went to one particular Internet site, where she could relax a little. There were stories there that she read again and again. Very special stories. From woman to woman.

Slowly, Kim let herself slip into the story. The woman with the chestnut brown hair sank back on the couch, and the other woman leaned over her –

"Ms. Wolff?"

Kim spun around. Her boss stood in the doorway. Silky chestnut brown hair fell across her shoulders, shiny and seductive. Kim swallowed.

"Are you working on something urgent?" her boss asked. "Or could you come see me right now?"

"I can . . . come," Kim managed with an effort. That was certainly true. She probably almost could've.

Sonja Kantner, Department Head and object of Kim's restless dreams, glanced briefly at the screen, but she was too far away, the screen stood at too sharp an angle, and the letters were too small. Kim thanked all the goddesses in heaven for that.

"I'll just save this quickly," Kim commented, feeling warm in the face. Hopefully, she hadn't turned beet red. But she didn't really tend to. That was lucky for her. At least at this particular moment.

"Good, do that," Sonja Kantner confirmed with a nod, then turned away.

Kim watched her luscious backside disappear from the doorway. Did she have to be so attractive? It was a daily torture.

SIX WEEKS EARLIER

When Kim had seen her new boss for the first time, at her introduction in the conference room six weeks ago, Kim had nearly fainted. She immediately worked out a plan for how, for reasons of strategic importance to the company, she could move the department head's office — normally immediately adjacent to her own — to the other end of the hall, or better yet, to another floor. Or even better still, to another building.

"Why don't you start by introducing yourself, Ms. Kantner," the CEO invited after relating a few of the career highlights of his new department head.

He drew back, and Sonja Kantner stepped forward. She repeated, in slightly different form, what he'd already said about her, but that didn't interest Kim in any case. What interested her, Sonja Kantner said right at the start: married, no children.

"Yet," she added with a charming smile.

She'd guessed right. Kim almost sighed when she received confirmation of what she'd already known anyhow. Sonja Kantner was straight, and solidly so. But what good would it have done if things had been otherwise? Kim brooded some more over her plan to ship her off to another building. Didn't they have branch offices in other countries, too? Couldn't Sonja Kantner perhaps be assigned there?

Kim knew one thing, at least: She wouldn't be able to stand having Sonja Kantner so close to her for long, everyday, almost every minute. Perhaps Kim would get used to her and the attraction would fade with time? Kim mustered Sonja Kantner's body once more from head to toe as she spoke. — No. — No, the chances of that were exceedingly slim. The opposite was more likely to occur.

When the assembly started to break up, Kim was about to leave when the CEO waved in her direction. "Ms. Wolff? Would you come over here for a moment?"

Kim took a deep breath and squared her shoulders. Courage! She went over to the two of them, and he introduced her with a smile. "This, Ms. Kantner, is your closest coworker, Ms. Wolff."

Sonja Kantner smiled likewise and offered Kim her hand. Kim would rather not have touched her, but she could hardly avoid that, after all. Sonja Kantner's hand was soft and warm in hers. For preference, Kim would never have let go, but Ms. Kantner drew back after the appropriate interval, as was proper.

"I'm glad to meet you, Ms. Wolff," she said. "I hope we'll work well together."

Work together? thought Kim, but aloud, she responded with what was expected of her: "I hope so, too, and I'm looking forward to it as well." She smiled in a way that she hoped came across as confident. The tingling that had slowly spread from her hand throughout her entire body somewhat hindered her ability to control her reactions.

"You'll take Ms. Kantner on a tour of the company and show her everything, won't you, Ms. Wolff?" her CEO surmised in a tone of friendly command.

Kim tried not to gulp. "Yes," she replied, the effort required to control her voice making it sound very soft, "of course. I'll show her everything." If only that were possible! What all Kim would've liked to show her . . .!

Sonja Kantner laughed. "But not until tomorrow! Today, I still have to tour the executive floor."

The CEO melted at her charming smile just as Kim had, only he was permitted to let that show; Kim wasn't. *One day's reprieve! At least she had that!*

"Then until tomorrow," Sonja Kantner smiled at Kim once more. "When will you be here?"

"At eight," Kim forced out.

"Good," smiled Ms. Kantner. "I'll be here at seven."

CB⪻

"This really wasn't necessary, Ms. Wolff," Ms. Kantner greeted her, beaming.

Already in such a good mood this early in the morning – this was going to be something! When had she gotten up? Kim had been punctual, but Sonja Kantner was already sitting at the desk when

Kim entered her office.

She came over to Kim and extended her hand. "Good morning," she said when she'd reached Kim, and her eyes delved into Kim's with an irresistible gaze.

She probably had no idea what effect that had on Kim . . . she had on Kim —

"You could just as well have come in at eight," Ms. Kantner continued. "I know I get on everyone's nerves by being such an early riser. But I like to catch up on things in peace and quiet first thing in the morning. When no one is here yet. Otherwise one never gets to some things." Her laugh was enormously likeable.

She'd only just started. What was there for her to catch up on? Kim nudged herself into an understanding smile and withdrew her hand, which Ms. Kantner still held. "You're right about that," she agreed. "Although I prefer to do it in the evening, when everyone else is gone."

Sonja Kantner laughed once more and went back to her desk. "To each her own," she said. She turned to face Kim. "How late do you stay at the office in the evenings?" she asked.

"Sometimes until ten," answered Kim, "but I usually don't come in until —" She broke off. Perhaps she shouldn't reveal to her new boss what time she normally came in in the morning.

Sonja Kantner smiled. She was too clever to be led so easily astray. "You don't normally come in at seven or at eight, do you?"

Kim sighed. "No," she admitted. "But I'll change that, of course," she added hastily. "If you're here at seven, I will be, too."

"That's not necessary," replied Sonja Kantner. "As I said at the beginning: I know I get on everyone's nerves by being such an early bird, but I don't demand it of anyone else." She kept smiling. "Although by ten o'clock in the evening, I'm usually already in bed. So we ought to agree on some time in between."

In bed? Kim looked at her. How seductive must she look lying in bed, if she was already this attractive during the day? She was sure to have wonderful negligees for nighttime . . . and if she wore nothing at all . . .?

"When's the earliest you can be here?" Sonja Kantner was now asking as she paged through a file on her desk, which her predecessor must've left behind.

Kim first had to tear herself away from her thoughts. "Eight-thirty?" she suggested then. She could probably just about manage that.

Sonja Kantner looked up. "Fine," she said. Then she smiled once more in that unbelievably likeable, almost loving way. "And if it's more like nine sometimes, that's not a problem. I suspect that was the time you really wanted to suggest, am I right?"

She must've graduated from a great many leadership seminars, to be this good. "Yes," Kim admitted.

"We'll thrash it out together eventually!" laughed Sonja Kantner. "Will you show me around the company now?"

Thrash it out together — what a nice image, Kim thought for a moment, before she yielded to Sonja Kantner and they left the office.

An excerpt from

Ruth Gogoll's Taxi to Paris
by
Ruth Gogoll

She stood a few steps away from me and looked out the window at a neon sign as it blinked on and off. She spoke into the empty darkness, "You can go quietly now. I won't hold you back." Her spine was straight as a board.

I took a step toward my clothes. But then I stopped. I didn't want to leave; that was perfectly clear to me. But what else did I want here? She was a hooker; she had expected me to pay for a "service" I had no idea I was getting. She conformed to my wishes when she saw that I wanted something different — as any good service is performed to suit the wishes of the client. The client? I suddenly saw myself in a very unfamiliar light.

She turned around and glared coldly at me. "Should I leave?" Her voice was icy.

I suddenly became aware of my nakedness. Embarrassed, I grabbed my shirt and threw it on. "No, that would be ludicrous."

She shrugged. "Most women want to be left alone afterwards. It's all the same to me." This icy voice somehow had a heart-softening quality. A contradiction in itself, but it seemed that way to me.

I buttoned my shirt and observed her. She had her arms crossed and stood there, legs apart, an unconquerable fortress. I went toward her. She followed my every move with her eyes, but she didn't stir. I stood in front of her and looked up. *My God. She was at least 6'2"!* "I don't want to be alone, and I don't want to go." I watched her, unshaken.

Mockingly, she screwed up her mouth and looked at me.

"Ah — the lady has developed a taste for it!"

She laughed. It sounded rather lachrymose. She bent down a bit. "Until just now you didn't know, and you were irritated. Now you know and already" – she snapped her fingers – "it turns you on, right? Until now it was just a somewhat exotic adventure. Something outside of the ordinary, am I right? But now, what an opportunity! What's it like to sleep with a woman who does it for money? You'd like to know, right? Why shouldn't you try it, now that we're already here?" She turned away from me and unbuttoned her cuffs. Over her shoulder, she added, "I hope you have your checkbook with you. I'm quite expensive."

With one jerk, she took off her shirt and tossed it on a chair. I saw her taut back and heard the scratching of her zipper. With a quick shake, she kicked off her boots, and her pants flew after her shirt. Now she was naked. With a crisp movement, she turned around and raised her arms for a moment. "There you are; I'm at your disposal."

Finally, I had the opportunity to look at her again and to establish what I had noticed at first glance, once more, she was unbelievably beautiful. I moved toward her and touched her. Her skin radiated the cold of a marble statue.

"No." I shook my head. "No, I won't do it. I won't treat you like a whore just so you can get rid of me more easily." I backed up.

"But sweetheart," she raised her eyebrows, as if to express her bemusement that I obviously didn't know the rules, "you're paying me. And I am a whore. Come!" She had put on a professional smile and came toward me. She reached behind my ear and stroked the sensitive spot under my earlobe with her thumb. I shut my eyes. "That's better," she cooed.

I wanted to forget it. I wanted to give in to the sensation of her stroking hand. But I couldn't. I opened my eyes. She was still smiling professionally. "What would you like? You can tell me, even if it's unusual. I'll fulfill all of your wishes. You needn't have any inhibitions."

She played it out like the opening credits to a movie. Suddenly, she smiled knowingly. She stopped stroking behind my ear and ran her hands down along my body until they rested on my buttocks. Then she knelt down. Only now did I realize what she had in mind. I'd been too busy with her show and my sensations. I pushed her head away. "Stop it!"

She wiped the smile from her face, stood with an indifferent expression, and looked at me coldly. "Whatever. It's your money. If you'd rather, you can abuse me for it, too."

I'd never before been in such an intimate situation with a woman who could switch herself off like that. She made me nervous; I wanted to know what she really felt. It enraged me how she took control of me in this way. And I'd never been able to conceal my anger. I blazed at her.

Promptly, she turned her smile back on and tried to pacify me. "But there must be certain things that you've never dared to ask from a woman." She laid her hand behind my ear once again. It would've been a wonderfully tender gesture if she hadn't done it so mechanically. Nevertheless, I enjoyed the moment of quiet. She bent down and kissed me gently on the lips. I wanted to believe for a minute, to imagine that she saw in me the woman, the beloved – not just the customer, the client.

She kissed me carefully, yes, that was the right word, carefully! She forgot nothing important! Her right hand ran down my body. Her left slid under my shirt and played with my nipple until it was hard. It was such an automatic routine; it almost made me sick. She must've done exactly this at least a thousand times before!

I wanted to push her away, but my hands landed right on her breasts. They were wonderfully soft. The velvet skin arched itself against my fingers. I began to stroke them. Instantly, she began to moan and pulled herself toward me. At first, I was surprised, but then it occurred to me what she was doing. Regretting that I had to give up the velvety softness of her breasts, I pushed her away. She looked at me with clear eyes. No trace of arousal.

"Didn't you like it?" she asked, professionally interested. I tried to hold her eyes, but she avoided me. She looked over my shoulder. "I'm sorry. I need some time to adjust myself to you. Most of my customers' demands aren't so . . . eccentric."

I couldn't help but smile. Her helplessness did more for me than the self-assurance she'd displayed up until now. I looked at her with loving affection. "You're beautiful."

Something flickered in her eyes, but then her face clouded over again. She asked coolly: "So why don't you want me then? You're paying for it. The others tell me what I should do, or if I shouldn't do anything . . ." She opened her hand in a gesture of helplessness.

An idea crept into my head. Under no circumstances did I wish to let myself fall into her game. But if she'd listen to me . . . She kept watching me, waiting coolly.

"Lie down," I ordered, with as much authority as I could muster. Astonishment flashed briefly across her face and disappeared again immediately. She spun around and took a step. Then she stood still.

"Where?" she asked flatly into the air. Her stiff back became even straighter.

"On the bed," I decided.

She set herself in motion. She strode gracefully to the bed. When she'd laid herself down, she stretched out her arms toward me. "Come," she said. She'd obviously decided to dispense with the professional expression. She looked honestly and deliberately indifferent.

I crossed the room and stood next to the bed. "Not like that," I contradicted. "Roll over." She hesitated. I waited. Then she turned herself over onto her stomach slowly, with an odd sidelong glance at me. I admired the soft, curving line of her back. She was really a beautiful woman. What could have caused her to . . .? Well, that was a pointless thought. She'd have her reasons. My fingers tingled with the desire to touch her, but I only traced the outline of her body in the air. I bent down and kissed her between the shoulder blades. She jumped. "Don't you dare moan," I warned. "We already had the show."

"The others like it now and then," she countered, shrugging, with her cool, indifferent voice.

"But I don't. So let it be."

I couldn't see her face, but I could've sworn she was smiling. "As I said before, you're somewhat . . . eccentric."

I kissed her again between the shoulder blades and noticed how she tensed up. She was trying to suppress the twitching. I smiled. That wasn't such a bad start. I began to cover her whole body with kisses. Slowly and tenderly, I wandered from her neck to her shoulders, then to her arms and back to her shoulder blades. My mouth glided along her ribcage and dawdled awhile in the hollow above her bottom. Although I took full advantage of this activity, I tried to observe her at the same time. At first, her hands lay next to her head. She seemed peaceful and relaxed. After the first kisses, she got goose bumps. She began to dig her hands into the pillow. Her knuckles became even tighter and whiter. As I came to her lower back, fine drops of sweat beaded up on her skin and shimmered, glistening like a fine rain. She breathed heavily, but buried her head in the pillow.

Again, my fingers traced very lightly the path from her neck to her ass. She jumped at many places this time. Her breath became heavier. She couldn't get enough air through the pillow anymore; she lifted her head and turned it to the side. Gasping, she sucked in air.

Although I believed her reactions were real, a little devil suddenly appeared on my shoulder. Perhaps the particular dynamics of this game I'd never played before, had taken hold of my brain and knocked out my normally attentive control mechanisms. In any case, I didn't think any more about it. Against my better judgment, I reprimanded her: "Don't act for me . . . I warned you!" It was only supposed to be a joke. I was firmly convinced she'd notice that, but she stiffened immediately. She was still gasping. After a few gulps of air, she began to tremble. Her hands pushed slowly under her head. "Please don't," she whispered flatly. Her voice was harsh with fear.

An excerpt from
Ruth Gogoll's Christmas Carol
by
Ruth Gogoll

It was late when Michaela headed home that evening. The streets were deserted. She entered her apartment where everything looked exactly as it always did. There were no Christmas decorations, no burning candles. Michaela missed none of it. What was all that humbug for anyway?

The apartment had only sparse furnishing; there was nothing unnecessary. Michaela's idea of superfluous included a coffee machine, a refrigerator and a television. She had none of those.

She had moved into the apartment with the few pieces of furniture remaining from the previous tenant. She had been forced to sell her family's house after she had inherited the company and discovered that she was nearly bankrupt. Her father had needed only a few months to ruin what had taken her grandfather decades and a lot of effort to build. At that moment, she had taken a solemn oath never to become like her father. Yes, he had always been everybody's darling. However, Michaela was not after that. Popularity had no value. Money was the only thing that counted, never having to rely on anybody.

She crossed her apartment in the weak light streaming through the window from a street lamp. Why should she turn on a light? She knew where everything was. There was hardly any furniture, so there was not much opportunity to run into anything. She did not have to pay for the street lamp – although, that was not entirely true either, her taxes paid for it, much to her annoyance.

She just wanted to change out of her clothes, brush her teeth and fall into her bed. She had no use for Christmas. She did not notice that the light through the window seemed to be brighter that night because the street lamp was supported by the many colored lights shining out from the surrounding windows. Had she noticed, she would not have cared. At worst, she would have gotten upset about people's wastefulness. Those people somehow felt the need to il-luminate the street, which was a waste if they were inside.

She yawned and went to bed, shivering when her body hit the cold sheets. There was no heat in her bedroom. It would get warm under the blanket in a moment, as always. She was still waiting for all of her toes to adjust to the surrounding temperature when she started to drift off.

She had a strange dream. What was even stranger: She usually did not dream at all. While she was dreaming, she was not aware of that, of course.

She was running through a long corridor, searching for some-thing, though she would not have been able to say what exactly she was looking for. She opened every door, of which there were in-credibly many on the seemingly endless corridor, and looked in-side. She found herself in front of storage rooms, bricked-up doors and windows, never finding what she was searching for. Once there seemed to be a room flooded with light behind one door, but when she wanted to look inside to see what kind of room it was, the door closed, and she was back in the dimly lit corridor. She no-ticed she was starting to panic. She knew, she had to find it ... it ... it ... whatever it was.

"Mike ... Mike ..." A voice drifted through her dream. "Mike ..."

She opened her eyes and peered into the darkness. Her bedroom faced the courtyard; not even the street lamps could cast a glow here. Still, her eyes adjusted quickly to the absence of light, and it was as if shadows populated the room, formless, faceless shadows.

"Mike ..."

It sounded like an echo, a faraway echo without any substance, as if coming from nowhere, as if it had no origin.

Michaela set up straight in her bed. It could not be that she was just imagining this! She had never had nightmares. There had to be some real cause. A burglar maybe?

She scanned the room — as much as she could see. She was not prepared for a situation like this. To be honest, she had always thought there was nothing to steal in her apartment — which was probably true — and that she could neglect any kind of security. She had an ordinary lock on her front door. That was it. She had no weapons, neither for defense nor for offense. She knew her grandfather had had a pistol, a souvenir from the war, and she knew that pistol still had to be somewhere. But, even if she were to find it, it was not likely that it would still fire.

A flashlight on her bedside table would have been very useful now. It would have provided light, and she could have used it as a weapon. Unfortunately, Michaela had thought that investment was unnecessary too.

She lay down again and tried to calm herself. She could hear the sound of her own breathing and her rapidly pounding heart. With difficulty, she tried to get both into a slower rhythm.

A rustle. She held her breath. She knew there had to be something in the room.

She stared into the darkness, unable to move. The little bit of light in the room seemed to change, as if suddenly a street lamp was switched on outside. This could not have been, after all, there were no street lamps in the courtyard.

No, the light did not come from outside, it came from inside. Michaela sat up again; and this time she got out of bed. If there was something there, she wanted to face it upright. The air was freezing, but she did not feel it, even though her feet tried to call her attention to it.

"Mike . . ." One of the formless shadows glided towards her.

Michaela shrank back, startled, but then stopped. She was hallucinating; that was all.

The shadow hovered in the air in front of her and then suddenly took shape — a female shape. A face peeled itself out of the darkness, strangely familiar and unfamiliar at the same time. Suddenly Michaela recognized something very familiar. "Karina?"

The shadow with Karina's shape smiled.

Michaela took a deep breath. What was that woman thinking? "Did you use your key again, even though I told you not to?" she asked with irritation in her voice. Then she scowled. Had she not taken the key from Karina?

With an unusual expression on her face, rather angelically innocent and a small halo around her head, Karina answered, "I didn't need to. Not this time." She smiled a shadowy smile.

Michaela wanted to say something but shut her mouth again right away. She was confused, because Karina was so different. She did not know her like this. "Why are you here, in the middle of the night?" she asked when the shadow did not seem to want to move.

"It is a very special night," Karina whispered, the angelic smile still on her face.

"It is a very cold night!" Michaela snapped. Suddenly she became aware of the frostbite threatening her bare feet standing on the bare floor. She fumbled for her slippers and put them on. Unfortunately, they were also cold.

"It's as cold a night as it has to be," Karina said. "As it always is."

"Why are you out and about then? Don't you have a bed at home?" A knowing smile spread over Michaela's face. "Or is your bed empty? Are you alone and looking for company?" Now she knew what was up. She recalled that Karina could not stand being alone. Her bed was rarely empty. And today – on Christmas – all of her lovers were busy elsewhere – all except Michaela. So Karina had come over.

"You are the one looking for something, not I," said Karina.

Michaela remembered her dream. "How do you –?" She started to feel spooked.

"I know everything," Karina replied, "but there's a lot that you don't know yet – or no longer. That's why you will have visitors tonight."

"What? More visitors? Do you want to have an orgy?" Michaela laughed.

"You just don't understand," Karina said. "I'm not the one you think I am. I'm just a messenger."

"I rather think you're a bad dream caused by my upset stomach," Michaela replied. "Or you're playing a trick on me." She waved her hand dismissively. "Leave me alone. I have to sleep. It'll be morning soon, and I have to go to work." She crawled into her bed and pulled the blanket up over her shoulders. My god, that was cold!

"Tomorrow can wait," Karina said, "but you might not."

"Don't talk in riddles!" Michaela got upset. "That's not your style." Indeed, Karina was the most direct person she knew. She never hid what she wanted. Why was she doing it now?

"You are capable of making even an apparition like me sigh," Karina said. "You don't believe in what you see. You walk through the world with your eyes shut, without looking around you. Do you never stop?"

"Stop and smell the roses, you mean?" Michaela laughed with chattering teeth as she shivered under her blanket. "Are you Satan offering me a single moment that's so beautiful I'd want it to last forever in exchange for the world?" She propped herself up. "All right, make me an offer. I'll think about it."

"I'm not the devil." Karina glided away. "Like I said, I'm just a messenger. The others will come. Be ready."

"The others? What others?" Michaela stared confused into the darkness that started to spread out again. The light coming from Karina's shape waned. "What others?" Michaela yelled into the silence that followed the darkness.

But there was no reply.

Check out these exciting books and more at

www.elles-books.com

www.ingramcontent.com/pod-product-compliance
Lightning Source LLC
Chambersburg PA
CBHW022032260626
47156CB00017B/1174